BORDER BLOOD

ALSO BY A.W. HART

Avenging Angels Series
Concho Series
Gunslinger Series
Legend of the Black Rose Series

BORDER BLOOD

CONCHO BOOK NINE

A.W. HART

**WOLFPACK
PUBLISHING**
— EST 2013 —

Text copyright © 2024 A.W. Hart
Special thanks to Michael A. Black for his contribution to this novel.

Published by Wolfpack Publishing
701 S. Howard Ave. 106-324
Tampa, Florida 33609

Paperback ISBN 978-1-63977-974-1
eBook ISBN 978-1-63977-415-9
LCCN 2023951079

BORDER BLOOD

CHAPTER ONE

A PAIR OF SHADOWS MOVED IN THE DARKNESS.

Concho Ten-Wolves lay on his stomach on the rough ground as he adjusted his night-vision goggles and surveyed the uneven field through the green-tinctured lenses as he keyed his mic. He was wearing a sleeveless, camouflaged Army blouse and dark pants.

"I got movement," he said.

"Roger that," came the reply.

By-the-book radio procedure, even though the standard ten-four would have sufficed. It was Carl Cate, one of the newbies on the Maverick County Police Department. The kid was green and right out of the Army—military police, which probably explained his radio terminology. He'd been paired for field training duty with experienced deputy Terrill Hoight to assist on this Special Auxiliary Border Surveillance—Joint Taskforce, or SABS—JT.

SABS—JT.

Leave it to the brass to come up with a moniker like that, Concho thought. But at least it wasn't SOBS.

He mulled over the possibilities for that acronym.

Sorry Ornery Bastards on Surveillance?

That brought a smile to his face.

Not that he was complaining. The sign-up sheets for the special overtime details filled up quickly at first, but the monotony and frustration and idiotic governmental bureaucratic procedures of the detail soon took its toll and the sign-ups dwindled quicker than a snow cone melting on the Fourth of July at a Texas parade. Concho had actually signed up for this one at the behest of his boss, Captain Dalton Shaw.

"You guys don't keep signing up, the brass upstairs will pull it permanently," Shaw had admonished.

Concho got along pretty well with him and actually liked the man. He saw Concho as being something of an iconoclast, or "a wild card," as Shaw often put it, he also recognized Concho's abilities and gave him prize assignments. Content with being the Ranger commander's "go-to guy," Concho wanted to stay on the man's good side.

"Before we know it, that damn border will be out of control and we'll be drowning in all sorts of problems if we don't watch out." The captain tapped the sign-up sheet.

Concho scribbled his name down volunteering for a night shift and handed it back to Shaw.

"There you go, sir," he said. "But as far as the border being out of control, I'm afraid it's already there."

"Tell me something I don't know." Shaw smirked. "So, in other words, you're just signing up to stay in my good graces?"

"That, and..." Concho grinned. "I can use the extra money. My girl wants me to buy her a plant for Valentine's Day."

"A plant? I thought you told me she has a real bad track record with them things?"

Concho thought about Maria's inability to maintain a healthy, watered plant for more than two or three weeks.

"She does," he said. "But it's what I call an easy gift. Not that expensive, and easier on her teeth and her figure than a box of candy."

Shaw snorted a laugh. "Well put, but having seen her, I

don't think she has to worry too much about either. Anyway, thanks for signing up. It's for the next two nights, by the way."

The thanks of a grateful boss had done little to ease the discomfort Concho was now feeling. The February night was chilly, but he'd been through worse. Much worse. This was a cakewalk compared to Afghanistan.

The sharp breeze brought the smell of the Rio Grande to his nostrils and he wondered how cold the water must be for those trying to cross. There hadn't been too much rain the past week, and it had to be relatively shallow. Probably good wading depth, or if not good, most likely passable except for a strong current.

But who knows, he thought. *Maybe this next group will have a raft.*

Another flicker of movement caught his attention, and he watched as the green images of two men appeared coming up from the arroyo. One of them looked like he was talking on a cell phone.

Probably won't be long now, Concho thought and keyed his mic again.

"I got two suspects moving by the arroyo," he said. "You got them?"

"Copy that. We do. We're ready to go mobile."

This time it was Hoight. Probably was feeling the standard trainer's anxiety. As an FTO you had to let your recruit do most of the work, but when things got down to the nitty-gritty, you also had to make sure things went smoothly.

"I'm going back to my vehicle," Concho said as he crawled back down the slight embankment and moved back to his F-150. The ground was pretty uneven along this spot and the declivity offered by the gently sloping ridge gave his pickup truck the perfect concealment from the prying eyes of the human coyotes. When he got to the bottom, he rose to his full height and did a quick jog to the truck, making sure he maintained a decent and less discernible crouch. At six-foot-six, he made a sizable target. If he'd still been back in the 'Stand, he would have been a sniper's dream. But this was Eagle Lake Texas and he was a Texas Ranger, not an airborne one.

He got to the pickup and yanked open the handle on the driver's door. He'd long since disabled the dome light connection so he wouldn't be illuminated as he opened the door. Sliding inside, he keyed his mic again, one extended click, indicating to Hoight that he was ready to roll.

"Okay," Hoight's voice said. "Looks like we got our group coming up now. Shit, it's a whole passel of them."

They were on a special sideband frequency that wouldn't bounce off any repeaters in the area, otherwise Hoight would have gotten reprimanded for using profanity over the radio. Tonight they were off the official books. They were SABs.

Maybe that stupid acronym was good for something after all.

Concho keyed his mic again.

"How many?"

After a few seconds of silence Hoight's voice answered back: "I'd say at least twenty."

A squawking sound from his mic caused Concho to wince. It was too close to his ear and Hoight and the kid had obviously both keyed their mics at the same time causing feedback.

"Ten-nine?" Concho said, asking them to repeat.

"My partner was going to correct me." Hoight's voice was laced with irritation. "He counts twenty-five. Looks like a mixed group. Lots of females, though."

Concho chuckled. There was nothing like training a rookie.

His window was down and the faint sound of a car's motor became audible.

No, wait…it sounded more like two cars.

He relayed this to Hoight.

"Damn," Hoight said. "Probably their rides. We've got to get off this road before they see us."

Radio silence followed. Concho started his truck and inched forward, still staying relatively secluded by the terrain. As long as he stayed blacked-out the chances of the occupants in the other vehicles noticing him were slim unless they too had night-vision goggles.

He caught a flash of red brake lights perhaps forty yards across the expanse. Obviously, Hoight hadn't remembered to tell the rookie to trip the kill switch for the brake lights on their squad car. Of maybe he did and was waiting to see if the kid did it. He scanned the road and saw two long shadows driving down the road. It had to be the pick-up vehicles.

"Terrill," Concho said into his mic, "kill your brake lights."

The sharp burst of static from his mic made him grit his teeth.

Feedback. Both of them pressed the transmit button at the same time again.

That rookie Cate was an eager beaver, all right.

The two cars drove past and Concho flipped his night-vision goggles down to get a clearer look at them.

One was a minivan. The other an SUV. A Lexus RX 350 Sport—a fairly good-sized vehicle, but certainly not large enough to cram in half of the illegals, if rookie Cate's twenty-five count had been accurate. That meant that this one was a two-part pickup: humans and drugs.

"You got an eye on them?" Hoight asked over the radio.

"They just went past our twenty," Concho said. "A minivan and an RX Sport."

"My favorite kind of bad guy car," Hoight said. He was obviously enjoying the freedom from proper radio protocol on this little-used side band.

"I've called for back-ups," Hoight said. "They're on the way. Maverick County and the border patrol. Let's wait until they get loaded up and grab them as they leave. While they're still on this back road. Before they hit the main highway. If they're all tangled together, we won't have to worry about chasing them in all the different directions."

Concho transmitted back an agreement, using a "Roger that" response which he knew would irritate Hoight, who was probably fed up with his rookie partner's by-the-book radio responses.

He pulled up the swatch of nylon covering the luminous dial of his wristwatch and checked the time.

0220 hours.

Hopefully, the stop would go smoothly and this whole thing would be over with by 0300.

But then again, Concho thought, *nothing good ever happens at three in the morning.*

* * *

CONCHO LEFT HIS PICKUP AND MOVED ON FOOT UP THE SLIGHT elevation so he could watch the progress of the loadings. From what he could tell, the two coyotes managed to cram nineteen people into the minivan and then had the remaining six, all females, get into the Lexus. The uneven spacing arrangement most likely meant that the six women had been selected for a separate and special destination. The nineteen others, mostly all males and a couple older females, would no doubt be released in the town and neighborhoods. He'd also seen them loading several large backpacks into the SUV. At least six or seven.

Fentanyl, probably.

That meant if stopped, both vehicles would run, but the van would be the one doing the blocking so the Lexus would have a clear getaway.

He wasn't going to let that happen. Recollections of the recent spike of fentanyl-related deaths he'd seen on the Reservation—mostly all teenagers and young people loomed large in his memory. Kids buying a pill they thought was safe, only to find out too late that it had been laced with the deadly drug. A line had to be drawn in the sand.

He relayed the information to Hoight and asked on the status of the back-ups.

"They're almost here," Hoight said. "In fact, I've just been advised they're turning onto the dirt road now."

"Have them come in blacked-out," Concho said, moving back to his truck. "And we better move in now. It'll be best not to let them get rolling."

"Roger that," Cate said, his transmission barely preceding another burst of feedback static.

Concho couldn't help but chuckle as he shifted into gear and pulled up onto the dirt road. Glancing to his left, he saw three vehicles coming toward him down the road with no lights.

Back-ups are here, he thought as he turned right.

The sudden screech of brakes broke the silence of the night as the Maverick County squad car occupied by Hoight and Cate screeched to a halt after almost colliding with Concho's truck. He didn't have to wonder who was driving. It had to be the rookie. Twisting the wheel, he swerved and kept going, now pressing down hard on the accelerator and hoping the coyote crew hadn't heard the loud mechanic squeal.

A second later he knew that they had as two pairs of bright headlights flashed on and started barreling toward him. Concho flipped on his lights too, as did the others. A sudden eruption of red and blue oscillating lights appeared in his rearview mirror. It was crunch time. The only question now would be how hard the coyotes were going to play it.

Real hard, Concho decided as a moment later the minivan began to head straight for him.

You want to play chicken, asshole? Concho thought and kept his truck running straight ahead.

Hoight's voice crackled over the radio advising the other converging units that they had the two suspect vehicles rapidly approaching.

The minivan swerved off the road to the right at the last second to avoid a head-on collision with Concho. The Lexus veered left and shot past him.

Swearing as he braked, Concho glanced in the side-view mirror to gauge how close Hoight and Cate were behind him. The bouncing reflection of their headlights danced in the mirror. In the split second he had to decide, Concho twisted the steering wheel around to the left, sending his truck into a semi-spin. He managed to straighten out at the last second and peel out going in the same direction as the fleeing adversaries. Hoight and Cate's squad crunched against the side of Concho's truck with the grating sound of metal against metal. The impact knocked them askew, but the heavier weight of the pickup allowed Concho to maintain his momentum with only a hint of variance. The taillights of the minivan and the Lexus showed that they'd veered completely off the surface of the road. The backup units were spreading out now, and seemed to be on an intercept course with both of them. The minivan bounced high and plopped down. They'd no doubt encountered some unexpectedly rough terrain. The Lexus, however, seemed to have been luckier. The big SUV swerved and cut between two of the backup units. Both of them stopped.

Suddenly the minivan dipped slightly and then rose upward, slamming down a few seconds later and then careening sideways for what looked like a good twenty feet before rolling over on its side and then its roof. As Concho roared past the crash site the minivan came to rest on its top, wheels still spinning and looking like an upside-down turtle. The three backup units all headed straight for it. Concho didn't slow down. The taillights of the Lexus were like two fading red dots against the inky blackness. Then they disappeared altogether.

"The Lexus is running with lights out," Concho said into his microphone.

"Roger that," came the reply, the rookie's voice sounding strained and nervous. "We've got your six."

My six? Concho smirked. More military jargon.

He caught a glimpse of them in the rearview mirror coming up behind him.

Ahead the Lexus became visible as the vehicle made a

sweeping right turn onto the pavement of the highway. About ten seconds later Concho did the same. He didn't look behind him to check on Hoight and Cate. Instead he pressed the accelerator pedal down and the big truck engine roared in response. As he was closing the gap between him and the Lexus, a quick red flash winked from the rear window. A millisecond later the crackling noise of the bullet smashing into Concho's windshield sounded like somebody crushing a walnut. Peripherally, he caught a glimpse of the spider web fracture with the neat, round hole in the middle a few feet to his right. He briefly entertained the option of shooting back, but decided not to do so. Despite the hazard of not returning fire, the danger of hitting one of the illegals was too great. The women had probably risked everything and then some getting to *el norte* in the hopes of a better life, only to take the first steps into a new nightmare. Still, despite the danger to them, Concho couldn't let them get away. Those seven backpacks of drugs alone probably had enough fentanyl to kill everyone on the Kickapoo Reservation and in Eagle Pass at least a couple dozen times over.

No, he thought. *They aren't getting away.*

Another winking red flash, followed by another smacking crunch against his windshield, convinced him that he had to end this as soon as possible.

Using the microphone for his police radio in the truck, he radioed his position, that he was in pursuit, and requested more assistance.

"Shots fired at the police," he added.

The engine in his big F-150 was sounding like a NASCAR racer closing in on the finish line as he pulled alongside the Lexus. The rear window showed a network of fractures from the rounds going through it, and the side windows were darkly tinted. Concho didn't know if the shooter was repositioning himself and didn't want to give him the chance. He veered right, colliding with the rear quarter panel of the Lexus.

The SUV shimmied and then straightened out.

Concho steered into the other vehicle again, this time giving the steering wheel a bit more of a twist.

The grating crunch was like the whining of a wounded beast.

The Lexus shook, moved back and forth a few more times, and then straightened out.

Hoight's voice boomed from Concho's shoulder mic. "You gonna pit 'em?"

Roger that, Concho thought as he gave the steering wheel a vicious right twist just as he accelerated and felt the truck's right side bumper collide with the left rear portion of the Lexus.

It was what they called a pit maneuver.

The SUV spun around ninety degrees as it smashed into the front portion of Concho's truck. He caught the frantic facial expression of the driver for an instant, and then the Lexus went into a yawing sideways slide, still maintaining its forward momentum and finally ending up on its right side in a shallow ditch beyond the left shoulder of the highway.

One Lexus in the side pocket, he thought as he sailed by, now stomping on the brakes and catching a glimpse of Hoight and Cate in the rearview mirror slowing down by the wreck on the side of the road.

Hopefully, the human cargo wasn't too badly damaged.

CHAPTER TWO

CONCHO SLAMMED ON THE BRAKES AND TWISTED THE WHEEL, bringing the pickup to a full stop. The wheel twist had angled his vehicle sideways across the two lanes of highway, and he hit the accelerator zooming back toward the scene of the wreck. As he approached he saw that the Lexus was nose-down in a slight ravine. The driver's door popped open and a male figure slipped out. He began running in Concho's direction. Hoight and the rookie were running in the opposite direction after a second occupant.

Concho was just about to radio it in when a yellowish flash flared in front of him about twenty yards away. The bullet pierced his already cracked windshield about five inches to the right of his position. He hit the brakes again, once more giving the wheel a twist so that the truck stopped with its right side facing the threat. Concho was out of the driver's door in a second and drawing his Colt .45 Double Eagle forty-five. A second burst of fiery brightness illuminated in the darkness and Concho heard the bullet strike the chassis of his pickup, exactly where, he didn't know.

Nor did he care.

His adversary was in the declivity of the roadside ditch.

Three strikes and you're out, he thought, bringing up the Double Eagle in a two-handed grip, acquiring a sight picture with the three green-glowing tritium night sight dots, and then squeezed the trigger. The big semi-automatic jerked with recoil in his huge hands and he was momentarily cognizant of the expended shell casing popping out of the ejection port.

Before him, approximately thirty feet away a body in a black outfit jerked forward and crumpled to the ground. Concho angled off to the left, trotting down one side of the depression and up the other. Still modifying his approach on an acute angle to the downed shooter to minimize the field of fire, he kept his weapon trained on the prone form.

"Ten-Wolves, you all right?" Hoight's voice blared through the radio mic.

Concho didn't reply. He kept his focus totally on the downed shooter.

The man lay still.

No movement.

It didn't appear that he was breathing hard, if at all, but that meant nothing.

It wouldn't be the first time a wounded subject might be playing possum.

Now a few feet away Concho kept his forty-five trained on his prone foe. The gun was nowhere in sight. Concho figured it was underneath the man's body.

Not a good sign.

With another two steps he was within reaching distance of the man's face-down form when he heard Hoight's voice again, this time calling out and not over the radio. He was about twelve feet away.

"Concho, you all right?"

Just as Concho was about to speak, the prone body twitched and came to life, rolling over onto his right side and extending a pistol, a dark colored semi-auto, in Hoight's direction. The Parkland Deputy's face registered shock and anticipation of terror.

Concho fired again, double tapping two rounds into the man's back and then following up with a third shot to the cranium.

The would-be shooter's body stiffened, his head jutting forward, and then back before slumping down. Concho figured the last shot had done the job, but kept his pistol trained on the adversary until he was able to place the sole of his boot on the man's outstretched gun hand. He bent down and pulled the gun, a Beretta 92F, from the slack fingers. Once he'd done that, he tossed the Beretta to the side and holstered his own weapon. Then he withdrew his cuffs and shackled the man's hands behind his back.

"He dead?" Hoight asked.

Concho checked for a pulse in the carotid, felt nothing, and nodded.

Hoight exhaled loudly.

"Damn, you saved my life," he said. "Thanks."

Concho nodded again.

"How's the other one?" he asked.

"In custody. Gave up without a fight, which means I'd better get back to my rookie. I just ran over here because you didn't answer your radio."

"Had better things to do," Concho said. He began patting down the body and was only semi-surprised to find the dead man was wearing body armor. He mentioned this to Hoight.

"Shit," he said. "I'd better get back and check the other one."

Hoight turned and jogged back to the Lexus.

Concho switched his radio back to the regular frequency and called the base.

"Go ahead, Ten-Wolves," the dispatcher said.

After giving his location and details of the incident, he finished with, "Better notify the duty officer and send out a shooting investigation team. One suspect DRT."

"Ten-four." The dispatcher's tone had taken on a more serious tone.

DRT, Concho thought. Dead Right There.

He decided to leave the dead man handcuffed where he was and not to disturb the scene any more. It was going to be a long night, stretching well into the morning.

Finding nothing in the man's pockets except a burner phone, Concho picked up the Beretta and slipped it into the pocket of his blouse before heading over to Hoight's position.

Cate was standing over a second assailant who was sitting on the ground with his hands secured behind him. The rookie smiled.

"Glad to see you're all right," he said.

"Put that guy in our squad car," Hoight said, "after you secure his weapon and search him twice."

"Twice?" Cate asked.

"Twice," Hoight said. "Remember, the gun you don't find is the one that kills you."

The rookie grinned, holstered his own weapon, and lifted the man to his feet.

"This guy's got on a vest," Cate said. He pulled the man's jacket down and undid the Velcro straps freeing the Kevlar garment. Cate found a small .380 in a holster sewn into the inner side of the vest.

"Look at that," the rookie said. "Looks like you were right, Terrill."

"Your training officer's always right," Hoight said. "You'd best remember that."

Cate's grin was ear-to-ear.

"*Chingate*," the man muttered.

"What'd he say?" Cate asked.

"It's a term of endearment in Spanish," Concho said.

Hoight laughed. "You don't really want us to tell you, do you?"

Cate compressed his lips and said nothing as he frisked the rest of the man's body. He came up with another burner phone similar to the one that Concho had found.

"All right," Hoight said. "Secure him and put that stuff in the trunk while we check on the people in the car."

He kept his weapon drawn, but at the ready. Concho withdrew his again and advanced on the crashed Lexus. After assuring there was no one in the front or back seats, they went around to the rear and opened the lid. There were six young, nubile girls huddled together in an impossible-looking tangle in the back section. They looked young, perhaps twelve to fifteen, their eyes opened wide in the moonlight.

"*Por favor*," one said. "*No matanos Señores.*"

Please don't kill us…these girls had apparently been through hell.

"*No se preocupe*," Concho said, in his most reassuring tone and told them no one would hurt them. He holstered his weapon and reached inside, helping the first one out. This seemed to do little to quell the girls' fear.

They were all fairly pretty girls but smelled like it had been quite a while since any of them had had a bath. Their clothes, loose-fitting T-shirts and blue jeans, were caked with sweat and dirt. Each wore a red-colored wristband made of some sturdy-looking plastic.

After all six of them had been removed from the Lexus Concho asked if any of them were injured. They all shook their heads.

Ah, the resiliency of youth, he thought.

But who knew what they had gone through to get here.

"*¿De donde son ustedes?*" he asked.

The girls glanced at each other, not saying anything.

Finally, the one who appeared to be the oldest replied. "*Nicaragua. Todas.*"

Cate came sauntering back, clapping his hands back and forth in a gesture that suggested a task well completed.

"He's all buckled in," he said, referring to the prisoner. "I still wish you'd tell me what that word means, though. What was it? *Chingate?*"

The heads of the six girls jerked in unison, and Concho chuckled. "*El puede hablar español solemente pequito.*"

This seemed to make them laugh a little.

Concho wondered what they'd been through to get here, and where they would end up now.

But wherever is it, he thought, *it'll no doubt be better than where they were bound for before we intervened.*

He was well aware of the abuses and sadistic treatment that young girls like these would be subjected to at the hands of predators.

"I seen them putting some backpacks into the SUV," Cate said, striding over to the vehicle and leaning inside.

He pulled up the back flooring section designed for storing the spare tire and other items.

"Un-huh," he said triumphantly. "Just like I told ya."

The rookie pulled out the two backpacks that Concho had seen being loaded into the vehicle and slammed them down onto the ground, his expression eager.

"I bet I know what this is," he said, pulling open one of the backpacks.

"Hey, watch it," Hoight said, but it was too late.

As Cate began to stand up the smile on his face faded and his head lolled to the side, eyes suddenly closing. His body twisted in sections, the legs first, his arms waggling in almost spasmodic fashion.

"Shit," Hoight said, stepping forward and dragging his now unconscious partner away. "It's got to be fentanyl."

Concho ushered the six girls off to the side and told them to sit on the ground, reassuring them again that no one would hurt them. He went over to the rookie, who was still unconscious.

"You got Narcan?" he asked.

Hoight was already pulling the small spray bottle out of his vest pocket and unscrewing the top. He placed the nipple-end into Cate's left nostril and squeezed the bottle. Cate's breathing started to come back to regularity and his eyes opened. He took another breath and started to smile and then his eyes rolled back into his head again.

Concho called for an ambulance adding that an officer was down with an accidental OD.

Hoight squeezed the spray bottle into Cate's other nostril.

The rookie's eyes opened again after a few seconds but then closed.

"Take it easy," Hoight said. "You must have inhaled some fentanyl dust. You're going to be all right. Ambulance is on the way. Just breathe normally."

Concho ran to his truck and retrieved his canteen. When he got back, Cate was still conscious but groggy. Pulling out his handkerchief, Concho poured some water on it and gently wiped around Cate's mouth, nose, cheeks, and chin. The kid's eyes danced like bouncing marbles, but he seemed to have regained control of himself.

At least he seems to have come out of it, Concho thought.

The six girls were still huddled together, their arms around each other, shivering in the cold night air. The two backpacks lay nearby.

Nothing good ever happens at three in the morning, Concho reminded himself.

Then, in the distance Concho could hear the wail of sirens, at least one of them with the steady, non-staccato beat of an ambulance. He looked again at Cate, who still seemed to be conscious and breathing almost normally. The rookie managed what appeared to be a smile.

"Man," he said. "That was quick."

"It usually is," Concho said. "But that Narcan brought you out of it."

"Thank God," Cate said.

Concho reached out and gave the rookie's shoulder a reassuring pat.

Well, he thought, *maybe something good finally did happen at three in the morning after all.*

CHAPTER THREE

CONCHO SAT IN THE AIR-CONDITIONED INTERVIEW ROOM AT THE Maverick County Sheriff's Police Station with his elbows resting on the table as he contemplated his current situation. It was windowless to the outside world, except for the big mirrored window section on the wall opposite to his chair. He knew the mirror was really a section of one-way glass allowing those standing on the other side in the hallway to observe the occupants of the interview room without being seen. That they'd placed him in a room normally reserved for interviewing suspects didn't bother him all that much. He'd been expecting it. The killing of a man in the line of duty, even one such as this, had to be investigated, especially in today's anti-police political climate. But he also knew he'd acted properly and had nothing to hide. Still, however, he felt exhausted.

Just as long as I don't go to sleep, he told himself.

Only the guilty fell asleep in interview rooms.

Rather than watch his flat reflection staring back at him, he buried his face in his hands and reviewed the incident one more time in his mind. After the arrival of the backup units and the ambulance, dispatch advised him that the shooting investigation team was en route and for him to remain at the scene. He'd confirmed receipt of those orders and went back to sit in his truck and collect his thoughts. Hoight waited as well in his squad as the site began to come alive with portable lights and evidence techs and police investigators swarming all over the place. What had been the scene of a lonely, isolated police stop only a little while before had been transformed into a human anthill. Concho reviewed the entire incident, from them first spotting the illegals, to the chase in the night, to the shooting itself.

Totally justified, he told himself once again. No other way to put it.

He'd walked the first members of the shooting team to arrive through all the steps leading up to and after the shooting. He didn't know these guys, but assumed they were from Ranger Internal Affairs. After listening to his account, and him showing them where the expended shell casings had fallen, they confiscated both of his Double Eagles and told him to go wait in one of the unmarked squad cars.

"I'd just as soon wait in my truck," he said. "I don't fit too well in a regular sized car."

The IA man assessed Concho's large frame and snorted.

"We'll see if we can drum up a Tahoe or something," the IA man said with a grin. "Your trunk's gonna have to be towed. It's part of the overall crime scene investigation now."

Concho had figured as much and wondered if the F-150 would even be drivable. That tactical police spin that he'd executed had caused some body damage.

At least I'll be giving some more business to John Gray-Dove, Concho thought, thinking that at least this would make the Reservation mechanic happy. And John, knowing the Department of Public Safety was picking up the tab, would be sure not to spare the expenses.

It'll be like having a new truck, Concho thought.

That had been hours ago and Concho felt he'd been cooped up in this room for way longer than necessary. He looked at his watch again.

0755.

Technically, he was still on duty since the detail didn't officially end until 0800. He had been hoping to shoot over to Maria's place and take her out to breakfast like he'd promised. She'd be leaving for work soon and he wondered if she'd tried to call him.

They'd taken his cell phone, too. Why, he didn't know. And both of his forty- fives, even though only one had been fired.

Just go with the flow, he kept telling himself.

But his anger was building, and he intended on getting back the unfired Double Eagle and his cell phone before he left.

Another pressing need asserted itself and Concho stood up. After giving his body a stretch, he went to the door and twisted the knob.

Locked.

"What the go to hell?" he muttered and debated whether to try and force the lock or throw one of the chairs through the glass window. Neither one seemed like a sensible option, so he raised his arm and gave the solid metal door a rhythmic pounding. After the better part of thirty seconds the door swung open and the same IA man he'd met out at the scene appeared.

"What's the problem, Ten-Wolves?" the IA man said.

"The problem is, I got to piss. And I need to make a phone call." He glared down at the man, who was about six inches or so shorter than Concho. "And what's the idea of locking me in here like I'm some kind of suspect?"

The IA man's eyebrow rose upward.

"Sorry," he said. "We're waiting for the rest of the investigative team to arrive."

"The rest of the team?"

"They're coming from San Antonio."

This wasn't making a lot of sense to Concho. He was just about to say something else, like he was now off-duty and was leaving, shooting investigative team or not, when he heard a familiar voice in the hallway.

"Let that man by, Rodgers," Captain Dalton Shaw said. "He's out of here."

Rodgers whirled.

"But, Captain, the rest of the—"

"I don't give a damn," Shaw said. "He's already given his preliminary statement and he deserves to get some sleep before he's interviewed any further."

Concho felt good about his boss's support, but this whole thing wasn't sitting right with him. He'd been in shootings before. Hell, at one time he'd singlehandedly wiped out a half dozen or so Aryan Brotherhood terrorists at a shopping mall. They hadn't kept him half this long back then, and that was when he was under the command of a boss that didn't like him. Shaw was fair and Concho knew that the captain held him in high esteem.

"Thanks, Captain," Concho said, pushing by Rodgers.

He made his way to the washroom and immediately went to the row of urinals, the feeling of relief sweeping over him as he relieved himself. When he'd finished, he went to the sink and washed his hands, then took off his hat, set it on an adjacent sink. Bending over, he cupped both of his hands under the faucet, filled them with cool water and tossed it over his face. When he straightened up he caught sight of Shaw's reflection in the mirror. Concho grabbed a handful of paper towels and wiped off his face.

"I think I just got rid of that gallon of coffee I had last night," he said.

Shaw didn't smile.

"So you want to tell me what's going on?" Concho asked. "This investigation thing's getting more complicated than a presidential colonoscopy."

That brought the trace of a grin to the captain's face, but only for a moment.

"It's complicated, all right." He took in a deep breath and

exhaled. "You've got to remember that this detail was a special, multi-agency task force affair."

"What's that supposed to mean?"

"It means, that as you said, it's complicated." He blew out another long breath. "In other words, we've got too many damn cooks spoiling the broth."

Concho wasn't liking the sound of this at all, but he said nothing, waiting for Shaw to continue.

"In other words," he said, "to ensure multi-jurisdictional integrity, it's been decided to bring in a multi-jurisdictional investigative team."

"Multi-jurisdictional?"

Shaw nodded.

"We've got Rodgers. He's a Ranger. A good man from our Internal Affairs division. They're also bringing in Maverick County IA, and somebody from the DA's office."

That didn't sound too outlandish to Concho. After all, Hoight was Maverick County and he and Cate had been in on the chase and the aftermath. Hoight had almost gotten shot, and the poor rookie had OD'd.

"They'll want to talk to you about what happened to that rookie, too," Shaw said. "There's concern that he wasn't properly supervised."

"That's bullshit, but what does that have to do with the shooting?"

Shaw shook his head. It was obvious he was almost as frustrated as Concho was. He held up his hands, palms outward.

"They're tying the whole magilla together, the illegals, the chase, the crashes, the shooting, and the kid's exposure to the drugs. Plus, since it was initially a federal violation, with the unlawful border crossing, the DOJ is coming in to take a look as well."

"The DOJ? Those assholes couldn't find their asses with both hands."

Shaw chuckled out loud this time.

"Concho, we're on the same sheet of music here, believe

me. But it's the times we're living in right now." He gave his head another little shake. "Believe me, I'm on your side. However, my hands are tied."

"Which means what? Hoight and me are gonna be squeezed through the wringer by a bunch of pencil-pushing geeks that don't have the faintest idea what it's like out here?"

"It's not that bad. I've reviewed the preliminary report and your statement. Off the record, of course, and it was a good shoot."

"You're damn right it was. The son of a bitch was going to shoot Hoight. Plus, he was wearing body armor. These guys weren't your run-of-the-mill smugglers. There's something more going on here."

"So leave it to the powers that be to investigate it," Shaw said. "In the meantime, you're on administrative leave."

Concho scrunched up his face.

"But—"

"No buts. Besides, you're up for your mandatory training cycle anyway."

All Rangers were required to undergo a certain number of hours of training each year. Concho had been notified about it, but had kept pushing it back.

Shaw reached up and clapped Concho on the shoulder.

"Go home. Get some sleep. Report to the range tomorrow morning."

"The range? You gonna give me my guns back? They took both of them, even though one of them hadn't been fired."

"I'll look into that. I know how attached you are to those Double Eagles. But ironically, we're transitioning to a new duty weapon anyway."

"A new weapon? What is it?"

"Wait and see." Shaw patted Concho's shoulder again and steered him toward the door. "Training and qualification's tomorrow. In the meantime, let's get the hell out of this place. We don't want people to start any ugly rumors about you and me hanging out in the washroom."

Concho grinned. If he hadn't been so irritated and so tired, he might have laughed.

Shaw reached into his pocket and held out Concho's cell phone.

"Here," he said. "I liberated this for you. You want me to loan you a gun until you get to the range tomorrow morning?"

"No, I want my Double Eagles back."

Shaw smirked. "You know, you are one stubborn Indian."

"Do you know any other kind? So don't be an *Indian giver* and get my damn guns back."

"You know the protocol on that," Shaw said. "Not till the shooting inquiry's finished."

"They don't need both my guns. I only fired one of them."

Shaw raised his eyebrows and considered this.

"Good point," he said. "But…"

Concho frowned. "And my truck's going to need some repairs. Any chance you can get me a loaner in the meantime?"

Shaw shook his head. "You won't need one since you're on administrative leave. I'll see if I can have a unit drop you off."

"And how the hell am I supposed to get around?"

Shaw flashed a grin. "There's always that ride service. What do they call it? Uber?"

"Yeah, right."

"Or maybe your buddy, Gray-Dove, can help you out. You're going to have your truck towed to his place anyway, aren't you?"

Concho took in a deep breath and nodded.

He glanced at his phone, which showed he'd had five unanswered calls from Maria Morales that morning. He didn't want to take the time to listen to the voice mail messages now. The time was 0826.

Still not too late to call her. Maybe she could swing by and pick him up. They could grab a quick breakfast and then she could drop him at Gray-Dove's.

"Go ahead," Shaw said. "Call your lady. And in the meantime, let me see about getting your unfired Colt back for you now. But don't forget that range training tomorrow. And you'll be doing your training and qualification with your new gun."

New gun, Concho thought. *No way.*

But he didn't say anything. The time wasn't right.

Shaw walked off down the hall as Concho scrolled down to Maria's number and pressed the CALL button.

CHAPTER FOUR

Maria answered on the first ring.

"Where've you been?" Her tone was somewhat angry, but also laced with a bit of concern. "I've been trying to get a hold of you all morning."

"Sorry, babe. I was working last night." He paused, debating whether to tell her more, then decided it was better to get it all out. "I was involved in a shooting."

Her gasp was audible.

"Are you all right?"

"Yeah," he said. "Just a little tired is all. I would've called you earlier but they took my phone. And my guns."

He heard Maria's gasp once more.

"So…is everything okay?"

Concho debated just how to answer that one. If he were honest, he'd have to tell her no, but he didn't want to worry her unnecessarily. Besides, he was convinced it was a good shoot, so his vindication would be forthcoming. He'd just have to wait in the limbo of administrative leave until the pencil-pushers finished their bean counting. In the meantime, hopefully Shaw could get one of his Colt Double Eagles back, and maybe Gray-Dove could loan him a truck.

"It will be," he said. "I just have to wait for the investigators to look over things."

But he silently wondered just how long that would actually be.

"So you haven't been to bed yet?" she asked.

"No, but I'm catching my second wind. In fact, I'm in need of some heavy nourishment." He checked the time again and saw it was now 0840. She had to be on her way into work by now. "You want to pick me up and I'll buy you breakfast someplace?"

"Pick you up?"

"Yeah. My truck's down for the count so I could use a lift."

"I wish I could," she said. "But I'm on my way in now. Have to go in early. That's why I called you before. Didn't you listen to my messages?"

From the sound of her voice, he could tell she was a bit miffed.

Honesty is the best policy, he reminded himself, and said, "I was about to, but I decided to call you first. Like I said, I just got my phone back a few minutes ago."

"Your phone?"

"Right. Why they took it is anybody's guess, but the brass has now called in a bunch of bureaucrats, state and federal, to go over everything with a fine-tooth comb. Maybe they wanted to download all my text messages to see who I voted for in the last election."

Maria laughed. "And who did you vote for? You never told me."

"Actually, I didn't vote. I was taught in the police academy to be apolitical."

"Why are the feds involved?"

It was Concho's turn to sigh. "Who knows? The overtime detail I was working involved the border. Illegals crossing with a bunch of fentanyl. Like I told you, it got a little messy—a car chase and the shooting. Because it's border blood, now the DOJ wants to poke its nose into things."

After several seconds of silence, Maria came back on the line.

"Sounds miserable," she said.

"That's kind of an understatement."

"Well, if you had listened to my messages, you'd know that I'm on the way in because there's a VIP coming to the mall this morning."

She paused, obviously waiting for him to inquire.

After what he felt was a sufficient amount of time to border on feigned apathy, he playfully responded.

"Okay, I'll bite. Who is it?"

"None other than..." Again, she paused to maximize the suspense before adding, "Vince Hawk. The movie star."

The name stunned Concho.

Vince Hawk had been known as Vincent Swooping Hawk back in the day when he was growing up on the Reservation. At least ten years older than Concho, he remembered Hawk as an aloof, sullen teenager who mostly ignored Concho's elementary school age youthfulness. It had been a tough time in his life. Although Swooping Hawk hadn't been among the other, slightly older young toughs who'd ridiculed and harassed and beat Concho with regularity, Swooping Hawk had not stepped in to stop the constant bullying either. It had been as if the plight of the half-Indian, half-Black young Concho Ten-Wolves had been beneath the older boy's notice or interest. A few times he'd watched and laughed at the proceedings. By the time Concho had matured and grown enough to stand up to the bullies, Swooping Hawk had left the Rez, heading for greener pastures. He dropped the "Swooping" prefix from his name, and shortened his first name to Vince, showing off a fairly impressive riding prowess on the rodeo circuit that had attracted the notice of a well-known White movie actor who was trying to resurrect the western. Vince Hawk, though not yet twenty years old, was given a speaking role as Taza, the son of Cochise, the great Indian warrior, in the White movie star's new motion picture. The studio publicity hounds immediately played up the fact that an actual "Native American" had been chosen for this role in the new film, and pointed out the dubious and culturally inappropriate casting of a White actor, Rock Hudson, who had played the same character in another movie decades before.

Yeah, the times, they were a changing.

Real Native Americans playing real Native Americans the movie heading had advertised.

It seemed to work wonders at the box office.

Hawk, for his part, immediately latched onto the publicity train by claiming to be half-Apache. Whether he was or not, Concho didn't know, but he did remember seeing the movie and thinking that someone he knew, somebody from the Rez, being in an actual motion picture was kind of cool. Hawk went on to become something of a minor celebrity by Hollywood standards, appearing in a few more movies and some television shows, usually playing, what else? An Indian. One thing about him, the man had never looked back, nor even mentioned his association to the Kickapoo tribe, or the Reservation.

Until now.

"What? Has he got a new movie coming out, or something?" Concho asked, not trying to conceal his indifference.

"Better than that," Maria said. "He's producing and starring in a new one about Geronimo. And he's going to be holding a big casting call right here in Eagle Pass. At the mall. He's promised to use a bunch of locals in the movie. Everybody's really excited."

The prodigal son returns, Concho thought.

"That's why I'm heading in early," she said. "We're having a big buffet in the mall office for him and he's going to be speaking in the center court section. I've got all my mall security coming in and Maverick County's sending a contingent over too, to help with the crowds. We're expecting a whole lot of people, especially with the casting call and try-outs being announced. Ah, it would be real nice if you could be there, too."

She'd added that last line rather quickly, slipping it in like an afterthought, although Concho figured it was anything but.

Five voice mails.

"All right," he said. "Let me find a way home and grab something to eat first. I might even take a shower and change my shirt too."

"That would be nice."

"Hey." The merriment came back into his voice. "I said *might*. I'll still have to find a loaner truck, you know."

Maria laughed too and told him to come by her office as soon as he could.

"Roger that," he answered, recalling Cate the rookie's formal radio protocol from the night before.

He made a note to stop by the hospital later to see how the kid was doing.

CHAPTER FIVE

CONCHO ESTIMATED THAT HE'D BEEN UP CLOSE TO TWENTY-seven hours straight and was feeling the strain as he watched as John Gray-Dove secured the mangled front end of Concho's F-150 in the sling and elevating the winch. The smile on his face spoke volumes. Concho had become one of his best customers. After securing the front wheels in the rubber stirrups, Gray-Dove gestured for Concho to get in the passenger side of the tow truck. He did so, having to leverage himself into the compartment. He had to remove his Stetson and banged his knees on the dashboard. Gray-Dove, who was about six inches shorter than Concho, slid behind the wheel with a practiced ease, although he too had to remove his cowboy hat exposing his short-cropped black hair. He'd kept it short after his military service, and even though he was over forty, it showed no trace of the gray that dominated his eyes. As soon as they were settled in the cab, Gray-Dove buckled up and told Concho to do the same.

The Ranger reluctantly complied, and the other man laughed.

"The way you drive," Gray-Dove said, "that should be an

automatic and unspoken commandment any time you get into a vehicle."

Concho adjusted the shoulder strap over his massive chest.

"This truck seems smaller for some reason." Concho glanced down as Gray-Dove manipulated a long gearshift. The gears made a ratcheting grinding sound and the truck suddenly lurched forward. "And I don't remember it being a stick, either."

Gray-Dove chuckled. "It's tow truck number two. You should be a detective."

"Very funny. What's the story on this beast?"

"I picked it up as a spare for a song and a dance," Gray-Dove said. "Now I got two, and the way you go through vehicles, both of them'll get plenty of use."

Concho frowned. "I'm going to need a loaner for a couple days."

Gray-Dove shifted into second gear and the tow truck continued to trundle forward.

"A big outfit like the Rangers can't afford another truck for their best man?" he asked.

"Their best man's on administrative leave right now. I was involved in a shooting last night."

Gray-Dove chuckled again.

"So? That's business as usual for you, ain't it?"

Concho was feeling ill at ease due to the cramped quarters and the lack of sleep. He debated again whether or not to go to the mall to see Maria. But then again, if Vince Hawk, the movie star, was going to be there...

"It was on the border and now the DOJ's involved."

"The DOJ? What do those assholes have to do with anything down this way? Hell, from the looks of it, they want to keep as far away from the border as possible."

"Little did I know when I signed up for some OT that it was a federally sponsored assignment."

"Sounds like a bunch of bullshit to me," Gray-Dove said.

"Yeah, but as you know, you got to play the hand you're

dealt." Concho shifted in the seat again and banged his knee on the dashboard again. "So what are the chances of getting a truck on loan?"

Gray-Dove smiled.

"Shouldn't be a problem," he said. "In fact, I can just let you use this baby." He reached up and patted the dashboard, which, in addition to being caked with dust, had a series of cracks creating an appearance of fragility. "Of course, I'll need you to be on call for any tows that might come up."

If Concho hadn't been so tired, he would have laughed, but fatigue gave way into momentary anger. He quickly dismissed the feeling. The truth was that Gray-Dove had always gone the extra yard for him, getting his vehicles fixed up and back in running order in an expeditious fashion.

The other man must have sensed Concho's irritation.

"Sorry, big fella," he said. "I didn't mean to make light of your troubles."

Concho waved his hand dismissively. "You know what the elders say. If one can laugh in the face of trouble, the evil spirits are kept away."

"Don't remember that one."

"Me either," Concho said. "I just made it up. Now what about that loaner?"

"As much business as you give to me," Gray-Dove said, "I'd be a fool not to take care of you. Maybe I can scrounge up a set of wheels for that old El Camino I been working on."

"What, did you steal some road signs and weld them over the holes in the floorboards?" Concho said. The El Camino was one of those perpetual repair projects that Gray-Dove was always working on and source of humor between the two of them.

"Hey," Gray-Dove said, "that ain't such a bad idea. Know where I can find some?"

Now it was Concho's turn to chuckle, and he thought how good it felt to be joking with his friend even though the overwhelming fatigue kept gnawing at him.

"So you got anything I could use or not?" he asked.

Gray-Dove shot him a quick glance accompanied by a mischievous grin.

"Sure do," he said. "And she's a beauty, too."

* * *

APPROXIMATELY FIFTY MINUTES LATER, CONCHO, HAVING JUST showered, and laid out his standard work uniform of white shirt, black jeans, and boots. The combination of the hot water, which he turned to icy cold at the end, had revived him so that he almost felt vigorous. He thought back to the long-ago time of his vision quest—the running, the endless fatigue, the visions…it had been an arduous path, but it had taught him the value of strength, rest, and renewal. It also had taught him how to push himself beyond the boundaries of what most men considered normal. He could reach deep down into those residual pockets of strength that few know they have. His vision quest had taught him much.

Although when he'd first driven back to his trailer in the cramped tow truck—Gray-Dove's self-described "beauty," he'd wanted nothing more than to crawl into bed, now he felt good enough to face whatever challenges were in front of him. Plus, he knew that Maria was counting on him showing up. Why, exactly, he didn't know. She'd hosted celebrities at the Eagle Pass Mall before, but none with the notoriety of Vince Hawk. There was also another reason why he wanted to make this event at Eagle Pass Mall. Concho was a bit curious to recon-nect with the man. It had been a good, long while since their paths had crossed…back to his early days on the Kickapoo Reservation. And while they'd never been what could be termed friends, Concho did hold a certain amount of respect and awe for what Hawk had accomplished.

Or was it merely envy?

That too, he thought as he put on his sleeveless, black T-shirt and then slipped into his black jeans and boots. His boots were highly shined, but he buffed the toes a bit by rubbing each one of them on the back of his jeans pant leg—an old Army trick when wearing Class A's or a dress uniform. "If a soldier looks sharp," one of his drill sergeants had said, "he feels sharp."

This outfit was his typical work uniform, but this morning he had selected a shirt that had been starched and pressed at the cleaners. After removing the plastic covering and looping the hanger on the top of the open door to his bedroom, Concho started to affix the circular Texas Ranger badge in place. Stopping, he instead went to his miscellaneous drawer in the kitchen and removed a small tube of polishing cream. After squeezing out a minute amount, he buffed the badge with a rag until it shone like a polished gem. Then he pinned it to his shirt and slipped the garment on, thinking he'd look very respectable until he reached for his double-holstered gun-belt. Then he realized that he had only one of his Colt Eagles. It wouldn't do to appear with an empty holster. That was the pejorative nickname the rank and files gave to the brass— "Empty Holsters."

No way was he going to project an image like that.

He set the gun-belt aside and went searching for one of his pancake holsters. Unbuckling his belt, Concho threaded his belt through the loops of the pancake and affixed it into place. Sliding the Colt into the holster, he secured it with the thumb-strap and also retrieved a detachable magazine holder and fitted that into place as well. Taking a moment to assess himself, he noticed that the silver belt buckle wasn't quite as shiny as it could have been.

Giving the buckle a quick dash with the same rag he'd used on the badge, he reflected on why he'd been going through the elaborate ritual. Certainly, he wanted to impress Maria, but he wondered how much Vince Hawk factored into his preening? A memory of Hawk's symmetrical face, replete with an aquiline nose, high cheekbones, and a chiseled jaw flashed in Concho's mind's eye.

Was he worried about the handsome movie star's effect on

Maria? She was hardly a wide-eyed schoolgirl. Or, deep down, was he a bit jealous of the regal looking and most likely very rich celebrity?

He and Hawk had both sprung from the same indigenous poverty of the Rez. He'd raised himself up through the military and then the Texas Rangers. Yet he was living in a trailer on the far reaches of the Reservation and using Gray-Dove's beat-up old secondary tow truck while Vince Hawk would most likely lived in a mansion and would be arriving in a long, black limousine

Glancing at his watch, Concho saw that ten minutes more had expired while he was doing his preening.

Aw, hell, he thought, smoothing back his long, black hair and slipping his hat on his head. Best get on with it. I'm close enough for government work.

As he moved to the door, he sensed something, and his hand lowered automatically to the Colt Double Eagle. Opening the door a crack, he took a quick peek around his yard. The tow truck was still in place, dented and splattered with mud, the large mesquite tree rustled slightly with an arid breeze. Everything else seemed in order…except the area by the fire pit.

Meskwaa sat in one of the lawn chairs smoking, his back to the trailer.

Concho closed the door behind him and walked softly down the steps.

"Has the eagle finished preening his feathers so that he may attract a mate?" the old man said.

He still hadn't turned around, and Concho figured that Meskwaa must have been alerted by the slight noise of the door closing. How he knew Concho had been preening was another matter, but the tribal elder's ways always defied an easy explanation.

"Welcome," Concho said, moving across the yard and taking a seat in the largest of the lawn chairs.

"How bad's your truck?" Meskwaa asked.

"Bad enough," Concho replied. He debated telling him about the shooting investigation.

"Figures."

Meskwaa drew in on the sparse, filterless butt of the glowing cigarette and let the smoke leak slowly out of his mouth. As the grayish vapor evaporated, he used his forefinger and thumb to crush out the embers and then dropped the residual bit of unburned tobacco into his shirt pocket.

Concho was feeling the strain of wanting to get to the mall, but he knew better than to dismiss the wise one. He'd obviously come here with a purpose in mind. Nor did Concho want to prompt him. Such was not the way of things. Instead, he merely sat back in his lawn chair and waited.

Meskwaa's ways were well known to Concho. The old man was not only one of the tribal elders who had watched over Concho during his vision quest many years ago, but Meskwaa was also a *Chupacabra*—a medicine man. His purpose for appearing here today would no doubt soon become clear.

The old man's eyes roamed over Concho's big frame. After a time, Meskwaa's head jerked with a fractional nod and a trace of a smile teased his lips.

"You look good," he said. "Shiny and new, like the clear and clean dawning a new day, despite not having had any rest."

This made Concho smile as well. How the old man knew that he hadn't slept was a mystery, but Meskwaa's ways were as mysterious and complex as they were legendary.

Concho said nothing, even though internally he felt a growing anxiety.

"I know you must leave soon, to see your woman," Meskwaa said. "But first, I must tell you. I had a vision."

CHAPTER SIX

CONCHO HAD LEARNED LONG AGO THE SIGNIFICANCE OF Meskwaa's visions. Although their meaning was not always initially clear, At times they defied any easy explanation, but Concho never disregarded them. He leaned forward and waited, as a sign of respect, for the old man to continue. In due time, he did.

"There's a storm coming," Meskwaa said. He closed his eyes and allowed his head to loll back a bit. "Dark clouds overhead, enveloping everything in a shroud of darkness. The sun is nowhere to be seen."

Concho wondered if the world was due for a total solar eclipse. The vision sounded ominous.

Meskwaa held up his hands.

"Lightning...thunder..." He paused, and then added, "The specter of death hangs heavy in the air." His head inched forward, slowly like he was bowing slightly. "I saw an owl—the worst of signs, and then a herd of wild horses chased by shadows."

"Shadows?"

The old man didn't reply and remained incredibly still for several more seconds, then his body relaxed, the tenseness dissipating, and he looked at Concho. The description had sent a warning chill racing up along Concho's spine.

Their eyes locked for a moment, and then Meskwaa smiled.

"I have delayed you long enough," he said. "You had better be on your way to the *Mall de las Aguilas*. Your fair lady awaits, does she not?"

Concho smiled too. "She does. And so does Vince Hawk."

Meskwaa's eyebrows rose for an instant in unison and a questioning expression formed over his lined face.

"Vincent Swooping Hawk? He has returned?"

"He has," Concho said. "I'm going to meet him this morning."

Meskwaa's head moved back and forth with a minute, nodding motion.

"I remember him when he was a boy," he said, "as I am sure you do as well."

"Yes," Concho said. Memories of the tall, slightly older and highly charismatic figure of years ago flooded his mind's eye once again.

"Then it's best for you to tread carefully," he said. "There is much yet to be revealed, and the hawk is always a clever and formidable adversary."

"I'm not looking for a confrontation," Concho said, but at the same time he did feel a bit uneasy about this Indian movie star being around Maria. Reports of the man's romantic conquests, whether true or not, were the stuff of constant attention in the press and the paparazzi followed him around like a pack of jackals. Concho knew Maria took her job seriously and guarded her professional reputation. The last thing she would want would be to be featured on the cover of some scandal sheet suggesting that she was Vince Hawk's new love interest.

"Confrontations may well spring from nothing," Meskwaa said, rising from the chair, "when two stallions vie for the same mare."

Concho did his best to swallow his growing anxiety.

I'm just being stupid, he told himself. Making something out of nothing.

He trusted Maria and knew that she could handle someone like Hawk, if he acted inappropriately. She was as smart as she was beautiful. Putting his feeling off to his fatigue and lack of sleep, he called on those reserves of energy and strength he knew he possessed to keep him moving forward on a steady course.

He glanced at his watch.

Nine-fifty-five.

It was time to get moving. He had just enough time to get to the mall before the early opening.

"I have to go," he said, getting to his feet. "Can I drop you somewhere?"

Meskwaa chuckled and gestured toward the tow truck.

"Being seen in that contraption would be bad for my reputation," he said and began walking.

Concho had known that Meskwaa preferred to get around by his own power. His perambulations were also a part of his character.

Fishing the keys out of his pocket, Concho headed for the tow truck.

"Take much care," Meskwaa called out. "The trail has many turns ahead."

It usually does, Concho thought as he grabbed the door handle and swung his leg up into the truck.

Time to meet the Hawk, he thought.

CHAPTER SEVEN

As Concho approached the *Mall de las Aguilas* he noticed the long line of cars lining Bibbs Avenue. Apparently, Vince Hawk's appearance and the pending casting call had attracted a lot of would-be movie actors. A couple of mall security guards had been stationed at the main entrance and were directing the flow of traffic to a designated parking area. A pair of long orange and white road-blocking sawhorses blocked the adjacent exit lane from the mall. Another set of barriers funneled the traffic to the right and toward the main parking lot. The long line was moving slower than a turtle crossing a four-lane Texas highway. Regretting that he wasn't in his F-150 with the special emergency lights he could activate to bypass the line, Concho once again checked his watch. It was now ten-twenty-five. At the rate this line was going, he would be lucky to get in there inside of fifteen minutes and the lot was filling up fast.

Then he got struck by an idea.

Scanning the ancient dashboard, Concho found a toggle switch that he assumed was what he was looking for. He flipped it on and heard the grating rotation of the yellow mars lights on top of the roof.

Not emergency red lights, he thought, *but close enough.*

He swung around the line of cars and sped toward the entrance, cutting in front of the first set of vehicles at the entrance and attracting a chorus of blaring horns.

One of the security guards ran over to the driver's window, his face twisting into a scowl.

"Hey," the guard said, "you can't cut in line here."

The scowl vanished as he drew abreast of the driver's door and saw Concho behind the wheel.

"Oh, Ranger Ten-Wolves," the guard said. "I didn't recognize you, sir."

The oscillating yellow lights alternately flashed on and off as the beams swept over the security badge on the guard's hat as he stood there smiling, adulation dominating his eyes and expression.

All of the mall personnel know Concho not only because of his frequent trips to visit Maria, but also for the one-man crusade he'd conducted several months ago when a group of Aryan Nation terrorists had taken over the mall and held people hostage. Concho had entered the mall and taken them out, one-by-one, saving numerous lives. It was an event not easily forgotten and had enhanced the Ranger's already substantial reputation.

A trio of auto horns continued to blare and the guard took several steps back and yelled at them.

"Will you knock it off," he shouted. "This is official police business."

Concho wasn't so sure he would go as far to agree, but he let it slide.

A few of the horns continued, but a couple of the others ceased. The guard motioned at them and made a simulated cutting motion across his throat.

As the horns faded into oblivion, the guard moved back to the driver's window and asked, "Are you here for the big event, Ranger?"

"Yeah," Concho said. "Vince Hawk get here yet?"

"He sure did. Pulled up in a stretch limo with four big buses behind him. They're all parked on the other side by the rear entrance." The guard smiled. "This sure is something, ain't it?"

"Sure is," Concho said.

"Say, how come you're driving this thing? You undercover or something?"

"Something like that." Concho smiled.

"Well," the guard said, "let me move that barricade and you can pull on through. Why don't you park on the other side with the rest of the Maverick County squads?"

Concho nodded a "thanks" and shoved the gearshift into first. The gears ground like an oscillating electric fan trapped inside a metal bucket but then slipped into first. Concho let out the clutch and the tow truck bounced over the center median strip and into the exit lanes. As he pulled past the guard who was moving the barrier, Concho gave him a wave and shifted into second. Going around to the far side had its advantages. If he had his F-150, he would have just parked in a fire lane and pulled down his visor indicating the truck's police vehicle status. The truck would be almost as good.

Down below, he saw the two massive brick pillars, flanked by a spaced copse of palm trees, rising upward in perpendicular fashion from the asphalt of the parking lot with the *Mall de las Aguillas* in blue lettering on the uppermost sign. The list of the anchor stores followed below it in descending order. Concho knew that the place had over 1800 parking spaces and figured, from the size of the waiting vehicles, they'd all be taken, and then some. By the main front entrance, a couple of news vans had pulled onto the expansive sidewalk area. The antennae were already elevated and most likely transmitting.

Better steer clear of those, he thought, and continued around the circular perimeter road.

As he rounded the corner, he saw the buses the guard had mentioned. There were four of them, looking all shiny and gleaming in the mid-morning sunshine. Each was the size of a tour bus, their glossy black exteriors adorned with and a stunning symbol of a bright red circle outlined in yellow with the black outline of a golden lightning bolt overlaid across the design. *Thunderhawk Productions* in gold letter gracing the sides. An elongated stretch limousine was parked in the fire lane, followed by four Maverick County marked squad cars lined up behind it along the back entrance side. Concho didn't see any officers and figured them to be inside. He pulled up behind the last of the squad cars and parked.

Leaving the tow truck in reverse, he shut off the engine and hopped out of the cab. The old vehicle shook with a post-ignition tremor and then was quiet. Concho hoped that it would start up again and last long enough to get him home.

He owed Gray-Dove for this ignominy, but now wasn't the time to worry about that. He strode purposefully toward the rear employee's entrance only to find it locked. He'd forgotten that you needed a key fob to gain entry. Maria had offered to give him one, but he'd never taken her up on the offer.

Glancing at his watch, he saw it was now ten thirty-three.

He thought about taking the tow truck around to the front but decided against it. The last thing he needed right about now would be to land on the five o'clock news getting out of Gray-Dove's tow truck after leaving it in a fire lane. Instead, he started a quick walk round the perimeter toward the front entrance. It was probably close to a quarter of a mile, but he kept a brisk pace and his long legs covered the distance quickly. On the way he pulled out his cell phone and hit Maria's number. It went unanswered and went to voice mail. Instead of leaving a message, he sent a quick text, which relayed, with a few misspellings due to haste, that he was here and en route to her office. Unfortunately, the elevating mid-morning temperature had also caused him to sweat a bit more than he would have liked.

It's been a morning full of miscalculations, he thought.

When he got to the main entrance, he saw a quartet of

Maverick County and mall security officers standing in the shade of the entranceway's overhang.

They straightened up when they saw his approach.

Concho was used to his appearance causing a rise in people. At six-four and close to three hundred pounds, he knew his size could be alarming. Add to that his dark skin and long black hair, which he had pulled behind his head forming a ponytail now, and he figured the officers had gone from low to mid-level alert. He hoped the shiny crescent Texas Ranger badge would put them at ease, and he was glad he'd taken the extra time to shine it. Plus, his reputation preceded him in these parts.

"Ranger Ten-Wolves," one of the Maverick County officers said. "Didn't know you were coming today."

"Neither did I," Concho said with a grin. "Where's the group at?"

"They're up in the mall office right now," one of the security guards said. "I'm sure you know the way."

The kid flashed a knowing grin. Concho and Maria had spent some quality time up there on more than one occasion.

"That I do," Concho said, grinning back. As he strode past them, he turned to one of the deputies.

"How's Cate doing?"

The deputy shook his head.

"Poor guy's in the hospital. Word is he's gonna be all right, but they want to keep him for observation just in case. Helluva scare."

"Good thing you and Terrill were on the scene," another one said. "Probably saved his life giving him that Narcan."

"It was a good reminder to all of us to be careful around that stuff," Concho said as he pulled open the glass door and stepped out of the hot sun and into the air-conditioned coolness. Inside the mall was devoid of shoppers and pedestrians, but as he walked down the center aisle, he saw a group of workmen putting the finishing touches on a stage in the center court area. It was a fairly large platform with a microphone on a stand near the front. He went immediately through one of the back corridors leading to a stairway to go up to the second level. The escalator was a distance away, and he was counting minutes now.

After trotting up the stairs two at a time, he walked briskly toward the mall offices and Maria's office in particular. He was almost there when he heard the abrupt sound of laughter coming from the large room adjacent to Maria's office. Glancing inside, he saw a crowd of about fifteen to twenty people standing around a long table with a big fruit layout—strawberries, orange slices, green grapes, slices of pineapple and watermelon. There were about half a dozen men in suits who had the look of corporate honchos. Isaac Parkland, the sheriff of Maverick County, was there, as were a couple of his undersheriff associates whom Concho knew in passing but not well. A heavyset guy in a suit that didn't quite fit his bulky frame was standing off to the side and Concho immediately saw the guy was wearing a shoulder rig.

Probably security of some sort, Concho thought.

But after catching a glimpse of the man's eyes, Concho decided this guy somehow had "cop" written all over him. He seemed to be giving Concho more than just a little notice.

Next to him was another good-sized man, but this one had the lean, muscular look of a heavyweight boxer in prime condition. His blond hair was swept back from his forehead giving his face an almost leonine appearance, and instead of a business suit he wore a tan sport jacket and expensive looking blue jeans. The collar of his light blue shirt was open at the neck and he had a red-and-white silk handkerchief, the ends of which were fastened by a gold ring, adoring his neck. From the first two oversized knuckles on his right hand, Concho pegged him as some sort of martial artist type. He stepped toward the expanse of fruit on the long table and with the smooth elegance of a big jungle cat, swept up a small tree of grapes and began devouring them.

Everyone's focus, except the heavyset guy in the ill-fitting suit, seemed focused on two other people.

One was Maria, Concho noticed, and the other was Vincent Hawk.

He looked superb in a tailored black jacket with patterns of Indian bead-work artfully showcasing his broad shoulders and narrow waist. His hair was glossy black and fashionably coiffed so that it fell in perfect continuity along the top of his shoulders.

The crowd shifted slightly and then Concho caught sight of Maria. She was wearing an elegant dark-blue business outfit, a blazer covering a white blouse, the skirt appropriately long, yet short enough to show off an exquisite pair of legs. Her head was lolling backward in laughter, and she hadn't noticed him yet, her face the exquisite portrait of blissful amusement. Hawk, a broad smile stretched across his face, was standing next to her, his right arm encircling her waist.

Feeling an automatic surge of proprietary jealousy, Concho stepped forward into the room. Most of the men's eyes remained on Maria, but Hawk, his head tilting slightly, turned his gaze toward Concho. A smile crested his lips.

"Well, I'll be damned," he said. "Concho Ten-Wolves, as I live and breathe."

Concho made no acknowledgment, but Maria glanced over at him and stiffened. She began to shift her body away from Hawk and he slowly removed his arm from around her and held out his right hand.

"Been a long time, Ten-Wolves," he said. "I hear you're a Ranger now."

Concho accepted the man's hand and shook it, noticing that Hawk's grip was exerting substantial pressure. Usually not one to demonstrate his own powerful hand strength, Concho in this instance tightened his grip commensurately, giving as good as he got. Hawk's lips drew back across a set of stunning porcelain veneers as his smile widened into something beyond a greeting. He emitted a grunt and pulled his hand away from the shake.

"Man, they should call you Iron Hand rather than Ten-Wolves," he said, giving his hand a quick shake. "You ought to register those things as lethal weapons."

Concho felt a surge of embarrassment at having succumbed to such a juvenile response.

"Sorry," he said. "I had something of a rough night."

"Oh yeah?" Hawk's grin was back to normal now. "What's her name?"

Without waiting for a reply, he snorted and half-turned toward the two men flanking him and said, "This is the guy I was telling you about. We grew up together on the Reservation. Of course in those days he was a little shit who used to get knocked around because his daddy was—well, let's just say he's only *half* Indian." Hawk's laugh was low and guttural. The others all laughed too, except for Maria and Sheriff Parkland.

"I can't tell you how many times I had to step in and save him," Hawk continued.

That wasn't quite the way Concho remembered it, but he said nothing. Better to let this jackass pontificate in front of his minions.

"But as you can tell," Hawk said, stepping back and moving his hand to emphasize Concho's big form, "he soon grew out of that phase. By the time I left the Rez, he was the one doing all the beatings."

Again, that wasn't quite the way Concho remembered things, but he still made no comment. He was, however, getting a distinct itch to get the hell out of this place as soon as he could. Glancing at Maria, he hoped his expression adequately conveyed his displeasure.

She averted her eyes from his.

Hawk slapped his open palm against Concho's back.

"I'm glad you're here for my local talent quest, Ten-Wolves," Hawk said. "I can use a big guy as one of my extras in the new movie I'm making. Of course, the makeup man's gonna have his hands full with the likes of you."

Another laugh.

Concho was growing more irritated by the moment.

"Let me introduce you to my guys, Ten-Wolves." Hawk pointed to the guy with the silk neckerchief. "This is my good buddy, my action coordinator, and all-around badass, Jim Dandy. He's also my stunt double whenever I have to do something that requires a bit of roughness." Hawk paused to emit a low-level laugh. "Except for the love scenes, that is. I usually refer to him as Tonto."

Dandy's face crinkled, too and he shifted the tree of grapes to his left hand while holding out his right for Concho to shake.

I wonder if he knows that tonto means "stupid" in Spanish? Concho thought.

Ready this time for another ultra-macho handshake, he was surprised that this one's grip was mild and barely more than a touch, like that of a concert pianist's.

Concho noticed a bit of jagged scarring along the man's left eyebrow mixed in with the hair follicles.

"Now don't let his good looks fool you," Hawk said. "He's as fast as a timber wolf and twice as mean, when he has to be. And he's got a spinning back-kick that could knock a piece of cake off the top of your hat."

"Maybe I'll do that as part of one of my demonstration shows," Dandy said. "Either that or the two of us could spar a couple of rounds."

Again, Concho said nothing.

"And you'll dig this guy," Hawk said. "May I present my personal bodyguard and head of security, Alexander Drum."

The heavyset guy stepped forward and shook hands with Concho. Again, the man's grip was firm, but not overbearing.

"You can call me Al," the guy said.

"You and him got a lot in common," Hawk said. "He used to be Chicago PD."

Concho gave the man another once-over.

Early fifties, around six feet or so, maybe two-sixty. The guy had the look of someone who'd walked the walk, all right. There was no reticence in this one.

"Yeah, twenty-five years," Drum said with a wry grin. "Spent the majority of it on the South Side. Second District, where all the shit lives."

"That sounds like quite a career," Concho said.

"It had its moments." Drum looked him up and down. "Rough night, huh? What'd you have? A shooting?"

Concho was a bit surprised at the question and wondered if Maria had mentioned the incident to Hawk and his buddies. His head swiveled in her direction, but once again she didn't meet his gaze. Instead, she edged farther away from Hawk and turned to one of the older guys in a suit and began a conversation.

Concho couldn't hear what she was saying, but at this point didn't give a damn either.

Why the hell had she asked him here?

Her insistence mystified him, but now he made up his mind that it didn't matter. He didn't intend to stay long. Later she'd have some explaining to do.

Aw, hell, he thought. *Does it really matter?*

He sighed, realizing that the fatigue was starting to catch up with him again.

"Hey, Ten-Wolves," Hawk said. "Have some of this fruit. It's delicious."

"No thanks," Concho said. "I just stopped by to say hello."

"Come on," Hawk said. "At least have a slice of watermelon. Or would that be something of a stereotype for you on your daddy's side?"

He punctuated his question with a tilt of his head, an ingratiating smile, and a shrug.

Concho flashed a smile of his own, although he felt like laying the man out.

"You have one for me," he said and started to turn away.

Isaac Parkland was there in front of him.

"Concho, I just wanted to say thanks for what you did last night," Parkland said.

Concho nodded. "No problem."

All he could think about was getting out of the door.

"Hoight told me what happened," Parkland continued. "Said you saved his life."

Concho shrugged. "I didn't do much. Thankfully, Terrill had some Narcan and saved Cate."

"Don't sell yourself short," Parkland said. "And I heard about the protracted inquiry. Anything I can do?"

"Not unless you can light a fire under somebody's ass in the DOJ," Concho said. "Get 'em to move faster."

Parkland laughed.

"The season for miracles was a couple of months back," he said.

Concho snorted a laugh and clapped the sheriff on the shoulder. He would have liked to inquire about Cate, but at the moment he just wanted to get the hell out of there.

Turning toward the door, he noticed that the crowd seemed to have grown a bit. Three more mall security guards had shown up as well as some Maverick County deputies.

Figuring that Hawk's appearance on the stage at center court was getting closer, Concho felt an increased sense of urgency to remove himself from these uncomfortable surroundings. Just as he made his way to the door, Maria was suddenly in front of him.

"You're not leaving, are you?" she asked. Her voice was a whisper.

He took in how beautiful she looked, brown eyes wide open, her luscious black hair arranged in an upsweep, her elegant blue business suit…

But then the ignominy of seeing Vincent Hawk strutting about and making his snide comments came rushing back. So did his anger.

"Why should I stay?" he said. "You obviously don't need me. You've already got your new Indian hero here."

That hadn't come out exactly the way he'd meant it, but he was too tired and angry to try to back his way out.

"That's not fair," she said, her voice rising slightly. After a quick glance over her shoulder, she resumed sotto voce. "I've got corporate here."

Concho resisted the immediate inclination to say something smart, like "Whoopty-do." Instead, he remained silent.

After a couple of beats he said, "I gotta get out of here."

Leaving it at that, he turned and strode through the door, not looking back and thinking that nothing, absolutely nothing, was going to keep him from going home and hitting the sack ASAP.

Let the chips fall where they may, he told himself, the anger still burning over Hawk's double-entendre quips.

Watermelon…

After slamming his hand against the push-bar on the door allowing access to the rear stairwell, he trotted down the stairs and then smashed a second push-bar on the lower door, sending it surging open against the pneumatic safety release.

Gray-Dove's tow truck sat right where he'd left it in the fire lane. He was in it in a flash and shoving the gearshift into first. The truck lurched forward as Concho popped the clutch, leaving a streak of rubber on the asphalt.

In his mind's eye, a juvenile Vincent Swooping Hawk stood smirking and holding a slice of watermelon toward him.

Once an asshole, always an asshole, he thought, but something told him he hadn't seen the last of Vince Hawk, and their paths would cross again.

CHAPTER EIGHT

ON THE RIDE BACK THE CONTENTIOUS MEETING AT *LAS MALL de las Aguilas* kept weighing heavily on Concho. It wasn't his rocky conversation with Maria that was bothering him the most, although that was bad enough. Nor was it all about the obnoxious Vince Hawk. The Indian movie star was obviously still a real horse's ass. Some things never change. His boorish and insensitive and borderline malicious quips hadn't stung Concho as much as the reminder of his status.

The term half-breed had never stuck with him. His father had been African American, his mother a full-blood Kickapoo. The old adage in the hood that "you are what your daddy was" never seemed to apply to him. He'd never known his father. Concho had grown up on the Reservation, had embraced the Indian ways, and had been tutored by Meskwaa throughout his vision quest.

At the time, it had all seemed like a natural progression.

But then years later, meeting his grandfather while Concho was still in the Army had proved to be a paradigm shift, although he didn't realize it initially. Slowly, the realization dawned on him, and the first time he'd understood that despite everything he'd accomplished—the vision quest, learning the ways of the elders, mastering the language, he didn't totally fit in either world. He was a man in metaphorical limbo. His path lay between the two worlds.

It always would.

Concho sensed something was amiss even before he turned onto the dirt roadway leading to his trailer. There was a beat-up old Ford Fiesta parked in front, and he saw someone seated by the fire pit and it wasn't Meskwaa.

No, this person was a woman. She was wearing a red-and-white print-colored blouse that looked so worn out it was almost pink and equally worn blue jeans that were riddled with patches and sewn-over spots.

She jumped to her feet quickly as he maneuvered the tow truck into the space where he normally parked his F-150. The plan was to leave the keys in the ashtray and Gray-Dove would pick up the tow truck when he left Concho's loaner later that day. Concho had told him not to make an issue of it.

"Don't bother to knock," he'd said. "I'll be sleeping."

But now it looked as if he wouldn't be.

As he got out of the truck, Concho saw the woman ambling toward him.

Kickapoo, he thought.

She appeared to be somewhere in her midfifties and walked with a noticeable limp. Her hair, once dark as a raven's wing, was now streaked with gray, and the deep lines in face made her look haggard and worn, as if life itself had worn her down. This wasn't a rare condition among the members of the tribe. Life was hard, especially those burdened with matriarchal responsibilities.

Although she looked vaguely familiar, her name eluded him.

His fingers brushed over the wide brim of his hat as she came over to him.

"Morning, ma'am."

"Ranger Ten-Wolves," she said, not waiting to introduce herself. "I need your help."

Once more fighting off the almost overwhelming fatigue, Concho took in a deep breath and stared down at the woman.

He wondered what kind of problem she had and why she'd come to him.

Questions…lots of questions.

And at the worst possible time for him.

"Yes, ma'am," he said. "What can I do for you?"

The corners of her mouth twisted downward and she looked about ready to cry, her breath now coming in sharp gasps rather than with steady regularity.

"Here," Concho said, gesturing toward the massive mesquite tree by the fire pit. "Why don't we step over to the shade and discuss things. Would you like some water?"

She shook her head, and a solitary tear wound its way down her weathered right cheek.

"I'm sorry to bother you," she said. "It's just that…I have no other place to turn. And I've heard so many good things about you—how you always help people in need."

Always?

Concho wanted to say that was a bit of an exaggeration but didn't.

"I do what I can," he said. "That's my job."

He couldn't help but speculate that this would shape up to be another irresolvable task. No doubt there was some type of incrementally destructive family problem—an abusive spouse, perhaps? Someone hooked on drugs?

He held his hand out toward the fire pit, and they walked there in silence.

Concho took his customary place in the largest of the chairs, proffering the one across from him that Meskwaa had occupied earlier that morning.

The old man's vision, Concho thought. *Could this be part of it?*

The woman sat down heavily and her lips twisted into a nervous scowl.

"Have we met before?" Concho asked.

He knew a great many on the Reservation, but he was known to far more people than he'd actually met.

"No," she said. "We haven't, but I've long known about you."

Oh great, Concho thought. *My legend precedes me. I wonder if she'll expect me to put on my cape and tights?*

"My name is Rachel Standing Bear," she said. "My husband was Daniel Standing Bear."

The "was" in her sentence told Concho a lot. No abusive spouse, and from the woman's age, most likely any children had long left the nest. The name had a vague familiarity to him, but he couldn't place it exactly.

He looked down, trying to remember.

"My husband was killed some years ago," she said. "At a county fair. Some drunken White men beat him to death."

Now the name and the incident clicked for Concho. He remembered Meskwaa mentioning it to him. It had been when he'd been on leave after coming back from overseas in the Army Rangers. "A tragic case," he'd called it. The man had left behind a family of a wife, daughter, and granddaughter.

"I remember," Concho said. "I was in the Army at the time, but my uncle told me."

He often referred to Meskwaa in that way, even though there was no actual blood relationship.

Rachel Standing Bear's head rocked back and forth in silent acknowledgment. No words passed between them for several seconds, and then finally she spoke.

"When Daniel was killed, it devastated our family." She swallowed hard and her dark eyes reflected a world-weary sadness. "Our daughter, Renee, died a few years after that."

This Concho did not recall hearing about, but then again, it was another lifetime ago.

The woman's eyes went to the ground between them and stayed there as she continued.

"Renee had—" She stopped talking and the cords in her neck tightened visibly. "A drug problem. She'd always been something of a free spirit—a wild child, you might say. When she died, her daughter, my granddaughter, was only two."

Concho didn't ask about the cause of death, but he assumed it was an OD. Instead, he sat in silence and merely nodded.

"I did my best with Renee," Rachel Standing Bear said. "But the…"

Her voice trailed off again, but she didn't need to complete the sentence. It was an all too familiar story for Concho. Drug usage was not uncommon on the Rez. And neither were unwed mothers.

"You said she had a daughter? Your granddaughter?"

She nodded. Her fingers came up and wiped at her nose.

"And she is why you've come to see me?" Concho asked.

Again, a quick nod, another swipe at the nose.

Concho leaned back and gave the woman a bit of space. He was tired as hell, and his patience was at an end, but he knew how hard it was to be totally dependent on someone else's largess. It wasn't the Kickapoo way to beg for a favor.

"I'm sorry," Rachel Standing Bear said. "It's just I have nowhere else to turn."

Her fingers dipped into the pocket of her jeans.

"I can," she began, "pay you for your time."

She started to extend her hand which had a thin, curled bundle of currency in it.

Concho held up his open palms.

"Please, that would never be necessary."

She stared at him a moment more and then slipped the bills back into her pocket.

I have to speed things up, Concho thought.

"What's your granddaughter's name?"

"Peskipaatei," she said. "It means—"

"Blue," Concho said, "like that of a peacock or a blue jay."

Her eyes widened for an instant, then she smiled and said, "You know our language."

It was a statement more than a question, but Concho nodded.

"Her grandfather, my husband, insisted that she be named that. He saw a beautiful blue bird on the morning of her birth. My daughter went along with it. She was only...fifteen when she gave birth. She wasn't married."

Another common story for a teenage girl on the Rez.

"Who was the father?" Concho asked.

Head shake.

"We never found out. Renee wouldn't say." Her eyes drifted downward again. "I don't think she even knew."

Wild child, Concho thought. An apt term.

But the fatigue was washing over him like waves on a lake.

"What exactly do you want me to do?"

She compressed her lips before she responded.

"Penny, that's what she calls herself." Pause, deep breath, and then, "She's fourteen now. The same age Renee was when..."

Concho didn't like the way this was shaping up, but he mentally started to review the list of female police officers he knew who might be able to be a distaff authority figure to try and get the girl on the right road. Nila Willow, the first female officer on the Kickapoo Police Department came to mind, although she tended to be a bit taciturn. Nevertheless, a positive female Indian role model would be more suited to the task than he.

"Mrs. Standing Bear," Concho began. "I—"

"She's missing."

"Missing? How long?"

She glanced downward.

"Since last night. I went to bed and she said she had to do some important schoolwork. I told her not to stay up too late because it was a school night. She said she wouldn't and then I went to bed and when I got up this morning to make her breakfast she wasn't there." The pained expression racked her face again. "Her bed hadn't been slept in."

"Is it possible she might have left early for school?"

She shook her head. "I told you, her bed wasn't slept in."

Concho was going to suggest that the girl might have made it but he decided to say nothing.

"I called the school," Rachel Standing Bear said. "She never showed up there."

"Have you made a police report?"

Her mouth twisted with an ugly expression.

"I went there this morning. They took their report, but I could tell by their faces they won't do nothing. That Robert Echabarri...said they would do everything they could, but I knew he was lying. I've known him since he was a boy. He's as useless as always. This never would have happened if Ben Deer Run was still alive. Even Daniel Alvarado would have been better."

Concho knew the parties she'd mentioned. Both men were former police chiefs of the Kickapoo Traditional Tribal Police Force, Alvarado only briefly, and both of them had been murdered. Echabarri had then taken over and despite his relative youth, Concho thought the man was a good choice. He considered bringing this up to Rachel Standing Bear, but he didn't think it would do much good. He had to figure an exit strategy that would ease this woman's anxiety and let her down easy without him engaging in a prolonged debate about the professionalism and dedication of Echabarri's police force.

"I don't really handle this sort of thing," he said.

The network of fine wrinkles deepened around her eyes.

Concho felt as if he'd delivered a devastating blow.

Before she could speak, he added, "But I will look into it."

The wave of relief washed over her face.

"Thank you." Her hands came together in a steeple-like gesture.

It was time for a bit of a reality check. The last thing he wanted to do was give the woman false hope. He was no miracle worker.

"But as I told you," he said. "I don't normally work with

juvenile matters as a Ranger. I can't make any promises that I might not be able to keep."

It was obvious that his last tempering words were falling on deaf ears. Her eyes were closed now, and she looked as if she were praying.

"In the meantime." He took out his notebook. "I'll need some information about Peskipaatei. And would you have a picture of her I could borrow?"

The woman reached into the pocket of her blouse and withdrew a folded piece of paper and a 3x5 color photograph. She handed them to Concho.

"Here," she said. "This is her eighth-grade graduation picture. She looks the same, except she has been wearing a lot of makeup lately. Trying to look grown up. And she put some blonde streaks in her hair."

Concho studied the photograph. The young Indian girl seemed to stare back at him with a halfhearted, photographer's prompted smile. No blonde streaks in this photo. Only jet-black hair artfully framing a rather delicate but pretty face. It was almost the picture of innocence, but the eyes told the story.

Fourteen going on thirty, he thought.

CHAPTER NINE

THEY WERE SEATED IN ROBERTO ECHABARRI'S OFFICE AT THE Kickapoo Police Station. The chief was leaning back in one of those ergonomic office chairs they advertised on TV. Concho's chair was less comfortable—just a standard metal frame with sparse padding on the seat and back, both covered with a faux leather-like material. It had groaned audibly when Concho had lowered his weight onto it. He noticed that Echabarri was looking sharp in his tailored uniform today. The walls of the office were looking sharp as well, decorated with his college degree, a certificate of completion from the FBI Academy, and a Staff and Command School certificate from Northwestern University. His big gunmetal gray desk was clear of just about everything except for a calendar, a telephone, a computer monitor, and his gray Stetson. Two open wooden boxes labeled "IN" and "OUTBOUND" sat off to the side. A framed photo of what Concho assumed to be Echabarri's family was on the side opposite the telephone. The young chief had divested the office of all the reminders of his two predecessors, and Concho couldn't blame him.

"Peskipaatei Standing Bear?" Echabarri said, rolling his eyes. "Her mother came to see you?"

Concho nodded.

"And this was after she'd already come here to make out a runaway report?"

Concho nodded again.

Echabarri shook his head and sighed. "I can't believe that woman. I guess she doesn't have much regard for my department."

Concho didn't say anything, but he was impressed that the other man had termed it, "my department." Despite Echabarri's relative youth and inexperience, Concho had high hopes for him. He also liked the young chief of police and was glad to see that he was enhancing his training and education. He'd gotten the job more or less by default after murder and corruption had tainted the last two leaders. Echabarri had inherited a department of three and had diligently worked to expand and professionalize it over the last several months, hiring a bunch of new officers including Nila Willow.

"She seemed pretty worried about her granddaughter," Concho said.

Echabarri frowned. "The girl hasn't even been missing twenty-four hours yet. Not that there has to be a time limit to report someone missing. But it's entirely possible that she just snuck out in the middle of the night. It wouldn't be the first time." He made a circling gesture with an extended index finger. "Of course, she did cut school today, according to the principal, but that's not an unusual occurrence either. She's what you might call a perennial runaway." After a snorting chuckle, he added, "Actually, perpetual might be a better term."

"Not her first rodeo, eh?"

Echabarri emitted another snorting laugh. "Not hardly. Not by a long shot."

"So I take it she's been entered in the computer as a minor requiring authoritarian intervention?"

"Yeah. I got Nila coming in on afternoons. I'll have her

nose around a little if little Miss Penny doesn't show up at home by suppertime."

This sounded reasonable to Concho. As he'd told Rachel Standing Bear at his trailer, the Kickapoo PD was actually better equipped to handle this matter than he was. But still, he felt obligated to at least verify that something was being done.

"Does Nila have any rapport with the girl?" he asked. "From what her mother said, Peskipaatei seems headed down the wrong path."

"Again, that's putting it mildly."

"I was thinking if a positive role model like Nila could talk to her, it might do some good." He tried to gauge Echabarri's reaction. The man looked skeptical.

"She's one of my best officers, but she's not a social worker. Or a miracle worker, either."

Concho thought differently but didn't say so. Sometimes cops had to wear a lot of different hats, and when dealing with a confused adolescent, he figured someone ought to at least try.

Echabarri seemed to read Concho's thoughts.

"All right, all right," the chief said. "I'll see if I can get Nila to give her a youth of America speech, or something. But don't expect miracles. I think little Miss Penny's pretty much a lost cause. It's probably hereditary. The way she's going, from what I've heard, she's probably going to be a teenage mother like her teenage mother was." He flashed a rueful smile. "You know how the cycle works. And then Rachel Standing Bear will be raising her granddaughter and her great-granddaughter."

Concho knew, all right, and what Echabarri was suggesting was the unfortunate reality of life on the Rez for so many young girls.

They sat in silence for several seconds and then Echabarri laughed. "But who the hell knows? If and when that happens, maybe the third time'll be the charm, and the kid will turn out to be a nuclear physicist, or something."

"Maybe." Concho stood. A lot of what Echabarri had said was probably true, and Concho was again feeling the fatigue of not having gotten any sleep for close to thirty hours washing over him. "You mind giving me a copy of the report?"

Echabarri grinned.

"Anything for my favorite Texas Ranger." He picked up the phone and called the record's clerk. "Yeah, Sherry, make a copy of the runaway report for Peskipaatei Standing Bear for Ranger Ten-Wolves. It'll be in the juvenile file." After listening for a reply, Echabarri grunted a "Thanks," and told the record's clerk that Concho would pick it up on his way out.

As he placed the phone back in its cradle, he turned his head toward Concho and raised one eyebrow.

Concho studied the gesture with a trace of envy. That was one facial move that he had yet to master.

"So I heard you were involved in a shooting last night," Echabarri said.

"Word travels fast."

"Just like the old days. Smoke signals. What happened?"

Concho gave him a quick summary, ending with, "I'm technically on administrative leave until the investigation is over with."

Echabarri shrugged. "It sounds like a good shoot. Shouldn't take that long."

Concho blew out a slow breath.

"Well, you wouldn't think so," he said. "But you know that old saying about too many cooks spoiling the broth."

The space between Echabarri's eyebrows showed twin creases as he looked up at Concho.

"I don't get you," he said.

"Since we were technically on a Special Auxiliary Border Surveillance—Joint Task Force, the feds are nosing into it."

"The feds?" Echabarri's face wrinkled. "Son of a bitch. Those assholes always drag their feet crossing every T and double-checking every I."

"Tell me about it. As I said, I'm technically on administrative leave."

"Well…" The chief got to his feet also. He was around an

even six feet and Concho towered over him. "At least it'll give you plenty of time to go look for Penny Standing Bear." Echabarri punctuated that with a laugh and he clapped Concho on the shoulder. "You look beat, big guy. You been to bed yet?"

Concho shook his head.

"That's next on my agenda. Look, do me a favor. If Peskipaatei does happen to return home, send me a text."

"Will do. And in the meantime, why don't you go get some rest. I'll call you if we need a tow."

It was Concho's turn to roll his eyes. Echabarri must have seen him drive up in Gray-Dove's truck.

"I'm planning on turning this damn cell phone off," Concho said. "Administrative leave, remember?"

Echabarri gave a slight shrug. "Just don't cheat yourself out of what might be your next career move. And if they fire you from the Rangers, I'll hire you here part time. A good man with a tow truck's hard to find."

Concho frowned. "Ha ha. You're about as funny as a cow turd in the punchbowl."

"What can I say?" Echabarri said, the grin still wide on his face. "It's a gift."

"Yeah, and one that I could do without."

Echabarri laughed and clapped Concho on the shoulder.

"It'll all work out," the chief said. "They say everything happens for a purpose. You want to grab some lunch?"

Lunch?

Concho hadn't realized that it was now approaching early afternoon.

Was this damn long night shift that had stretched into the daytime ever going to end?

"No thanks," he said. "I've got a date with my pillow, remember?"

After accepting a standard-size business envelope from the records clerk, Concho thanked her, stuck it in his pocket, and headed out to the tow truck. Echabarri's barb about calling

Concho in case they needed a hook still grated on the big Ranger as he shook loose the ignition key and slid behind the wheel.

At this point, he was ready to accept even that ancient El Camino that Gray-Dove was always working on. Of course the floorboards were so rusted he'd have to do a Fred Flintstone braking effort by digging his heels against the roadway.

He shoved the key in the ignition, depressed the clutch, and started it up. The engine shook and rattled before cycling into a smooth rhythm. Concho took out his cell phone to call Gray-Dove and ask about obtaining another loaner but then recalled that they'd already discussed that. Gray-Dove had said one was going to be dropped off as soon as it was available. Whenever that might be.

Too long without sleep, he thought. *Too many mistakes being made.*

Just as he was putting his phone back into his pocket, it vibrated and chimed with the notification of an incoming text. It was from Captain Dalton Shaw.

> *Ranger Ten-Wolves, you are hereby ordered to report to the range tomorrow at 0800 hours for mandatory training. At this time, you are on administrative leave pending the conclusion of the shooting incident you were involved in. Official investigation is still pending at this time. Please text your confirmation of this message upon receipt.*
>
> *Captain Dalton Shaw*

Concho reread that second to last line again

Official investigation still pending at this time.

It's all horseshit, he thought.

The truth was there was nothing substantial to investigate. The shooting was justified. It was just that a bunch of bureaucrats who were more concerned with optics than what actually happened were drawing things out so they could put the proper spin on things. It was long overdue for some of those gutless wonders to grow a set of balls and take a walk in the real world.

Concho considered texting Shaw back what might be an appropriate response, but in the end, decided against that. Too little sleep mixed with a healthy dose of anger and resentment didn't add up to what could be called a wise move.

Besides, it wasn't the captain's fault. The higher-ups were probably leaning on him too, and Concho had no doubt Shaw was somebody he could count on when the chips were down. And in this case, they could bounce up or down at a moment's notice.

Instead of fashioning a textual response, he just hit the automatic reply button and dropped the phone back into his pocket.

One should never overlook an opportunity to keep one's mouth shut, as Meskwaa was fond of saying.

Shifting into first, he popped the clutch and took off with an accompanying metallic cacophony of meshing gears, wondering if the old tow truck had enough spunk left to leave a spoor of rubber on the pavement.

It was time to sleep and nothing was going to keep him from that.

CHAPTER TEN

THE NOISE WOKE HIM UP.

Or was it the dream?

It was the same one that had started way back when he'd been in the Army. Life in a combat zone...the dream first visited him at a base camp in Afghanistan and had followed him after he'd come back to the States and joined the police force and then the Rangers. The old ghost, he called it, periodically slipped into his slumber whenever he was under some kind of stress. Although the circumstances of the dream always varied slightly at the onset, it always came down to that same set of unalterable circumstances, that same feeling.

He was facing down somebody with a gun or weapon of some sort. This particular time he was in a dark place, whether it was inside or outside he didn't know, nor did it matter. A phantom figure ahead of him, large and menacing, was advancing, refusing to obey instructions. Everything was hazy, like they were in the middle of a fog, or a smoke-filled building, but somehow he knew there were people watching. He didn't know who they were, but he knew there were a lot of them.

Something shifted and the parameters narrowed considerably without warning and the phantom raised a large semi-automatic pistol. The muzzle was a huge circular black hole and it seemed to eclipse everything.

"Drop the weapon," Concho found himself calling out in his dream, but the phantom kept moving forward.

Concho brought his own weapon up and acquired a sight picture.

"Drop it."

Nothing.

He lined up the front sight in the V between the two halves of the rear sight.

Flat across the top, just the way they'd taught him in basic training in the Army.

The large phantom was getting closer and suddenly Concho knew the man was going to kill him.

He didn't know why, but that didn't matter. Nothing mattered in this dream except firing his own weapon. It was one of his Colt forty-five Double Eagles.

His index finger squeezed the trigger.

It wouldn't move.

He squeezed harder.

Still the trigger wouldn't budge.

He brought his left index finger into play to join his right and squeezed with all his might.

Frozen.

It was somehow very apparent to him that the phantom's gun was in perfect working order and was going to fire it in another second.

Danger and terror overwhelmed him.

And then he woke up.

It was always like that.

Waking up, covered with sweat, wringing with anxiety, right before he heard the shot in his dream.

But this time there was something more.

The noise.

As he lay in the darkness, he strained his ears to listen.

Nothing, then something. The sound of a door being gently closed.

Rolling out of bed, Concho's right hand was already reaching for his Colt forty-five that was still in the pancake holster he'd worn earlier. His left searched for his pistol-belt with his other forty-five and the extra magazines and the mini-mag flashlight, but it wasn't there. Then his brain shook off the residual fog of his deep slumber and he remembered that they'd confiscated the other Double Eagle. He'd left the pistol belt on the dresser.

The clock next to his bed showed the time in glowing red numbers: 23:58. He'd taken to keeping this clock on the 24-hour clock cycle.

Regardless, it was almost midnight.

He'd stripped down to just his underwear and headed for bed soon after getting home from talking with Echabarri. It was about 1400 when he'd lowered the shade and gotten into bed, perhaps another twenty minutes before he'd drifted off to sleep. Damn near ten hours. He should have felt rested, but he didn't. His gnawing periodic bodily functions had seen to that. He'd awoken several times to go to the bathroom, and then the onset of the dream had left him feeling exhausted. Restful sleep had been an elusive entity.

Of course, now he had the surge of adrenaline flowing through him.

Standing, he moved to the door and peered through the crack.

The rest of his trailer was dark, but he could discern movement.

How many and who were they?

Footsteps, soft yet unhurried scuffed over the flooring of the hallway and approached the bedroom. He flattened against the wall and waited as a hand came through the opening and the door pushed silently open.

Without hesitating, Concho grabbed the dark figure's left

arm and yanked. Someone spilled onto the bed with an accompanying huff of air.

Pushing the door open wider, he did a quick peek down the hallway.

No one.

"Move and you're dead," he yelled, his words having a grating sound to them.

"Concho?"

A woman's voice, soft, frightened, and totally familiar.

Maria.

He heaved a sigh, lowered his weapon, and reached over to flip on the lights. The soft overhead glow captured her beautiful face, fraught with alarm, her left hand drawn up in a guarded position next to her mouth.

"I—I'm sorry," she said. "I was trying not to wake you."

He studied her for a moment in the harsh light. Even though she was sprawled out on the bed, lying on her side, she looked beautiful. Her long black hair was still fastened up on her head by a maze of bobby-pins, but a strand had come loose and now partially covered the left side of her face like a raven's wing.

"You didn't," he said, stepping over to the bed and sliding the Colt back into the pancake holster. "My dream did that. And I'm the one that should be apologizing. I didn't hurt you, did I?"

She shook her head.

After sliding the now holstered gun back into its crevice, he sat on the bed next to her. She had on the same outfit as this morning. The blazer was missing, but the white blouse and dark-blue skirt were the same. He admired the textured smoothness of the skirt over her legs and the lyre-like swell of her hips.

"You sure?" he asked. "I didn't mean to manhandle you."

"I'm fine." Her fingers brushed the errant hair away from her face. "I've been trying to call all day, but it kept going right to voice mail."

Concho realized he'd turned the phone off just before he'd lain down.

"Sorry, it was a rough day. A rough night, actually. I just wanted to be dead to the world." He grinned. "And I guess I was, until you came in."

"Don't joke about that." Her fingers brushed over his lips. Her touch was soft, yearning.

He put his hand on her hip, his fingers gently rubbing the curve of her pelvis, then drifting upward to her waist.

"I wanted to come before this," she said, "but corporate insisted on hosting some sort of big dinner at the hotel for Vince."

So it was "Vince" now?

Concho figured Hawk would use his celebrity status to leverage a room at the Kickapoo Lucky Eagle Casino. Knowing the man's reputation, and judging from his bombastic behavior earlier, Concho was willing to bet it was the swankiest room in the place—the presidential suite.

"Long day's journey into night," Concho said, remembering the title to an old play.

"You don't know the half of it." Maria's hand settled on top of his for a moment and she straightened up and sat facing him on the bed. Her fingers traced over his jawline. "You need a shave."

"And a shower, too." Concho realized he hadn't attended to any basic hygiene since before his previous night shift surveillance. He wondered how he smelled. Maria's scent was intoxicating, tempered with a dash of fading perfume.

Their faces edged closer to each other. Neither one spoke, and then Maria leaned forward and gently kissed him.

"I've been going all day, too, and could use some freshening up," she said, her tone becoming a seductive whisper. "Ever heard the expression, you wash my back and I'll wash yours?"

"It'll be a tight fit," he said and cupped her face in his huge hands before kissing her again.

CHAPTER ELEVEN

THEIR LOVEMAKING HAD GONE ON FOR MOST OF THE NIGHT, and despite the absence of a full night's sleep, Maria had insisted on leaving early—very early, so she could go home and get ready for work. It was barely five a.m., and Concho got up as well and offered to make her breakfast, but she declined.

"Shower here," he said with a grin. "I won't look."

She returned the smile with a wicked one of her own, but shook her head.

"I have to be in early to make sure everything goes smoothly with the talent quest," she said. "Plus, I have to fix my hair and change clothes. I can't be caught wearing the same outfit two days in a row."

At the mention of the talent quest, Concho frowned. It reminded him of the only negative specter that had come out of their interlude the night before: Vince Hawk.

He'd sensed it from the onset when they'd first gone to bed. She seemed tense, her timing bit off from their normal pace, her lovemaking somehow more tentative than usual. He said nothing at the time, and it wasn't until later, much later, that Concho managed to get the truth out of her. After a long day of activities and announcements about the talent quest Hawk was sponsoring, the corporate executives had set up a big soiree at the Lucky Eagle Hotel and Casino, which Maria said she was obligated to attend. It dragged out and just as it was breaking up, Hawk had insisted he had just thought of something he needed to show her regarding the talent quest. They went up to his room, the presidential suite in the six-story hotel structure, and once inside, Hawk then made a pass at her, telling her how beautiful she was and trying to get her to spend some "special time" with him and his two female companions who were already in a somewhat inebriated state of undress in the suite.

She frowned and shook her head as she related the story.

"They were both young," she said. "Way younger than me, but they had a hard look to them. Ladies of the evening would be my guess, or rather girls. I'd be surprised if they were both over eighteen, all tattooed and prancing around practically naked and giddy. And they both looked high and acted like they'd just shorted something. They tried to pull me to this big hot tub, and Hawk said it was a great way to relax."

Concho felt his jealousy and anger rising.

"So what happened?"

She heaved a sigh. "I told him I wasn't interested, and when he grabbed my arm, I pulled loose."

"He grabbed your arm?"

She sensed his growing ire and placed her palm flat against his chest.

"Nothing happened," she said. "I told him I was in a committed relationship and that was it."

Concho wondered how much of it she was downplaying.

"And he didn't grab me hard or forcefully or anything," she said. "It was just like a little tug, is all."

"A little tug" was one tug too many.

Concho thought about getting dressed and going to the Lucky Eagle right then, and smashing down the door of the suite, and giving "a little tug" of his own to Vincent Swooping Hawk.

"That son of a bitch," Concho said. "When I see him, I'm going to—"

"No." Her protest was sharp and immediate, but her tone softened when she added, "You'll do nothing of the sort."

"Like hell," he said, his blood still boiling.

She put her face close to his, her dark eyes staring into his own. "Please. You can't do anything. If something happens to jeopardize this talent quest thing, after all the money corporate has sunk into the project, and all the revenue their planning on raking in, I'll be out of a job."

"Job or no job," Concho said, "that asshole stepped over the line."

"I told you nothing happened."

They stayed locked in a naked embrace for several more seconds, neither speaking. Finally, Maria broke the silence.

"Promise me," she said. "That you won't do anything."

Concho didn't want to make a promise he didn't intend to keep.

"Promise," she repeated, pressing down on his bare chest.

After a few deep breaths, he nodded. Nothing would be changed or settled by him acting like a jealous fool, but he also sensed that a reckoning down the road was most likely inevitable between him and Hawk.

Now, several hours later, he pulled up to the gate at the police range on the outskirts of the city and listened to periodic cracks of gunfire that were already emanating from the series of dirt berms beyond the entrance. The red flag was at full staff and Concho glanced at his watch.

Eight thirty-five.

He was a bit late, due to him stopping by Gray-Dove's place to check on the status of that less conspicuous loaner.

"Sorry," Gray-Dove had said. "I ain't got nothing ready for you yet. Had a couple of emergency repairs come in."

Concho felt like asking him what constituted an emergency over his F-150 that was also a police vehicle, but instead inquired about changing out the tow truck.

Gray-Dove shook his head, a grin plastered on his face. "I still haven't gotten the El Camino running yet, but in the meantime, you're looking real good in that tow truck. I'll call you if I need you."

"You're all heart."

The officer stationed at the checkpoint came strolling over, eyeing the vehicle suspiciously until he saw Concho holding out his ID.

"Ranger Ten-Wolves?" the gate guard said. "You're running kind of late. We got started at zero-eight-hundred."

Concho blew out a slow breath remembering the text from Shaw.

"Why you driving this thing?" the guard asked.

"Long story," Concho replied. He was in no mood to relate it.

The guard didn't inquire further and lifted the barrier, waving him through.

The sounds of the gunfire grew louder as Concho drove down the gravel road, passing a smattering of prefab buildings and a set of bleachers. A group of about ten men all wearing their white Stetsons and holstered side-arms stood in a circle with one other man, obviously in charge, giving them what looked like a final set of instructions. A wooden picnic table sat off to the right with a bunch of cardboard containers and a stack of papers piled on top of it. The crowd of men was all holding dark plastic boxes—the kind handguns came in. The instructor was a tall, rangy sort with a leathery-looking face. His head swiveled left, shooting a quick, squinty-eyed glance at Concho as he exited the tow truck. After a few more words to the group, the instructor waved the group away, and they headed toward the array of berms, each putting on ear muffs or inserting earplugs. The rangy man sauntered toward Concho, who was taking his time getting out of his vehicle.

Captain Shaw had texted him earlier asking if he was on his way to the range and Concho had texted back with a simple, *Affirmative*. Things were all starting to culminate in a collection of irritating events that was making his life miserable: Vince Hawk hitting on Maria, her admonition to Concho not to do anything, the protracted shooting investigation, and his promise to Rachel Standing Bear to look for her granddaughter…

Sometimes a man must walk through a gauntlet of misfortune, Meskwaa would say.

Concho thought about the old man and smiled, hoping he'd see him again soon. He felt he could use a bit of Meskwaa's cynical humor mixed with his cogent wisdom, especially in this current period of troubling circumstances.

"You Ranger Ten-Wolves?" the rangy man asked. His tone had an undercurrent of irritation. He was several inches shorter than Concho and appeared to be in his midfifties, but with a textured hardness that exuded competence.

"Yes, sir," Concho said, figuring that imbuing a little bit of official protocol might go a long way here.

The other man frowned.

"Don't call me 'sir.' I work for a living. Name's Sergeant Crawford." He extended his arm and at first Concho thought the man was offering to shake hands, but instead Crawford brought his arm up and scrutinized his watch. "Didn't you get the captain's directive to report here at zero-eight-hundred?"

No nonsense in this guy, Concho thought. He debated how to respond and decided on honesty, for the most part.

"I had a rough night," Concho said. "Wasn't able to sleep, Sarge."

Crawford squinted at him.

"That sounds like a piss-poor excuse."

"Agreed," Concho said.

"Ten-Wolves," Crawford said slowly. "Were you involved in that mall thing some months back? With those white supremacists?"

"Yeah, that was me."

Crawford's eyebrows twitched and his expression seemed to soften.

"Captain Shaw told me you were involved in another shooting recently."

"Very recently. Night before last. In fact, I was kind of surprised when he told me to report here today. I'm on administrative leave pending the investigation."

"Shaw said it was a good shoot, but they got a bunch of muckety-mucks from the DOJ sticking their noses in. How the hell did *that* happen?"

Concho felt his reputation and his current predicament had somehow scored points with Crawford.

"The shooting occurred when I was working a special overtime detail on the border," Concho said. "Luck of the draw, or in this case, the unluck."

Crawford snorted and held up a calloused open palm.

"Say no more. With those assholes breathing down your neck I can understand why you couldn't sleep. Been there myself a time or two."

Concho allowed himself a hint of a smile. Crawford had obviously jumped to the wrong conclusion about the lack of sleep, but Concho wasn't about to tell him the real reason.

Crawford turned and motioned for Concho to follow. They stopped by the picnic table and Crawford picked up what appeared to be the last of the triangular plastic gun containers. He flipped up the two clips that held the container tightly closed and opened the lid. Concho saw a large semi-automatic pistol that resembled a 1911 in design. The weapon appeared to be single-action and had a glimmering black finish and an extended magazine. A miniature black and white emblem of the American flag was on the frame of the weapon next to the upper curvature of the grip. Picking up the gun, Crawford flashed a grin.

"This is the new weapon the rangers are going to," he said. "The Staccato XC. If Joaquin Jackson woulda had one of these…" He let the rest of the sentence trail off, then his head jutted outward as he looked Concho straight in the eye. "You do know who Action Jackson was, don't ya?"

"What Ranger doesn't?" Concho replied. He'd been hearing about the legendary Texas Ranger ever since he was a boy. Jackson was so famous that a movie, *Extreme Prejudice*, had been made about his exploits back in the 1980s. Concho had a DVD copy of the movie.

Crawford grunted an approval.

"Good. You ask way too many of our newbies, and they don't know nothing about him." Crawford's nostrils flared. "Damn shame."

"That's like a marine not knowing who Chesty Puller was," Concho said in agreement.

Crawford's eyebrows rose in unison. "You were a marine?"

"Army Ranger. But I served in Afghanistan with a lot of devil dogs."

"Semper fi," Crawford said, using the Marine Corps greeting even though Concho was an Army vet. "Anyway, this is got to be the sweetest weapon you'll ever fire."

He released the magazine from the Staccato and pulled back the slide. After double-checking the chamber, he handed it to Concho.

The gun was all metal and lighter than Concho would have imagined.

"Work that slide," Crawford said.

Concho did so and was surprised at the smoothness of the action.

"Ain't she sweet?" Crawford asked. "A five-inch barrel and the frame is machined aluminum, which explains the lightness. Thirty-seven ounces without the mag, and a two-point five-pound trigger pull. Lemme see your hands."

Concho lifted his arms and spread his palms open.

Crawford emitted a low whistle.

"With mitts like that, you probably don't have to worry about recoil," he said, "but those vents along the front of the slide disperse the gasses to reduce it substantially and allows the shooter to stay on target. The front sight is built onto the frame, not the slide, which also allows for more rapid target reacquisition. Seventeen rounds, plus one. Well, whaddya think?"

"Actually," Concho said, "I've never cared much for nine-millimeter. I've always had better luck with a forty-five."

Crawford's face scrunched up. "All that stuff about a lack of stopping power with a nine is a bunch of bullshit. Shot placement is where it's at, and the Staccato gives you seventeen and one without a reload."

Concho didn't want to get in a debate about his Colt Double Eagles, but had to admit the Staccato was an impressive weapon. Plus, he was down one gun anyway, and moreover, he liked this old-time Ranger.

"So," Crawford said, a sly grin on his face. "You ready to try it out?"

Returning the grin, Concho said, "Sure am."

* * *

CONCHO BREEZED THROUGH THE MANDATORY QUALIFICATION courses with both his remaining Double Eagle and the Stacatto, and then spent another hour on the Hogan's Alley portion of the range. It was an elongated wooden structure with open windows and doors, into which various target would rotate into view. Some of them were full-color depictions of hostile offenders holding various weapons, while others were similar renditions of confusing looking non-threatening items such as cell phones or open wallets. The shooter had to walk the gravel lane in front of the wooden structure and engage the appropriate targets as they appeared, and also taking cover at various points behind junk cars, fireplugs, and mailboxes for tactical reloads. You never knew what kind of illustrated individual was going to pop up next. It was a timed event and with his long legs, Concho always did well in both accuracy and timing and this session was no exception.

Crawford, who was at the controls, took him through his

paces and pointed out that he was able to make the entire walk with only one load in the Stacatto.

"See what I mean?" Crawford said. "It's one helluva weapon, ain't it?"

"You got stock in this company, or what?" Concho retorted.

The old Ranger laughed. "It's made in Texas. That ought to persuade you, if nothing else."

Concho didn't mention that his belt was set up for the Colt forty-five caliber sized magazines, but he was down one gun as it was. Carrying the Staccato in a shoulder rig might come in handy.

"You convinced me," Concho said. "Looks like your stock investment will be paying off."

"I wish." Crawford grunted a laugh and dug out a box of nine-millimeter ammunition from his large backpack.

"Here." He handed the box to Concho, who jammed it into his pocket.

Crawford took out another box. "And you'll want some forty-five too, I expect."

Concho grinned. There wasn't much getting by this sly old fox.

After thanking Crawford for his time and instruction, Concho took both weapons to the series of picnic benches where a variety of gun-cleaning equipment was laid out.

A clean weapon was an effective weapon, they'd taught him the Army, and adhering to that policy had never failed him yet.

After disassembling the two guns, he laid the parts out on a blue cloth and began scrubbing the barrels of each. The smell of the acrid gunpowder solvent was stinging his nostrils when a shadow appeared on the surface of the bench and Concho glanced up. It was Captain Shaw.

"I see you did well with your new weapon," he said.

"Yeah, I'll be anxious to start carrying it, along with my

other two guns, speaking of which, when is this bullshit gonna be over with?"

Shaw's eyes shot downward toward the ground as he took in a deep breath.

"Hopefully, sooner rather than later," he said. "They'll be calling you in later in the week to take your statement."

"Take my statement? I already gave one yesterday morning."

"Not to the feds," Shaw said. "And I'd like to remind you that you can have legal representation with you for that. I recommend you take advantage of the—"

"Dammit, Captain," Concho said, standing up so that he towered over Shaw. "This whole thing's a bunch of prime, grade-A bullshit. You know that was a good shoot, and so do they, if they did any investigation. What the hell's this all about?"

Shaw shrugged and wouldn't look him in the eye.

"I already made my feelings known," he said, "and believe me, I'm on your side. But this whole federal Special Auxiliary Border Surveillance—Joint Task Force thing gives them an excuse to assert their authority. You know it as well as I do."

"SABS," Concho said. "It should be SOBs—sons of bitches."

Shaw managed a chuckle. "Again, you're preaching to the choir. I don't like it any better than you do, but until those tight-assed sons of bitches we're talking about do get off their soft behinds and clear the investigation, we're stuck."

"And I'm still on administrative leave."

Shaw jerked an extended index finger in a mock pistol-like fashion at Concho and made a clucking sound.

"You got it," he said. "Stay ready, remember what I told you about having legal rep if you want or need one. I'll keep you advised." He turned to go, then stopped. "Nice shooting, by the way."

"It was easy," Concho said. "All I did was imagine there might be a fat-assed federal bureaucrat behind every corner."

Shaw snorted a laugh.

"Stay out of trouble," he said. "And enjoy your vacation while it lasts. Valentine's Day is coming up, ain't it? Take your lady out for a nice romantic dinner and a movie. I heard Vince Hawk's in town rounding up extras for his new picture. Maybe you can get a part playing an Indian, or something. It's supposed to be about Geronimo."

Shaw continued walking, and Concho jammed the wire brush forcefully down the barrel of his Colt.

Geronimo, he thought. *You don't know the half of it.*

CHAPTER TWELVE

AFTER A QUICK TRIP HOME TO GRAB A BITE TO EAT, CONCHO then slipped on a vest made from one of his old Army BDU blouses and a shoulder rig that more or less fit the Staccato. Suited up in fresh black jeans and a black T-shirt, he felt almost normal. Since his regular duty belt had two holsters for the twin Double Eagles, he used the same pancake holster of the sole remaining Colt and slipped the forty-five caliber mag holders on the left front of his belt. The shoulder holster had two magazine holders on the right side and he stuffed the two nine-millimeter mags into those. He was loaded for bear with over seventy-seven rounds total between both guns. While he didn't anticipate being involved in anything requiring that much firepower, he lightheartedly recalled that old military adage about never having enough ammo. The BDU vest was big and it concealed both weapons pretty well. He also left his Texas Ranger badge affixed to the left side of his chest and let the blouse cover that as well.

Technically, he was on administrative leave, but he was still a Ranger. No two-bit, overblown, bureaucratic investigation was going to change that. While he still had a generally optimistic feeling about the outcome, the whole matter wasn't sitting well in his gut. But how could they not rule that it was a justified shooting?

He checked his image in the mirror before heading out.

Just your average John Q. Citizen, Indian style, he thought as the reflection stared back at him. But also a very well-armed Indian.

Pushing back his long hair, he slipped his black Stetson on his head and checked the mirror one more time. He'd thought about wearing his regulation white one, but decided against it.

Rebellious or merely iconoclastic, he was going with black, his favorite.

He went out and hopped in the tow truck. He took out his phone and debated whether or not to call Maria and check on her to see if Vincent Swooping Hawk had hit on her again. Her admonition not to interfere hung heavily in his mind, but he decided to give her the benefit of the doubt that she could handle a creep like Hawk. But he still felt that eventually at some point, he was going to have to set the conceited movie star back on his heels.

Concho took in a deep breath, held it for about eight seconds, and blew it out slowly. He repeated this three times. It was a stress reducer that he'd learned in the Army. The theory behind it was taking conscious control over an involuntary bodily function—breathing, for a few seconds and thus reducing anxiety, which was fostered by a feeling of an escalating loss of control. Sometimes it worked, sometimes it didn't.

Today it didn't.

The problem with Hawk the masher, the shooting investigation, the federal agency sticking its nose into things, the administrative leave...all of them still swirled in his mind.

Concho recalled Meskwaa's vision from the day before: Dark clouds overhead, enveloping everything in a shroud of darkness. Lightening, thunder, and the specter of death hanging heavily in the air. And not to forget the owl—the worst of signs and the herd of wild horses chased by shadows.

There was a storm coming, all right. In fact, it had already started.

And he was on good old administrative leave.

But as long as he had to deal with this forced vacation, he figured he might as well make the best of it. There was a lot to do, but the first thing he did was give John Gray-Dove another call. That was another disappointment.

"I'm still working on yours," Gray-Dove said. "I got two emergency jobs that came in. Both KTTP police cars."

"What the hell is mine?" Concho said. "A chopped liver mobile?"

Gray-Dove grunted a laugh.

"Don't give me any shit," he said. "The chief told me to do his two first. Said you were on administrative leave, so yours got shuffled to the bottom of the deck."

"I'll have to thank him for that." Word had spread fast and Concho wondered who else knew about his status?

Gray-Dove's laugh continued. "Tell you what, write up any tows you do and I'll put you on commission. And don't go too far. If my regular tow truck breaks down, I might need that one back in a hurry."

"What am I going to drive then? A bicycle?"

"Now that you mention it, I do have one of those and with the right cable, you might still be able to pull off a tow or two."

"It's a good thing you're such a hot-shot mechanic," Concho said, "because you'd never make it as a comedian."

He terminated the call and tossed his phone down on the seat. He shoved in the clutch and twisted the key. The engine ground on and on without catching, so he pumped the gas a few times and finally it caught. Concho rammed the gearshift into first and took off, swearing and promising himself that he'd get Gray-Dove back for this.

His anger had dissipated by the time he pulled up to the hospital and then another idea occurred to him. Pulling into a fire lane, he shut the truck down and grabbed the *ON TOW— OFFICIAL BUSINESS* sign from behind the visor and shoved it onto the dashboard. If any overzealous meter maids noticed and gave the truck a parking ticket, Concho knew what he'd do —nothing.

What the hell, he thought, *Gray-Dove probably wouldn't pay them anyway.*

He sauntered to the front entrance of the hospital and went directly to the front desk. After getting Cate's room number, he went to the elevators and pressed the button. As the doors opened, Terrill Hoight stepped out, gaze low and with an expression that looked as dejected as all hell.

"Hey, Terrill," Concho said. "How's our boy doing?"

Hoight glanced up and a slight smile graced his lips.

"Concho, how you doing, man?" Hoight's tongue swept over his lips and he extended an arm to keep the elevator door from closing. "You here to see Cate?"

Concho nodded, wondering why his friend seemed so down.

"Why the long face?" Concho asked. "He not doing well?"

Hoight gave his head a quick shake.

"He's fine. They're just holding him for investigation—I mean observation." The slight smile twitched a bit. "I'm the one under investigation."

"You? Why?"

Hoight shook his head again and the elevator doors lurched forward, striking his arm. The doors then automatically retracted.

"The sergeant in charge of the FTO program is saying I violated field training protocol." Hoight frowned. "He says I didn't take proper precautions and put my trainee in a precarious situation."

"That's a load of bullshit. You tell him we were getting shot at?"

"I will," Hoight said. "I've got my hearing coming up this week."

"I saw Sheriff Parkland yesterday morning, and he didn't

say anything negative about you. I told him you did a good job."

"Thanks, I appreciate that." He took in a deep breath. "And I heard they're dragging you over the coals about that shooting. What the hell's going on with that?"

"Your guess is as good as mine. The feds are sticking their noses into it."

"What? The FBI or the DOJ?"

"Does it make a difference?" Concho laughed.

The doors automatically closed again and bounced back after striking Hoight's arm.

"No, I guess not." Hoight's expression turned serious. "Hey, listen, if there's anything I can do, let me know. I'll be glad to testify. That was a good shoot, not to mention you saved my life."

"And I appreciate you as well," Concho said.

The two of them shook hands as some kind of alarm bell rang from inside the elevator.

They both grinned and Concho stepped inside as Hoight exited.

A rough time for the good guys, Concho thought as the doors slid closed.

* * *

THE SIGHT OF CATE LYING ON HIS BACK WITH THE OXYGEN tubes in his nostrils and the IV line inserted in the crux of his left forearm lingered in Concho's mind as he walked back to the tow truck. As he'd anticipated, there was a parking ticket affixed under the windshield wiper. He plucked it off and glanced at it.

UNAUTHORIZED VEHICLE PARKED IN A FIRE LANE.

The fine was listed as a whopping two hundred and fifty dollars.

That was a bit too hefty to pass on to Gray-Dove as part of a payback, and this wasn't a particularly good time to ask Parkland to void it either. Not with the feds nosing around and looking for any little irregularities attached to his life and the shooting.

Ranger Ten-Wolves, the mimicking, off-putting, irritating imitation of some anonymous federal agent's voice inside Concho's head said. *Tell us again about why you went to Sheriff Parkland and asked him to fix a duly authorized ticket that you incurred...*

All he'd wanted to do was visit a fellow officer who was in the hospital.

The irritating voice continued inside Concho's head: *And you couldn't take the time to park in the proper area of the lot, like every other regular citizen? You have an aversion to following rules, don't you?*

Concho blew out a breath as he jammed the ticket into his pants pocket making a mental note to pay it later. It would be his good deed for the day.

And as they say, no good deed goes unpunished, he thought. *I can't win for losing.*

The subject of good deeds brought his mind around to his other charity project of late—Peskipaatei "Penny" Standing Bear. He'd meant to check with Echabarri earlier to see if the girl had returned home as the chief had predicted. Taking out his phone, he punched in the number for the Kickapoo Traditional Tribal Police Department. Sherry Garcia, the day shift records clerk, answered.

"Hey, Sherry, it's Concho. The chief around?"

"No, he's over at the Eagle Pass Mall at some kind of meeting."

"The mall? Does this have to do with that stupid talent search thing that Vince Hawk's putting on?"

He heard her giggle. "Stupid thing? It's kind of a very big deal, you know. They even canceled school today so the kids could go try out. It's going on today and the rest of the weekend. Sheriff Parkland's over there too."

"Parkland? What's he doing there?"

"Who knows," she said. "I'm just the records clerk around here, but if I had to guess, I'd say Roberto's thinking about a second career as a movie star."

"I'll have to start saving some rotten tomatoes to throw at the screen. In the meantime, maybe you can help me. I was wondering about the status of a juvenile case."

Sherry made a tsk-tsk sound. "You know those are confidential. I can't divulge any information about juveniles."

"And I'm not asking you to," Concho said. "But I happen to know Peskipaatei Standing Bear was reported missing and I was hoping she'd come back home. Can you at least tell me if she's still listed in the computer?"

After a few seconds delay, Sherry asked him to spell the girl's first name and her date of birth. Concho did so.

He could hear her fingers dancing over the computer keyboard. After another few seconds, Sherry came back on the line.

"Nope, she's still listed as a runaway. Why? You seen her?"

"No, her grandmother stopped by my place yesterday and told me about her."

"Rachel?" He could hear Sherry's sigh over the phone. "She's such a nice lady. A saint really. Does seamstress work for everybody on the Rez. That's how she supports herself and her granddaughter. Well, that and the casino stipend. She was calling here all day yesterday and then again this morning asking if we'd found Penny yet. I got so I was dreading answering the phone."

Concho was glad Rachel Standing Bear didn't have his cell number, but that would change if he called her now. He debated what to do for a moment and then asked, "Is Nila working?"

"Not yet. She's on afternoons. Want me to have her call you when she gets in?"

"Yeah." Concho started to recite his phone number, but Sherry stopped him.

"I've got it here on my screen," she said. "We do have

caller ID and all those technological things, you know. We're a regular official police department now."

"Sorry," Concho said. "Force of habit."

He thanked Sherry for her help, terminated the call, and debated what to do next. He thought about calling Maria to see if she was coming over tonight but then decided not to. From the sound of things, she was pretty busy. Still, he didn't feel like going back to his trailer and relaxing. He wanted to do something, but what?

No good deed, he thought and took out his notebook to look up Rachel Standing Bear's phone number.

CHAPTER THIRTEEN

RACHEL STANDING BEAR LOOKED EVEN MORE WRETCHED WHEN Concho visited her. When he'd called before dropping over, her voice on the phone had been laced with desperation.

"This is the second night and I haven't heard from her," the frantic woman said. "She's not answering her phone either. She's never done that before. Even when she was away before, she always at least answered."

"I just checked with the Tribal Police," Concho said. "They have an officer working on this, and I'm going to meet with her this afternoon."

"They're doing nothing. Peskipaatei means nothing to them."

Rachel Standing Bear's derision was obvious in her tone.

After trying unsuccessfully to try and buoy the woman's spirits, Concho switched tactics and asked if he could stop by to get some more information.

"Of course," she said. "You're my last hope."

The trailer where she and Peskipaatei lived wasn't all that different than the one Concho had lived in growing up. He too had been raised by his grandmother until she'd been murdered. This trailer was comparatively small and not in very good condition. A bedraggled row of flowers, petunias, decorated one section of exposed dirt near the front entrance, looking sort of like a cheap broach on a worn-out dress. Numerous rust spots lined the metal frames of the windows and door, and the once sturdy cement steps were badly broken and chipped so badly that some cement blocks had been haphazardly placed into them to augment the decrepit steps. Concho briefly entertained the altruistic notion of getting a bag of cement and coming back to do some patch work.

But one step at a time, he thought. *First, I'll have to see if I can find Peskipaatei.*

Rachel Standing Bear welcomed him inside and offered to make him some coffee.

"No thanks," Concho said. "I can't stay long. I asked if you could write up a list of Peskipaatei's friends."

The woman's face took on a sad expression.

"I tried to think of some," she said, looking down at the threadbare carpet in what must have passed for a living room. An old TV sat across from a dilapidated sofa and a couple of equally decrepit chairs. "But I'm afraid I only came up with a few first names."

She handed Concho a list of five names, all apparently female, on a torn-off sheet of notebook paper.

"Does she have a regular boyfriend?" he asked.

Rachel Standing Bear gave her head a vehement shake.

"I don't allow her to go out on dates with boys," she said.

Concho wondered about the effectiveness of that order but said nothing. He was getting a clearer picture of the situation now: a young girl living at about the poverty level and under the control of a loving, but restrictive grandmother...a good candidate for perpetual runaway status, as Roberto Echabarri had put it.

"I wonder if I could look at your granddaughter's room?"

"Sure. This way."

Concho followed the woman past a small but ultra clean kitchen area and then down a narrow corridor. They passed one bedroom, which he took for Rachel's, and on to another one adjacent to the rear door.

An easy escape hatch for a perpetual runaway.

The girl's room was an austere version of what Concho imagined a typical teenage girl's room might look like, although the bed was so tightly made you could bounce a quarter off of it. Concho suspected that was due to the grandmother's insistence or intervention. It was small and, except for the bed and a card table, devoid of furniture. Stacks of neatly folded clothes, mostly tank tops, a few blouses, underwear, and jeans were in a wooden box that he guessed substituted for a dresser. Another wooden box, set on its end to provide greater height, had a mirror, makeup, and a bunch of other feminine items. A small plastic jewelry box was on an inside shelf next to a couple of bags of unopened purple Taki bags. Concho checked the box and found an assortment of cheap jewelry composed mostly of earrings and necklaces. It also had a false bottom under which he found a nickel bag of weed and a feathered roach clip.

"What's that?" Rachel Standing Bear asked, and then frowned and added, "Oh, my god."

Concho said nothing. At least he saw no other signs of drug use, but that was far from a certainty, and he had no intention of doing a thorough search.

A pile of school books sat on the small card table along with a laptop computer, a single notebook, and a couple of pens. He opened the notebook and saw that the pages were covered with a free-flowing handwriting and numerous crude sketches, mostly of exaggerated hearts and flowers in purple and green ink. Most of the notations seemed to be nonsensical musings and notes to girlfriends rather than school lessons. He lifted the lid of the laptop and pressed the button to turn it on. When nothing happened after a good minute, he checked the connection and found it was not plugged in. The battery was evidently dead as well.

"Do you know the password for this laptop?" he asked.

Rachel Standing Bear shook her head.

"I bought it for her with the monthly casino check a while ago," she said. "Peskipaatei insisted on having one. She needs it for school, or so she says. I don't know anything about those things."

"Does she have a tablet too?"

The woman's eyebrows twitched and her hand swept toward the top of the table.

"Just that one."

"No," Concho said. "I mean an iPad. Another computer, a smaller one that she carries around?"

"Oh, that thing. Yeah, I bought her one of those, too." Rachel Standing Bear glanced around. "I don't see it here. She must have it."

"You notice anything else missing?"

The woman looked around, and she started to shake her head, but stopped.

"Her backpack's gone. It's a blue and white Tilly bag." Her lips twisted in apparent disgust. "Another thing I bought her that she said she had to have. She said all the girls have them, especially her friend, Holley."

Her finger pointed to a framed picture on the table next to the laptop.

Concho scanned the photo of two young girls, their heads pressed together and smiling in what appeared to be a "selfie photo." One was Peskipaatei, the other a White girl with red hair, freckles, and braces. They both appeared to be in their midteens and both were holding matching blue and white backpacks. The photo appeared to be more recent than the eighth-grade graduation photo that Rachel Standing Bear had given him yesterday. The lettering, *BFFS, decorated* the top of the frame.

"This her?" Concho asked.

Rachel Standing Bear nodded.

"She's rich. Lives in one of the ritzy places in Eagle Pass.

Don't ask me where because I've never been there. Peskipaatei knows her from school."

"Do you know Holley's last name?"

The woman thought for a moment.

"Cameron, I think. Like I said, I've only met her once when her father dropped Peskipaatei off here after they both tried out for the cheerleading squad. Holley made it, Peskipaatei didn't."

"You remember anything else about them?"

She shrugged. "Drove a real fancy car—one of those ones with that V inside a circle emblem."

"A Mercedes Benz?"

"Yeah, that was it. Silver colored."

Concho made a mental note of that and asked if she remembered anything else about them.

She shook her head. "I just seen them that one time. They seemed polite enough, but I could tell they couldn't wait to leave and probably wanted to wash their hands after being here." Her eyes shot downward. "Peskipaatei was so embarrassed she didn't even want to show them around our house, like she was ashamed of our home. And her grandfather had worked so hard to try and make this place nice."

A solitary tear wound its way down her left cheek.

"What's her email account?" Concho asked.

Rachel Standing Bear heaved a sigh and recited a g-mail account name.

"I don't know her password," she said. "At first I was keeping tabs on her, but she kept changing her password. I guess I should've kept up with it more."

Again, Concho didn't comment. Regrets were always plentiful and apparent. He decided not to take the laptop. Although the tech group could probably crack it, he didn't really have any legal standing to ask them. Plus, if this thing went sour and an official investigation was opened for a more serious matter, like kidnapping or homicide, there was no way Concho could explain his involvement in interrupting the chain of custody of any evidence. He turned back to the woman.

"You mentioned your granddaughter has a cell phone," Concho said. "Whose name is on the account?"

"Mine. She's only fifteen, after all."

"I'll need the number. And I'll also need you to sign a release so I can get the phone service company to release the information about the phone."

"You can find her through that?"

Her tone sounded suddenly optimistic, and Concho hated to fill her with false hope.

"Maybe," he said. "If she's got it on, it could give us an idea of where she's at, if we can trace it. Or at least who she's been talking to."

"I've been calling her constantly, but the phone just goes to voice mail right away."

Concho figured that it must be turned off, which would limit the chances of establishing triangulation fix, but it could provide a history of the girl's recent locations. He told Rachel Standing Bear this and gave her one of the standard release forms. She scribbled her name on it without even reading it.

"So you think you'll be able to find her?" Rachel Standing Bear asked.

Again, her voice was imbued with hopefulness.

"I'll do my best," Concho said, reaching down and picking up the *BFF's* photo. "You mind if I borrow this?"

"Sure. Anything. Whatever it takes to find her." The woman's breathing was rapid now, as if she'd been walking at a brisk pace for several hundred yards. She looked up at him. "Ranger Ten-Wolves, please...you've got to find her. She's not a bad girl really, and she's all I've got now. She's smart, too. She was doing real good in school this past month. Wants to be a nurse someday."

Concho knew better than to make some sort of optimistic promise he might not be able to keep but repeated that he'd do his best.

"That's all I can ask of you," Rachel Standing Bear said. "Thank you."

And that's all I can do, Concho thought as he took one more glance at the photo and slipped it into his pocket, wondering how this was going to turn out.

Unfortunately, he couldn't shake the feeling that it wasn't going to have a happy ending.

CHAPTER FOURTEEN

CONCHO WAS DEBATING HIS NEXT MOVE WHEN HIS CELL PHONE rang. He glanced at the screen and saw it was one of the Kickapoo Traditional Tribal Police Department numbers so he answered it.

"Ranger Ten-Wolves?" a feminine voice asked. "It's Officer Nila Willow. I heard you wanted to talk to me."

Her use of both formal police titles immediately put Concho on notice. She was also on a departmental line, which was no doubt being recorded, so whatever they said to each other had no expectation of privacy. Although he'd known her for a while, her demeanor was still a bit stand-offish. The woman didn't say much and Concho wondered if she was just shy or if she didn't like him for some reason.

"Yeah," he said. "I did call earlier. Thanks for calling me back."

"No problem." She left it at that.

This lady was all business, that was for sure. Concho had been glad when Echabarri hired her, the first female officer on the KTTP, and he'd heard she'd been a standout at the state police academy. First in her class in both academics and physical fitness.

The dead-air silence on the phone made him wonder if she'd terminated the call, or something, and then he recalled her taciturn nature and cleared his throat. Given that it was a recorded call, he had to be careful what he said and what he asked of her. Plus, word of the shooting and his administrative leave status could make things a bit complicated.

Better be straightforward, he thought.

"I was talking to the chief yesterday," he said. "I heard Peskipaatei Standing Bear's missing."

His comment was met by the sound of more dead air.

He cleared his throat again, hoping to spur some conversation on her part, but that didn't work.

"The chief said he was going to have you look into it," he said.

Again, the silence.

"So?" he left the word dangle a bit before adding, "Have you found anything out?"

Nila Willow offered no response.

He began to wonder if this woman ever muttered more than one or two sentences an hour. Getting her to talk was like pulling teeth.

Or maybe she was afraid to talk. It was an ongoing police case and giving out information about juveniles was a touchy matter.

He tried one more tactic.

"Her grandmother stopped by my place and asked me to look into things for her."

"Oh?"

A one-word response. At least he was making progress.

"Yeah," he said, thinking of trying a different tactic. "I suppose you heard that I was involved in a shooting a couple of nights ago. I'm technically on administrative leave until the investigative hearing clears me to return to duty. So, I figured I'd help Rachel Standing Bear out a bit, and you guys as well, by looking into the matter."

After he stopped talking, he realized how hackneyed that

sounded, but he thought he heard a slight giggle of amusement on the other end.

"That's the most absurd explanation I've heard in a while," Nila Willow said.

"Yeah, well, absurd or not, it's the truth. The chief said the girl's kind of a regular runaway, and I was hoping she'd return home on her own, but that's not the case. I saw Mrs. Standing Bear a little while ago and she still hasn't heard from her."

More silence.

So we're back to the silent treatment again, he thought.

"From what I've gathered from the grandmother," he said, "I think the girl could use the advice of a good female role model. Too many young girls on the Rez run into trouble without the right guidance."

"And you think that's me? The right guidance?"

"Well, you're a lot closer to a good female role model than I am."

That elicited another faint hint of amusement from her, but after a sigh, her tone stiffened once again.

"Ranger Ten-Wolves, what is it exactly that you want me to tell you? You must know that giving out information in juvenile cases is restricted for patrol officers. You'll have to talk to one of our juvenile officers."

"Okay, but I got some inconclusive information from the grandmother about her friends. I was hoping you might fill things out a bit more."

"I'll leave word for one of our juvenile officers to contact you," she said. "Now I really have to get going. Roll call's coming up. Goodbye."

"Nila, wait."

But he could tell the connection was gone. Sighing, he shook his head and scrolled down for another number.

Raul Molina, Concho's best friend on the Rangers, answered his personal cell phone even before the second ring. They'd gone through their Ranger Training together and now Molina was working dispatch.

"What's up, big man?" Molina's voice said over the phone.

"A bit of this and a bit of that," Concho replied. It was quickly becoming their standard greeting exchange.

"Hey, I heard you were involved in a shooting," Molina said. "How's that going?"

"Could be better," Concho said. "The feds are involved and you know how they love to drag things out."

"The feds? Why the hell are they sticking their noses into it?"

"Courtesy of the Special Auxiliary Border Surveillance— Joint Task Force, or SABS—JT," Concho said, injecting a heavy note of sarcasm into his words. "Puts it under their purview."

"Shit. And to think I was considering scarfing up some of that easy overtime. All they usually want to do is to drag good police officers through the mud every chance they get."

Concho was always hesitant to subscribe to the clichéd anti-federal agency stance so many police officers adhered to, but it was hitting pretty close to home in this case. He still hoped there would be a quick resolution, though.

"Well," Concho said. "That remains to be seen. Anyway, I need a favor."

"Don't you always?" Molina chuckled. "One of these days you're going to have to make good on all your promises to buy me a beer sometime, you know."

"You got it. What I need is for you to run a Sound-Ex on someone named Cameron."

"Okay." Molina cleared his throat. Common spelling?"

"I believe so."

Molina's reply was slightly hesitant. "Okay. First name?"

"I don't know."

"Huh? You got any idea how many people with the last name of Cameron there are in the state of Texas?"

"Probably more than just a few," Concho said, "but this is most likely a White male and he drives a Mercedes. And he lives in Eagle Pass."

Concho heard his friend's loud exhale.

"All right, that gives me something to work with." The sound of computer keys being pressed came over the phone connection. "You got anything else, like an approximate age?"

"Maybe thirty-five to fifty."

Molina snorted.

"You're gonna owe me a lot more than a beer for this one." He paused and his voice took on an inquisitive tone. "Hey, what's this all about anyway? Ain't you supposed to be on administrative leave, or something?"

"Or something," Concho replied, trying to keep his tone light. "I'm looking into something for a friend."

"A friend? This ain't some kind of child custody thing, is it?"

"Not hardly." Concho debated how much to tell him but then figured as long as they weren't on a recorded line it wouldn't hurt. "A young Indian girl from the Rez is missing. I told her grandmother I'd look into it. This guy Cameron's daughter is a school chum of the girl."

Molina didn't respond, but Concho could hear the man's fingers dancing over the keyboard. After the better part of a minute, he grunted and cleared his throat again.

"Okay," he said. "Here we go. Reginald P. Cameron, Eagle Pass, Texas. Drives a new Mercedes Benz." He read off the address and the man's date of birth. "That him?"

"Sounds like it," Concho said, writing the information down in his notebook. "Run one more for me, will ya?"

Molina made an audible groan. "Now what?"

Concho recited Peskipaatei Standing Bear's information.

He heard more clicking of the keys, followed by, "She's still listed as a Minor Requiring Authoritative Intervention. No mention of her being endangered though."

So the KTTP was still treating her as a standard runaway. Apparently the case was still on the back burner, even though the girl had been missing for well over twenty-four hours. He made a mental note to talk to Echabarri about upgrading her

missing status to endangered if he couldn't get any solid
leads.

For all the good that would do, he thought. He was following a
cold trail.

The sad fact remained that dozens of young girls, way too
many of them Indian or Native American, disappeared each
year, never to be heard from again. He hoped for a better
outcome in this instance.

Maybe this administrative leave is a good thing, he thought. *At least
it gives me a little time to try and find her.*

For now, though, it was time to see what Holley Cameron
had to say.

CHAPTER FIFTEEN

THE CAMERONS LIVED IN AN UNINCORPORATED MAVERICK County section of Eagle Pass called El Dorado. It was near the more upper-class areas of the city, although not of the same caliber as the ultra-rich, like Lucio Zapatero and his wife. But Concho knew that money and a big house was no assurance of legitimacy. He'd dealt with the Zapateros a few months back while investigating a bank robbery and knew of Lucio's dubious business connections south of the border. Concho circled the block once, spying the silver Mercedes in the long driveway next to a burgundy Cadillac XT5 SUV. The garage itself had three overhead doors so the possibility of another vehicle was a distinct possibility. Perhaps it was reserved for daughter Holley, who was probably too young for a driver's license at this time. The house itself was two stories and was well kept. A green lawn was expertly cut and the row of bushes under the front picture window was artistically coiffed as well. He debated whether or not to park and observe for a bit. Sherry Garcia had mentioned earlier that school had been canceled due to the big talent quest, so there was a possibility Holley Cameron would be home. There was also the equally logical possibility that she was out with friends.

He pulled the tow truck over to the curb and glanced at his watch. Sixteen-thirty-five.

Close enough to the standard five o'clock dinner time of most rich, affluent, upwardly mobile white families. Plus, if he sat here in this contraption and maintained a surveillance he was bound to attract the attention of some neighborhood watch group. Then he'd be answering questions from the local police.

Better to get it over with, he thought, and shoved the gearshift into first and eased out the clutch, turning onto the long spotless cement drive and wondered if the old oil pan would leave any telltale dribbling on the immaculate surface. He'd noticed a few droplets documenting some of his previous stops.

Oh well, he thought as he pulled up behind the Mercedes, it'll be job security for Cameron's maintenance staff.

A scenario of a bunch of harried brown men with bottles of gasoline, cleaning solvent, and baking soda trying to remove the stains floated around in his mind's eye.

The front door had an overleaf of fine wood, oak, he guessed, outlining the frame of the jamb. A decorative doorbell, ringed in gold, initiated audible chimes inside the house when Concho pressed the button. He half-expected a butler to open the door, but instead it was a middle-aged man with dark-brown hair and a bit of a paunch whom Concho assumed to be Holley's father.

"Good afternoon," Concho said, holding up his identification. "I'm Ranger Ten-Wolves. Are you Mr. Cameron?"

The man's skin was pale, and the skin around his eyes looked puffy and tight.

Either plastic surgery or Botox injections, Concho thought. The elusive quest for eternal youth.

"What do you want?" the man said. He glanced toward the decrepit tow truck in the driveway and his face stiffened as he looked from the ID to the tow truck and back again to Concho.

It was a great temptation for Concho to parrot one of those

old bumper stickers mottos like, *My other car is a Mercedes,* but he felt that might not go over too well in this instance.

"I'm investigating a missing person case and I need to speak with your daughter, Holley."

"Holley?" The space between the man's eyebrows furrowed. "What for?"

Concho took a silent but deep breath before he answered.

"As I told you, it's a missing person case. A young girl. One of Holley's schoolmates. They're friends."

"What? Who?"

This runaround was getting to Concho. He tried a different tactic.

"Is your daughter home right now, sir?"

Answering a question with a question seemed to throw the other man off track.

"Why, yes. She is. We're about to have dinner."

"Good." Concho nodded and began a subtle shift in his posture, edging forward a little. Cameron immediately took a step back to maintain his personal integrity zone. "This won't take long, if I could speak to her now, please."

Cameron's face had taken on an expression of mixed anger and alarm. His jaw gaped and his body stiffened. Before he could speak, a woman and a girl appeared in the foyer behind him. The woman was tall and slender and appeared to be in her early forties with red hair. The girl was wearing a long-sleeved lavender top and those "distressed" blue jeans with the prefab fabricated holes in them. Her red hair was long and held back by two gold barrettes. A matching gold necklace with a reddish stone in the center of a charm graced her neck. These fine jewelry pieces stood in contrast to the raggedy jeans and scarlet rubber bracelet around her left wrist. There was some writing on it but Concho couldn't discern what it was. He did know, however, from the photo that she was Holley Cameron.

Smiling, the big Ranger tipped his hat to the women.

"I'm sorry for the interruption," he said, first glancing at the mother and then centering his gaze on the daughter. "But I'm working a missing person case and it's someone you know."

The girl's eyes widened.

"Who?" she asked.

Concho reached into the pocket of his BDU vest and withdrew the BFF framed picture.

"Peskipaatei Standing Bear," he said, showing the photo. "I believe you and her are friends."

He phrased it like a statement of fact rather than a question. The girl started to answer when Reginald Cameron lurched forward and tried to grab the framed photograph.

"Let me see that," he shouted.

His fingers curled around it but Concho's big hand held it securely. He turned his head and gave the other man one of his "Don't mess with me" stares.

Cameron's face blanched and his fingers retreated.

"Penny's missing?" Holley Cameron said.

"Yes." Concho turned back to look down at her. "When was the last time you saw her?"

The girl pressed her lips.

"Un…I don't know. It was at school, I guess. A couple of days ago I think."

"Can you narrow it down a bit more? Did she confide in you about any plans she might have had?"

Holley was about to answer when Reginald Cameron inserted himself into the conversation again.

"Is this that Indian girl I told you I didn't want you hanging around with?"

His daughter's gaze immediately went to the floor.

"Please, Mr. Cameron," Concho said, trying his best to sound non-threatening. "I just need to ask a few more questions."

The other man's mouth opened and he started to speak when Mrs. Cameron interjected.

"Reg, please. He's only trying to do his job and if Holley can help."

"I told her not to hang around with that—"

Whatever word he'd had in mind was never uttered. After a few seconds of awkward silence, the wife said, "What if it was Holley that was missing? Wouldn't you want someone to help?"

Reginald Cameron's mouth worked, but no words came out. He looked away and remained silent.

"She was real excited about the big talent quest starting," Holley said. "All of us were. I know she was planning to go to that."

"Did you see her there?"

The girl started to answer when her father cut her off again.

"You went to that thing?" His voice boomed. "After I told you not to?"

"I didn't go," she said. "I just heard she wanted to go."

Concho doubted the veracity of that statement, but figured this wasn't the right time for a third degree. Not if he wanted to get any more cooperation.

"Did you two speak on the phone at all the past few days?" he asked.

Her eyes shot to her father, and she shook her head.

"Would you mind if I looked at your phone real quick, Holley?" Concho said.

"Wait a minute," Reginald Cameron said. "What right do you have to look at my daughter's phone? You got a warrant?"

That last refrain labeled the man as one of those ignorant TV educated lawyers parroting a phrase made popular on cop shows. If Concho had had a nickel for every time some misinformed jackass had said that, he would actually be driving a Mercedes himself.

"I'm just asking your permission, sir. Perhaps your daughter can show me the names and phone numbers of some of their mutual friends." He tried his disarming smile again, but knew it probably looked more feral than benign. Directing his next question to Holley, he asked, "Does she have any other friends I might talk to? A boyfriend, maybe?"

Holley started to say something and then stopped. She shrugged her shoulders and shook her head.

"I can't think of anybody," she said.

Concho could tell the girl was most likely lying, or at the very least holding back.

"There," Reginald Cameron said. "Satisfied? Now I'll have to ask you to leave."

"Reg," his wife said.

He shot a glaring look her way that ended any further conversation. Turning back toward Concho, he asked, "What's your badge number?"

Concho took out two of his cards and handed one to him and then one to his daughter.

"My information is on that card, sir. Now, if I may…" He turned to the girl. "I'd like you to think about any mutual friends that I might check with. And if she does call you, please tell her that her grandmother is very worried and ask her to call me right away."

She gave a quick nod.

Concho could absolutely tell that she was holding back, intimidated by her father's untoward rage.

"Okay," Reginald Cameron said. "That's enough. You've already ruined our dinner."

Concho glanced at him and said, "My apologies for the interruption, sir, but there's a young girl your daughter's age that's missing. Her family's very worried about her." He shot a quick glance at Holley and noticed a slight twinge around her eyes. If only he had a few more minutes with her, preferably alone or out of the earshot of her father.

His hopes were dashed when he saw the father rip the card out of his daughter's hand.

So much for this lead, Concho thought.

"And we've already told you we know nothing about that

—" Once again, he left the sentence unfinished. Twin blushes colored his cheeks.

"Thank you for your cooperation," Concho said, keeping his tone neutral as he turned and stepped back toward the door. Pausing, he said, "Please give me a call if you do think of anything else. Anytime."

"She has nothing else to say," Reginald Cameron spat out. "We've already told you all we know."

Maybe, maybe not, Concho thought as he stepped through the open door.

He still had a vestige of hope, but more than just a few things were bothering him about the encounter, some of which he couldn't quite put his finger on.

As he got into the tow truck, he caught the quick sight of someone, he couldn't tell who, pushing aside the drape in the front window.

Holley maybe?

Or perhaps it was her father, making sure the big intruding Indian Ranger was in fact leaving.

Have to wait and see, he told himself and shifted into reverse. As he backed the tow truck he saw the vehicle had left an appropriate parting gift. Three dark speckles of oil now decorated the concrete.

He was grinning as he backed out of the driveway.

* * *

CONCHO PULLED UP IN FRONT OF THE KTTP STATION JUST IN time to see Roberto Echabarri walking out of the front door and heading for his white SUV with the tribal police emblem on the side. He was wearing a brown suit and tie and looked very dapper. When he saw Concho, he stopped, knocked his Stetson back on his head, and smiled.

"I was wondering when you were going to drop by again," Echabarri said. "You get back on regular duty yet?"

"Close, but no cigar," Concho said, getting out of the truck. "Still waiting to be officially interviewed."

Echabarri shook his head and laughed.

"Well, I gotta say, you cut a very fine figure behind the wheel of that…" He paused and grinned. "What exactly do they call that thing?"

"It's called a tow truck." He reached out and gave the solid metal door an affectionate pat. "So how'd your screen test go?"

"My what?"

"I called earlier and got the word that you and Parkland were over at the mall sucking up to Vince Hawk, trying to get a couple roles in his new movie."

Echabarri's smile transformed into a frown.

"Hey," Concho said, flashing a rather wicked grin. "What's wrong? They already cast the parts of the Lone Ranger and Tonto?"

The chief emitted a snort.

"That'll be the day. And for the record, the meeting was strictly business. He wants an extra watch overnight on his tour buses while they're parked on the far side of the casino. And Hawk also wants to film part of his new western on the Rez. And Parkland was there about maintaining the sheriff's security detail through the whole weekend. The thing's really a big hit."

"That's good to know. You're turning into a real dedicated civil servant."

"Which is why the Tribal Council appointed me chief. Now what brings you here, or should I say, what favor do you want now?"

"How do you know I want a favor?"

"I'm psychic."

"Well, now that you mention it…"

"Hurry up. They got the stew pot cooking for me at home."

"Then I'll be brief," Concho said. "I just need permission

to use your departmental fax machine. And one of your computers to type out the cover letter."

"Who you sending a fax to?"

"The phone carrier for Peskipaatei Standing Bear's cell."

"Penny? She's still missing, ain't she?"

Concho nodded.

Echabarri put his hands on his hips and blew out a long breath.

"Nila mentioned it to me. I told her to nose around some." His face assumed a thoughtful expression. "It's been over twenty-four hours, hasn't it?"

"Closer to forty-eight, if her grandmother is right about her leaving the night before last."

"Shit," Echabarri muttered. "We'd better update her status to missing-endangered."

"That's what I was thinking. And I've got a release form signed by Rachel Standing Bear for the phone info. The account's in her name."

Turning back toward the front entrance to the station, Echabarri said, "Let's go."

"I can handle this as long as I've got your blessing," Concho said. "No need for you to be late for supper."

"Nah, who knows when they'll get back to us, and this way there'll be somebody here twenty-four-seven to monitor. I'll leave word for dispatch to contact you if and when the phone company replies."

"A list of calls made and received as well as locations would be much appreciated."

"No sweat. I'll call Nila in and have her help you." Echabarri heaved a sigh. "We should've been more attentive to this in the first place. It's just that…well…" He took in another deep breath. "No excuses. We dropped the ball, or rather I did by not pushing it. Do you know how many Indian girls disappear each year and nobody does squat about it? Nobody even cares. Plus, I shouldn't need you to tell me how to do my job."

Concho said nothing but clapped his friend on the shoulder and they walked into the station together.

Maybe now, Concho felt, they were starting to get somewhere.

CHAPTER SIXTEEN

THE TWO SUBSEQUENT PHONE CALLS UNDERMINED WHATEVER satisfaction Concho felt as he drove away from the KTTP station. The first was from Maria, and she sounded a bit distraught.

"What's wrong, honey?" he asked, but he was afraid he already knew the answer.

"Are you home? Can I come over?"

From the tone it sounded like she was a step away from tears. He hoped against hope it was nothing serious.

"Are you going to tell me what's wrong?" he asked.

"I will. Where are you?"

"Just pulled out of the KTTP."

"I'll meet you at your place," she said. "Okay?"

"Sure. But now tell me—"

"I will," she broke in. "But not over the phone. I'm on my way too."

With that, she ended the call.

He dropped his cell phone on the seat next to him and downshifted to third, hitting the accelerator to get some more speed from the old truck as he raced down the road. As he shifted back into fourth, his cell rang again. Thinking it was

Maria calling him back, he immediately grabbed it and answered without looking at the screen.

"Honey?" he blurted out.

"Don't you usually say 'hello?' " a male voice said.

It took Concho a second to place it.

"Captain Shaw?" he asked.

"You sound upset. Everything all right?"

"As good as could be expected," Concho said, "for being on administrative leave."

He heard Shaw chuckle.

"Well, when it rains, it pours sometimes," the captain said. "But hopefully we're edging closer to the sunshine. Your preliminary hearing's been scheduled for tomorrow morning at the Maverick County Sheriff's Headquarters Station. Nine o'clock sharp."

"My preliminary hearing? You make it sound like I'm being charged with a felony."

"Nothing like that. Poor choice of words on my part. I told you, I reviewed your report. It looks like a good shoot to me."

Concho felt like asking how it looked to the damn feds, who were seemingly making a mountain out of a proverbial molehill. But instead, he asked, "So what's the latest?"

Shaw made a clucking sound. "You know those tight-sphinctered feds. They like to play everything close to their vests. You got the right to have a legal aid rep with you, you know."

Concho mulled this over.

"Do I need one?"

"Not in my opinion," Shaw said. "But it's your call. Anyway, Internal Affairs will be assisting as well. They're going to open up with the standard bullshit by saying you don't have to make any statement, but refusing to do so will constitute insubordination and you'll be subject to dismissal."

"This ain't exactly my first rodeo, Captain."

Concho had been through shooting reviews before but never one with the DOJ involved.

"Yeah, I know," Shaw said. "And you and I both know that this whole thing stinks. But you got to play the hand you're dealt sometimes. Just know that I'll be pulling for you. Just use your head, tell the truth, and watch your ass."

The captain's somewhat conflicting comments made Concho feel like Shaw knew a lot more than he wasn't saying.

But what?

Before Concho could inquire further, the captain abruptly ended the conversation with, "So as far as this conversation we just had, it never happened. I just notified you of the time of the hearing. Nothing else. Got it?"

"Yes, sir."

"Good luck, then," Shaw said and hung up.

It sounded like his boss was covering his tracks, which brought more anxiety into the equation.

What was he holding back?

A double-barreled set of worries, he thought.

Concho reviewed the events leading up to and through the shooting in accelerated playback in his mind. Would he have done anything different?

No, he thought. *I wouldn't have.*

He'd have to stand by that and hope the board of inquiry didn't try to twist the facts. But if they did, he'd be ready.

* * *

MARIA'S CAR WAS PARKED IN THE USUAL SPOT ADJACENT TO THE entrance to the fire pit. He glanced around and saw her sitting on the steps to the trailer's front door. She had a key. He wondered why she hadn't gone in. After shoving the truck's gearshift into first gear, he shut off the engine and stomped on the emergency brake. There was a slight incline and the last thing he needed was the tow truck somehow slipping out of gear and rolling into Maria's car. It was a small chance, but the way his luck had been running lately, he didn't want to gamble about anything. As he got out of the vehicle and strode toward her he took a moment to admire her exquisite beauty.

Her hair was still fastened up on her head, but two errant strands on either side framed her face in ebony. She was wearing one of her professional, dark-blue business outfits—a jacket and matching skirt, and a white silk blouse. He felt his passion rising within him and the growing tightness in his groin and could hardly wait to get her out of her outfit and into his bed.

"Hi," he said as he stopped in front of her. "How come you didn't let yourself in and get comfortable?"

"If by that you mean why I'm not naked already, I figured I'd take the luxury of having you undress me."

Her smile was provocative.

"Say no more," he said.

Concho reached up and unlocked the front door to his trailer and shoved it open. Then he slipped his keys back into his pocket, bent down, and slid one arm under her knees and the other around her back. Lifting her was easy. As he ascended the steps her face brushed against his and her tongue darted over his lips. She knocked his hat off his head. Pressing her body close to his, he marched straight through the living room, down the narrow hallway, and into his bedroom. Lowering her slowly onto the bed, he straightened up and removed her high-heeled shoes. Her feet felt stiff and tight so he gently massaged them.

Maria moaned softly.

"Oh, that feels so good." Her voice was hardly more than a whisper.

Concho continued with the foot massage for a bit more, and then let his hands move up her lightly tanned cinnamon legs. Stopping at her hips, he lifted her and reached behind to unfasten the metal clasps of the skirt and pull down the zipper. As his fingers moved with slow precision, Maria first raised her hips to allow him to remove the skirt, and then she shrugged off her jacket. Her white lace panties came into view. By the time he'd removed her skirt, she'd finished unbuttoning her blouse and tossed that off as well.

"I thought you were going to let me do that?" he said.

She reached behind her and undid her bra with a seemingly effortless flick of her fingers.

How did women always manage to make it look so easy?

His eyes were fixed on her breasts as she slipped out of the brassiere and dropped it over the side of the bed. She now had on only the underpants and Concho felt like tearing them off of her. His large fingers gripped the lacy edge of the elastic and he started to pull but her hands caught his.

"Un-un," she said. "Not till you're undressed."

"What?"

"You heard me," she said. "I want to watch."

"Oh? You turning into a voyeur now?"

Her tongue swept over her full lips.

"It's all in the anticipation," she said. "And don't forget to go back and lock the front door."

He let his fingers trace over her pubic area as he straightened up.

"You sure know how to put a damper on the mood," he said.

Her smile was wicked as she rolled onto her side, her breasts rolling slightly, her nipples stiffening.

"I just don't want anybody disturbing us when it's my turn to undress you," she said.

* * *

THEIR LOVEMAKING HAD BEEN QUICK AND INTENSE, BOTH OF them surging forward like two wild, hungry beasts, kissing, exploring, tasting, and finally consummating the act. Afterward they lay naked in each other's arms, a thin sheen of perspiration covering both of them.

"So what's troubling you?" she asked.

His head jerked slightly.

"How'd you know something was troubling me?"

Her finger made concentric circles on his chest.

"I can tell," she whispered.

He chuckled. "You know, I was just about to ask you the same thing. You told me you had something you wanted to talk about in person."

He felt her ribcage expand as she took in a deep breath, but didn't reply.

"So?" he asked.

"You first."

It was his turn to inhale copiously.

"I've got my shooting review tomorrow morning. Captain Shaw called and more or less advised me to bring a lawyer."

"Are you going to?"

He shrugged.

"I don't really think I have to. I mean, it was a good shoot. Even Shaw said so."

"Then why's he suggesting a lawyer?"

Concho shrugged again.

"Don't know. Maybe because the feds are sticking their noses into things."

They lay entwined together, neither moving or speaking. Finally, Maria said, "Maybe you should. I can make a call to corporate. I'm sure they have lawyers on staff that could—"

"Absolutely not. I don't need one and if I did, it wouldn't be some pencil-necked geek from the *Mall de las Aguilas*."

Her head elevated off of his chest.

"And what's wrong with the *Mall de las Aguilas*?" Her tone sounded haughty and he couldn't tell if she was joking or not.

"Well," he said, grinning. "For one thing all their lawyers will be too busy bending over to kiss Vince Hawk's ass, won't they?"

Her body stiffened for a split second and Concho picked up on it.

"It's your turn now," he said. "What's bothering you?"

When she didn't reply and started to move away he used his big arm to tighten his embrace.

"Huh-un," he said. "You don't go anywhere until you confess."

"Confess? That's bullshit. Now let me go. I have to use the bathroom."

He held her fast.

"Nope."

"I told you. I have to go."

"I don't believe that for a minute."

"Concho!"

"I'll reach under the bed for the chamber pot," he said with an accompanying laugh. "Now what is it?"

Her body strained to push away from his, but to no avail. Just when he was getting worried that he really might be keeping her from using the facilities he felt her body relax and collapse against his.

"I had another rough day," she said.

It took only a moment for him to connect the dots.

"Hawk?" he asked.

She nodded.

"What did he do this time?"

Her teeth closed over her lower lip.

"Nothing," she said. "He just…"

"Tell me."

She took a quick breath and related the story. It had been another long, grueling day dealing with the ongoing talent quest. Meetings, planning, luncheons…Hawk had waited until the end and then said he had some release forms he needed duplicated by tomorrow. Maria told him she'd send someone from security up to his suite when one of the big wigs from corporate interceded and told her to see to it herself. Hawk had grinned and winked at him surreptitiously. That's when she knew the whole thing must be part of a preplanned ruse.

"Just the good old boys," she said. "Never meaning no

harm, getting the female mall manager in a position to do a little extracurricular activity."

The ends of her mouth twisted downward.

"Did you go?" he asked, feeling the rage building within him.

"Yes, I did, but I only went up to his room. I maintained a proper distance and when we got inside he flashed his leering grin and said, 'Alone at last.' "

"What happened then?"

"I asked him where the forms he wanted copying were, and he just laughed." She stopped and caught her lip between her teeth once again.

"What else?"

"He tried to be glib, and then he put his hand here." She took Concho's wrist and guided his palm to her buttocks.

Concho felt the red-hot anger burning within him. His exhalation came in a snort and he relaxed his grip on her and started to get up.

"Looks like I'm going to go have a little talk with that son of a bitch, Hawk," he said. "And that corporate asshole, too. What's his name?"

She straddled him, keeping both hands pushing downward on his massive chest.

"No you won't," she said.

"The hell I won't."

"Please, please, please." She lowered her face to his chest and began sobbing. "I'd lose my job. And there's nothing more that happened. Really."

He waited a few seconds, then reached over and brushed the tears away from her exquisite cheeks.

"I just want to help," he said.

A laugh burst from her mouth and despite the flow of tears, she smiled.

"Actually, you already did," she said. "I told him you were my boyfriend and that you were a Texas Ranger and you wouldn't like him copping a feel."

"Boyfriend? Is that all I am?"

"No, of course not, but—"

"I figured I'd at least rate being called a significant other, or something." She stared at him for several seconds and then her lips curled into a sly smile. Leaning forward, she kissed him and then said, "Significant other...I like that. Why don't I show you how significant you are?"

Her open mouth closed over his.

After a long, sensuous kiss, her lips withdrew and she asked, "What does that tell you?"

He shrugged. "That you should have said you've got a two-hundred-seventy-five pound badass that would be coming for him. But anyway, did it work?"

"Did it ever." She brought her right hand up and wiped away a tear. "He backed off like a scared rabbit. Or a rebuked tom cat. Anyway, he apologized profusely and walked me to the door. I almost had to laugh as I rode down in the elevator. Alone, leaving Mr. Hawk to play with his bag of tricks. I was still a little disappointed in Bob Otis—he's the guy from corporate, though. That he'd set me up like that."

"I'll have to have a little talk with him, too."

"No you won't," she said. "I'll deal it. There's no way I want to disrupt this talent quest thing, but I intend to make a full sexual harassment complaint later."

"You go, girl," he said. "I guess I'll let you handle it then."

"You really mean it?"

Her expression was so perky that he didn't have the heart to tell her that he already knew he'd let her corporate HR deal with Bob what's-his-name, but Concho also knew he was on a collision course with one, Vincent Swooping Hawk.

CHAPTER SEVENTEEN

MARIA HAD SET THE ALARM FOR FIVE O'CLOCK AGAIN AND insisted on leaving without even eating breakfast, saying she had to drive home, shower, do new makeup, and change clothes. Concho didn't object and after watching her depart against the yellowish glow of a nascent sun, decided to go for a run to clear his head and shake off the residual anxieties of the pending shooting investigation and the coming confrontation with Vincent Hawk. One was as inevitable as the other.

After changing into his sweats and running shoes, he slipped on the shoulder rig and fastened the new Staccato into the holster. He didn't bother to take any extra magazines in the corresponding pouches on the right side, figuring seventeen plus-one rounds would be enough protection on a casual training run. Hopefully, he wouldn't encounter any feral hogs or predators of the two-legged variety. But the area looked serene and peaceful as he slipped out his back door and down the steps.

A couple of jackrabbits scurried away as he ran along the edge of the arroyo. Maybe the coyotes were late sleepers, and the early morning temperature was most likely discouraging to any snakes. He still kept an eye out as he passed over the dusty terrain. The ground was uneven in most spots, but he quickly adjusted, appreciating the cushioning support of his well-designed running shoes. He's been surprised back in the Army that they allowed the recruits to run in gym shoes, especially during airborne training. Back in the day, he'd heard the old veterans complaining that they'd done it all in their jump boots —running, marching, jumping.

Times change, he said back then. My ancestors ran these same plains barefoot or maybe in moccasins.

He went what he estimated was two about two miles and then turned back and reversed course. By the time he got back to his trailer, he was covered with sweat but felt great. It was not yet six and the grayish sky was tinctured with an orange glow rising over the eastern horizon.

Something flickered in the fire pit and Concho saw a familiar figure sitting in one of the lawn chairs. A wisp of smoke drifted upward from Meskwaa's shaggy head. Concho strode over to him, his breathing returning to normal by the last few steps.

"She left you early this morning," Meskwaa said. A sly smile traced over his lips as he brought the twisted cigarette away from his mouth and looked at Concho's sweat-soaked garments. "And apparently you had surplus energy that you didn't get to expend. How do you call it? Sublimation?"

Concho grinned at that thought.

"Something like that. But we both have busy mornings scheduled."

The old man nodded and drew in more smoke from the crinkled butt. There was barely anything left of the cigarette. After taking one more draw, he let the smoke drift slowly out of his nostrils as his calloused fingertips ground out the burning embers. He then methodically removed a small, cream-colored envelope from his shirt pocket, opened it, and dropped the extinguished butt inside. Replacing the envelope in his pocket, he glanced up at Concho and then to the extra-large lawn chair opposite him.

Concho took his seat.

"I had another vision," Meskwaa said. "This one more disturbing than the first."

Concho leaned forward, waiting.

Instead of continuing with the description, Meskwaa's eyes narrowed and settled upon the Staccato.

"You have a new gun," he said.

"I do." Concho undid the snap, removed the Staccato, dropped the magazine, locked back the slide, and used his left hand to secure the ejected round before it fell to the ground. He handed the weapon, butt-first to Meskwaa.

The old man inspected the pistol, turning it to and fro, then hitting the slide release and easing the slide forward. He pulled it back a few times, nodded, and held out his left hand for the magazine. Concho handed it to him and Meskwaa inspected it as well.

"Seventeen rounds," he said. "Eighteen with the one in your hand. Quite a formidable weapon. You know, if Geronimo would have had a couple hundred of these, he would never have had to surrender."

"Probably not," Concho agreed.

Meskwaa smiled and looked over at him. "He regretted that surrender, you know. On his deathbed he said that he wished he'd fought on to the death."

"Yeah, well, sometimes discretion isn't the better part of valor."

"It seldom is," the old man said. "It is wise to remember that today. In your trials."

Concho wondered how the old man could possibly know about his upcoming hearing. A trial was a good way to describe it. He knew better than to inquire how Meskwaa knew the things he knew. Knowing such things was the way of a *Naataineniiha*, a medicine man of the Kickapoo Tribe. But Meskwaa had used the plural: *trials*.

What else can you tell me?" Concho asked. "About your vision?"

"There is much deception, trickery, and danger. There are those who lie in wait, their hands ready with weapons. Expect that they will strike at you from out of the darkness, from behind the next corner, the next arroyo. But do not fear. You will have some help."

"I will? From who?"

The old man's head gave a fractional shake and he said nothing more.

Concho waited for Meskwaa to elaborate, but when he didn't Concho knew the warning concerning the vision must be pretty much complete.

"You're making me glad I took that gun with me this morning," Concho said.

Meskwaa nodded, locked back the slide, and handed the gun back to him.

"You would do well not to be baited in your dealings with Vincent Swooping Hawk," Meskwaa said.

Again, Concho was surprised, but realized he shouldn't have been. Word of Hawk's triumphant return was already old news on the Rez.

"I've been around too long for that," he said.

"Still, the hawk is a clever adversary. While no match for the wolf in combat, the bird uses speed and trickery when it strikes."

"I will be careful. And I don't expect it'll come to much. He's too interested in making his new movie." Concho held up his big, clenched left fist. "And running into something like this could ruin his movie-star profile."

Meskwaa chuckled. "I hear he's making a movie about Geronimo. Filming it on the Rez and down in Mexico."

"So I've been told. Production costs are supposed to be a lot lower down south of the border."

The old man's chuckle deepened. "I wonder if he knows that the real Geronimo hated Mexicans. Killed a lot of them."

"Let's hope he pays them a decent wage instead."

Meskwaa smiled as he got to his feet and placed a hand on Concho's shoulder.

"Beware of the treachery in your first trial today, too," he said. "The spirit of the truth is on your side, but make sure you are at your best. You have a rough journey ahead."

Concho pondered the astuteness of Meskwaa's preternatural wisdom and prescience as he watched the old man walk away.

* * *

BEING AT HIS BEST MEANT LAYING OUT A FRESHLY DRY-CLEANED white shirt and black jeans as well as taking the time to shine up his boots and use a healthy dose of Brasso to make his Texas Ranger star gleam. Just like going up for Soldier of the Month at Fort Lewis back in his Army days. He remembered the old sergeant's advice: Look your best—when a soldier looks sharp, he feels sharp. And he definitely needed to feel sharp today, especially after Meskwaa's warning. Concho was just starting to pin it onto his shirt when his cell phone rang. Glancing at the clock he saw it was barely 0800. Plenty of time to get to the hearing site by a little before nine. He debated whether or not to answer the phone when he saw the screen showing the number for the KTTP station.

Maybe it's Echabarri, he thought and grabbed it.

"Ranger Ten-Wolves?" a feminine voice asked.

"Speaking."

"This is Nila Willow, KTTP."

A worst-case scenario shot through Concho's mind. Had they found Peskipaatei? And was she all right?

He asked Nila the question.

"No," she said. "We haven't found her yet. But the phone company came through with the information we asked them for. They emailed everything over here to my departmental account. I just got it."

"I thought you were on afternoons?" he asked.

"I am," she said, "but Sherry called me this morning at home to tell me this stuff came in. So I came in early."

He glanced at his clock again.

Afternoon shift started at 1600 hours.

She came in very early, he thought.

That was an unusual sign, but a positive one. His and Echabarri's encouragement for Nila to take more than just a passing interest in this case seemed to have taken hold, and he didn't want to upset the applecart or do anything to change that. He still felt that she was a crucial part in maybe turning Peskipaatei's confused and misguided life around. But that was replete with a lot of maybes...if they could find her...if she was still unharmed...if she was still unspoiled...if they could reach her. She'd been missing probably somewhere near the 72-hour mark, which meant that this was probably more than just a causal collusion with friends. Thoughts of her falling in with some real rough company had been tiptoeing on the edge of his consciousness since he first started looking into this case, and now that seemed more and more likely. Somehow this missing runaway had taken on an enhanced significance for him. His mind flashed back to his own humble beginnings, a half-Black, half-Indian misfit kid being called "half-breed" by the older punks who beat him up every day because he was somehow "different." He'd been a young boy walking the path between two cultures, two worlds, one completely unknown to him and the other totally familiar but never quite accepting. His grandmother doing her best to shelter him, Meskwaa taking the time to lead him through his vision quest...the path had solidified before him and he'd found himself, but even now, sometimes on rare occasions, in his dreams he would be back on that old, uncertain trail, walking the same path, although his essence was much clearer now, thanks to the wisdom and guidance of Meskwaa.

"Hello?" Nila Willow's voice said. "Are you there?"

"Yeah, sorry. You get anything useful?"

"That depends. I've got a bunch of phone numbers she

called and received and some locations that can be triangulated, for the phone anyway."

"Does it show where she might be now?" Concho asked.

"The last designated location was the day before yesterday at the *Mall de las Aguilas*. After that the phone was turned off."

That put her at the talent quest event at Eagle Pass Mall. It fit with what little he'd gotten out of Holley Cameron, and it was a place to start. He glanced at his clock again.

0806.

"Listen, Nila, would you have time to go over to the mall and ask them to pull their surveillance videos from the other day? For the talent quest thing."

His request was met by silence.

"I'd do it myself," he quickly added, "but I'm due to appear at my shooting review this morning."

"Oh, I did hear about that."

When she didn't add anything more, Concho repeated his request that she check with the mall security about the videos.

"You think we'll find anything?" she asked. "I mean, there were a lot of people there for the start of that talent quest event."

"It's worth a shot, and I'd like to make sure we get a copy before they tape over it and it gets erased."

"This may seem like a stupid question, but will they give it to me without a warrant?"

"I'll grease the wheels," he said, thinking he'd give Maria a call now. "I know they have state-of-the-art equipment and all kinds of cameras. Pan, tilt, and zoom types. Gives high resolution. They got a government grant a couple of years ago and part of it was they had to be cooperative with the local law enforcement agencies."

"Which wouldn't necessarily include the KTTP."

"Don't sell yourself short."

It was now closing in on 0808 and he was feeling the urgency to finish getting ready and get to the hearing.

Late doesn't rate, he thought.

But knowing what he knew about Nila Willow, he figured he'd better lay on a bit of saddle soap.

"Look," he said. "I know you came in early and you're devoting a lot of your time to this matter, but it's very much appreciated."

She didn't immediately reply, and then said, "I don't mind. Having had time to think about it, I kind of caught a glimpse of myself a few years back. What might have been."

What might have been applied to him as well.

She said she'd try and nail down some of the listed phone numbers after going to see mall security. Concho thanked her, hung up, and dialed Maria.

"Concho?" she said, sounding mildly irritated. "What do you want? I told you I had to get ready."

"Maybe I just wanted to hear your voice once more before I ride into battle."

Her tone softened.

"Oh, that's sweet. But are you expecting a battle? I mean, the person you shot was shooting at you, wasn't he?"

Not wanting her to worry, he said, "Shouldn't be too bad. Anyway, there's another reason I called. I need a favor."

He gave her a quick rundown of the missing girl and why he needed the videos.

"How long do those videos last before they're recorded over?"

"Well," she said. "I'm not totally sure, but I think they last about a week."

"Good. I'll need the ones from two days ago. The talent quest."

"Sure, I can do that," she said. "How old is she?"

"Fifteen. I'm sending an officer over from the KTTP. I told her to ask for you."

"Okay," Maria said. "I'll be expecting him."

"It's a 'she.' Her name's Nila Willow."

"Oh, I see." Her voice was imbued with what he assumed was mock indignation. "A *female* officer."

"Relax. She's like the sister I never had." The clock was showing 0825 now and he still hadn't finished getting dressed and wanted to run the brush over the toes of his boots one more time for luck.

Maria laughed.

"I can't wait to meet her," she said, and then turned serious. "And good luck with the hearing."

"Thanks," he said, still fingering the badge.

I'm going to need it, he added mentally.

CHAPTER EIGHTEEN

CONCHO NOTICED THE ARRAY OF OFFICIAL GOVERNMENT vehicles in the side lot to the Maverick County Sheriff's Police Headquarters when he pulled up. He parked the tow truck in the official section, got out, and stretched. One of the deputies who was getting out of his squad car looked at him and did a double-take. Glancing around, the deputy made his way over and stopped by the tow truck's left rear fender. He was young and slender and nervous.

"You're Ranger Ten-Wolves, ain't ya?" he asked. His name tag read *EGGERT*.

Concho nodded.

The deputy's eyes shot around again with a wariness and he said, "I want you to know we're all pulling for you. We heard what they're trying to do. They called Terrill and Carl in for this thing too."

"How's Cate doing?" Concho asked.

The deputy nodded. "He's good. They're already inside."

Concho nodded. "Guess I'd better get in there myself. Don't want to be late."

He resisted adding the tag of "for my own funeral." There

was no sense being negative. He took a deep breath and started for the front entrance.

"Good luck, Ranger," Deputy Eggert called out after him.

Concho gave him a quick wave.

It didn't surprise him that they'd summoned both Hoight and Cate to be interviewed. Concho and Hoight had already given preliminary statements the morning after, and Hoight had mentioned that he, too, was under investigation for his alleged lack of field training supervision concerning his trainee. Concho wondered that if they'd question him about that, too. He really didn't recall Hoight doing anything wrong. Both he and Hoight had tried to warn the rookie to use caution around the suspected drug cache. Pulling open the front door, he stepped inside and caught sight of three men standing together engaged in a conversation. One was his boss, Captain Dalton Shaw, and the second was Maverick County Sheriff Isaac Parkland, both of whom Concho knew. The third man towered over the other two and was dressed in a dark suit. He was broad-shouldered and appeared to be in his late forties with a curly crop of blond hair that was thinning at the crown. He looked like a pro football lineman perhaps a couple years past his playing prime. And the shoulders and upper arms of his suit jacket fit snugly, indicating the athletic bulk of his physique. As Concho entered the foyer, the three of them stopped talking and turned toward him.

Shaw nodded, as did Parkland. The third man showed no reaction.

"Ranger Ten-Wolves," Shaw said. "This is Special Agent-in-Charge Donald Welch, DOJ. He'll be taking part in the proceedings this morning."

Welch immediately stepped forward and Concho noticed the man was tall enough to look him straight in the eye.

A big bastard, Concho thought, *just like me.*

The man's posture was very erect and Concho took that to mean that this Special Agent Welch used his size as an intimidation factor. He extended his hand. Concho accepted it expecting a perfunctory shake. Instead, he was surprised by the amount of pressure Welch was applying to a simple handshake, as if he were trying to squeeze hard enough to make Concho wince.

But that wasn't going to happen. He returned the pressure in kind, which made Welch grunt slightly.

"Damn," the man said. "That's one hell of a grip you've got there, Ranger."

"I could say the same about you, Special Agent."

Concho watched closely for a reaction, but Welch's light blue eyes betrayed nothing. Instead, the DOJ man turned toward Parkland.

"Sheriff, why don't you escort Ranger Ten-Wolves to one of your interview rooms until we're ready for him."

Despite the interrogative preamble, it had been phrased as a statement, not a question.

And they were taking him to an interview room?

Concho knew from experience that those were generally reserved for offenders or those under suspicion. And Welch was basically ordering Parkland around in his own police station. Like a big mountain lion urinating on a bush to designate his territory, the apex predator was asserting himself. If this was any indication of what was to come, it was going a rough ride, all right.

Meskwaa's words of warning echoed in Concho's head: *Beware of the treachery in your first trial today.*

I'd better be at my best, Concho thought. He's already trying to intimidate me.

Parkland's expression was neutral, and he placed his right hand on Concho's arm while extending his left toward the door leading into the internal area of the building.

"On second thought," Welch said, "if you can have one of your underlings do that, I have one other matter I need to discuss with you. Privately."

The sheriff stopped and his mouth gaped ever-so-slightly. Then he pressed his lips and took in a deep breath. Turning toward the Plexiglas window behind which sat a female receptionist, Parkland told her to have one of the station deputies step out. The woman nodded and picked up a phone.

"And make sure that he speaks to no one until we're ready for him," Welch added. "Please."

The final word was posed as an afterthought, a superfluous adverb. Welch's disregard for the others around him was as clear as the rather thick and bulbous nose on his face.

Again, Concho managed to show no emotion or apprehension. A jumble of the rest of Meskwaa's words came back to him: *You have a rough journey ahead, but the spirit of the truth is on your side. Make sure you are at your best.*

* * *

As Concho walked down the hallway in the interior of the station house escorted by another deputy, the electronic entry control lock buzzed behind them, indicating someone else had been admitted. Concho rounded a corner and saw Deputy Hoight being ushered into a room farther down the corridor. He was dressed in full uniform and his face had a grim expression on it.

"Hey, Terrill," Concho said.

Hoight turned, saw Concho, and smiled.

"Concho. They got you in here this morning too, huh?"

They were still about twenty feet away and before Concho could respond, a loud voice came from behind them.

"No talking, please. We'll be getting to you each in turn."

Concho glanced back over his shoulder and saw the trio, Shaw, Parkland, and Welch striding toward them. It had been the big fed who'd shouted the "no talking" command.

Concho debated whether or not to tell Welch to go to hell, but held back. It was standard operating protocol for this type of investigation. Keep the witnesses separated and interviewing them separately. No doubt Welch probably wanted him to know that they were going to grill Hoight and probably Cate, too, before talking to him.

Classic interview and interrogation, he thought. *Keep your primary target wondering what the others had said.*

Hoight's face twitched with a faint but fleeting hint of a smile. He looked like he'd already been fed through the wringer.

"Oh," Welch said, holding up his hand, his index finger extended. "Would you two mind putting your weapons and cell phones in the lockboxes? Standard procedure for DOJ interviews."

The finger pointed toward the open drawers on the wall. A key dangled from each.

Concho figured it was probably bullshit and glanced at Shaw. The ranger captain's jaw muscles were bunched up, but he said nothing.

"You going to leave yours in the box too?" Concho said, pausing to take the Staccato out of the pancake holster. He hadn't wanted to bring the Colt just in case they claimed they needed to hold it for examination for some reason. They still hadn't given his other one back.

Welch raised an eyebrow as he stared at Concho.

"Captain Shaw," he said. "I suggest you have a little talk with your man about his attitude. This is, after all, a federal investigation at this point and as we all know, federal statutes supersede those of mere state statutes."

Looks like the big mountain lion's *decided to piss on another bush,* Concho thought.

"I think his attitude is just fine," Shaw said. "And may I remind you that it's a joint investigation and he and I are both Texas Rangers."

The corners of Welch's mouth turned downward slightly, but he said nothing.

Score one for the Rangers, Concho thought.

He was feeling better already.

However, his ebullience didn't last long. It soon faded as he sat in the relatively small, box-like interview room for the better part of an hour. It was stuffy in there, almost on the borderline of being uncomfortably hot. A large wooden table was in the middle of the room, with three chairs on one side and a single chair on the opposite side—the hot seat. Concho knew once the interview started, that was where he'd be instructed to sit. For the moment, however, he sat on the edge of the table and put his foot on the seat of one of the chairs. Crossing his arms on top of his elevated knee, he looked down and checked the sheen on his leather boots.

It was holding up well.

If you look sharp, you feel sharp, and right now he was a straight razor.

But that didn't mean he wasn't anxious to get this fiasco over with.

If he had his phone, he could have called Nila to check on her progress, or Maria to verify that she was able to pull the mall surveillance videos. He knew that keeping him isolated and waiting and incommunicado was just another standard interview tactic, but that knowledge did little to ease his irritability. Why had he even signed up for that damn special overtime detail? Of course at the time, who would have expected it would evolve into a full-scale mess?

Lots of questions and few answers, he told himself. Nothing to do but sit tight and wait.

Welch was going by the book, all right, and Concho didn't like being treated like he was a run-of-the-mill suspect. He'd been through shooting investigations before, but this was the first with the feds involved. The stories he'd heard and his own dealings with the FBI came floating back to him. It wasn't totally unexpected or unfamiliar. Police were police and feds were a different animal. That was the way a lot of law enforcement officers termed it. Concho had never wanted to believe that. He recalled his sometimes contentious relationship with Della Rice, the female FBI agent who'd put him through his paces a few times before recognizing that he was a straight shooter. Their relationship had gotten off to a rough start due to his limited association with Lucio Zapatero. Rice had been suspicious that Concho was dirty because he'd helped the drug czar's wife when she was involved in a bank robbery and some other shady goings on. Eventually, nothing came of Rice's inquiry, and he and the FBI agent had parted company as friends in a professional, interagency sort of way.

Inevitably, Concho's thoughts came back to the shooting on that fateful evening a few nights ago. He started reviewing the sequence in his mind and wondered if he'd have the opportunity to review his report before the interview started? Figuring that Shaw would have a copy of it, he rose and went to the door.

The knob only moved a fractional click and froze.

Locked in.

This really pissed him off and he thought about pounding on the door to get someone's attention, but how would that look?

In fact, he thought, *this was probably by design.* Welch had all the earmarks of a head-hunter and would probably like nothing better than to be able to write in his report that "Ranger Ten-Wolves proved most vociferous and uncooperative during the lead-up to his interview."

In the meantime, the plan was to make him feel as uncomfortable as possible.

Concho glanced over at the mirrored panel on the opposite wall to his right. It was one-way glass, and he'd stood on the other side of it many times watching a suspect's actions before an interview. It usually told him a lot. Guilty people were fidgety initially but oftentimes settled down and went to sleep. It was strange, but well-documented behavior. The thought ironically made him yawn, and he looked at the mirror and grinned. If Welch or his counterparts were on the other side watching, Concho wasn't going to give them the satisfaction of losing his cool or going to sleep. Instead, he tipped his hat at his reflection in the mirror and went back to his chair. There was a dark plastic globe mounted at the juncture between ceiling and wall that Concho knew contained a PTZ camera. He wondered if it was recording him now.

If so, he was determined to give them nothing special to look at. He used the old Army trick of extending the shine on his boots by rubbing the insteps against the back of each leg, then checking the result.

Certainly no spit shine, but close enough for government work.

He went back to his chair, removed his hat, and set it on the table. After resuming his seated position by the table, with both feet on one of the chairs he did his best to relax. A few deep breaths later, he managed to place himself in a meditative state and replayed the events of the shooting in his mind once more, recreating every detail to the best of his ability.

Time continued to drag along, but he paid no attention to it. Approximately fifteen minutes more, the door to the interview room opened and Welch stepped in, a lips-only smile on his face. Behind him were three other people, one of whom Concho recognized. It was Sergeant Bill Elliot, who was part of the Texas Ranger's Internal Affairs section. Concho had expected Elliot would be there. The other two were a male dressed in a suit almost identical to Welch's and carrying a chair and a woman who had a stenographer's machine and a tray with folding legs. Concho pegged her as a civilian. Obviously, the other man was another fed—Welch's partner, no doubt. They always operated in pairs, like the raptors in those dinosaur movies. But this time they were going up against a T-Rex.

Concho smiled and said, "Nice of you to join me. And thanks for locking me in."

He made a point of not moving.

Welch said nothing. He pointed to the far corner opposite the door, and his partner set the chair over there. The stenographer unfolded the legs of the tray and took her seat, setting up in a far corner. She was looping a new spool of that special paper through the machine as Welch glared at Concho.

"Ranger Ten-Wolves," Welch said, "if you don't mind, we'll need you to sit on that side of the table."

He indicated the chair opposite them.

Concho grunted and removed his feet from the seats of the other two chairs and rose to his full height. Since he and Welch were about the same height, Concho made a point of moving slowly and looking the other man directly in the eyes. A quick, fleeting, humorous image of himself putting on war paint flashed in his mind.

No wild Indian moves are gonna cut it, he thought. *And I can't let them bait me.*

As he moved around the table, Concho noticed Welch making a show of dropping his thick, manila folder onto the table.

He figured that most likely half of the papers were probably blank, but he had no doubt that Welch would use the stuffed folder to his advantage by periodically paging through it after Concho had answered a question.

That was another standard interview trick to unnerve the interviewee.

Or the suspect, Concho thought, which is what he felt like.

After everyone had taken their seats, Welch shot a questioning look at the stenographer, who gave a quick nod.

"Very well," Welch said, initiating the proceedings. After reciting the time, date, location, and subject matter, he turned to Elliot.

"Officer Ten-Wolves," Welch said, "Sergeant Elliot of the Texas Department of Public Safety, Internal Affairs Division, will now read something to you."

"It's *Ranger* Ten-Wolves," Concho said.

It was a minute point, but Concho knew he'd broken the DOJ man's rhythm—like a boxer throwing out a fast jab to bounce it off of his opponent's nose. It wasn't meant to do much damage, just to throw the opponent off his game a little.

Welch emitted something akin to a growl as he cleared his throat.

"Very well, *Ranger* Ten-Wolves. This proceeding is being recorded, as you can see by the presence of our stenographer."

"What about the camera?" Concho flicked a finger toward the PTZ globe above them.

Another jab.

Welch frowned and blew out a long breath.

"It is being videotaped as well, so I advise you to curtail your adversarial attitude and cooperate. Are we clear?"

Concho nodded without an oral response all the while resisting the temptation to use the line, "Crystal," from that old Tom Cruise movie, *A Few Good Men.* But despite his height and build, this guy Welch was no Jack Nicholson.

"Please respond orally for the stenographer," Welch said.

Concho did so and smiled at the woman.

Her reaction was a slight twitch at the corners of her mouth. He didn't recognize her from any of the times he'd testified in court, but that didn't mean anything. The support staff was extensive and even then tended to blend in with the wallpaper.

After Elliot issued the instructions to Concho about his right to remain silent under the Constitution regarding the Fifth Amendment and his failure to cooperate with the investigation constituting willful insubordination and grounds for dismissal, Concho said he understood and signed the form. Elliot asked him to recount the events of the incident in question, and Concho did, explaining it step-by-step.

"And," Elliot said, "you believed at the time that your life and the lives of our fellow law enforcement personnel at the scene were in jeopardy?"

"Absolutely," Concho said.

After a fleeting second of silence, Concho was filled with the false hope that it was over and the G man would fold his tent and go harass someone else.

That hope lasted only as long as it took Welch to clear his throat.

"*Ranger* Ten-Wolves," Welch said, stressing the word *ranger* again. "You claim that you were engaged in a running gun battle with the subject, is that correct?"

"Yes, sir," Concho said, resorting back to his military correctness. It would look good on the transcript.

Welch showed no reaction to the formality. Instead, he elevated the folder so Concho couldn't see what was in it, and began examining, or pretending to examine, the pages.

Concho waited.

"And you weren't wearing a body camera during this incident, correct?"

"Yes, sir."

"Are you aware of any video recordings of the incident?"

Concho wondered where the government man was going but decided to just keep it simple. "No, sir."

"How many shots do you claim he fired at you?"

Concho thought for a moment. He hadn't specified that number before.

"I'd say four or five," he said.

Welch raised his eyebrows slightly, paged through the sheaf of papers again, and then said, "Four or five times?"

"That sounds right."

Welch made a show of taking in another deep breath.

"And you are aware," Welch continued, "that only three shell casings from the subject's gun were recovered at the scene." It was another question phrased as a statement. "How do you explain that?"

"Well, the first shots occurred during a vehicular pursuit," Concho said. "We traveled a fair distance so perhaps the search grid wasn't expansive enough."

Welch said nothing.

More paging through the folder...

"And you said you returned fire how many times?"

"Four."

"Four times?"

"Yes."

Welch let out a laborious breath.

"And how many times and where did you hit the subject?"

"After the vehicle crashed," Concho said, taking his time replying. "The offender exited the vehicle and took cover in a shallow trench, where he fired at me at least three times. I waited until I had a clear shot and fired. I'm not sure where my round hit, but he went down."

"And then you approached him?"

"That's correct."

"And you had your weapon trained on him while he was down?"

"I did," Concho said.

"And why was that?"

It was a stupid question, and Concho felt like telling the big fed just that. But he didn't, Welch was obviously trying to bait him.

"He was laying face down with his arms under his body," Concho said. "I couldn't see his hands or his weapon."

"And were you issuing verbal commands during this time?" Welch asked.

Sergeant Elliot's mouth was a tight line, a disgusted look on his face.

Concho figured he wasn't enjoying the government man's idiotic tactics either.

"I don't recall," Concho said. "It was a confusing time because Deputy Hoight was advancing from the opposite direction and was yelling to me."

"And it was at this time you say the subject jumped up with his weapon?"

"That's correct."

"And you shot him?"

"I did."

"How many times?"

Concho blew out an exasperated breath. He'd already

given those details. He wished there was someone, anyone, to jump up and object, stating, "Asked and answered already."

But no one did.

Concho longed to say he'd shot the son of a bitch Mozambique style—twice in the torso and once in the head, but instead he said, "Three times."

"You're absolutely sure?"

Concho didn't know exactly what trap Welch was trying to set.

"As best as I can remember."

"Without any warning?"

"There was no time for a warning. He was going to shoot Deputy Hoight."

"And you know this how?"

"He was bringing his gun up to do so."

"Did he declare he was going to shoot Deputy Hoight?"

"What? No, of course not."

"Then how do you know he wasn't going to surrender?"

Concho snorted a laugh. The stupidity of the question made that inevitable.

"Is something funny?" Welch asked.

"Just your questions," Concho replied.

He regretted his felicitous retort immediately after he'd said it. On the transcript, it would look as if he was being a smart-ass.

Not good.

He inhaled, hoping to get a chance to elaborate. Welch made the mistake of paging through his bogus file again, giving Concho the opportunity to assert himself.

"Look," he said. "It was dark, and the subject had already shot at me numerous times. He jumped up and started to point his gun at Deputy Hoight, and I fired to prevent the offender from shooting him. End of story."

"Not quite the end." Welch smiled. It was one of those Cheshire cat smiles. He evidently thought he'd scored a point, or was about to. "Where did you shoot him? What area of the body?"

"I shot him twice in the torso and once in the head."

"More specifically," Welch said, paging to another portion of his sheaf of papers, "Twice in the back, and once in the right rear quadrant of the skull."

Right where I was aiming, Concho thought.

He nodded.

"Once again, please give an audible response for the recorder," Welch said.

Before Concho could answer, the door suddenly opened and Captain Shaw burst in, followed by a tall, thin man in a buckskin jacket. Concho had seen this man before both in court and on TV—Spencer Givens, one of the best defense attorneys in the state of Texas.

"I believe my client has answered your question in his previous testimony, Special Agent," Givens said.

His client?

This was news to Concho. He glanced up at Shaw, who was smirking.

"What's the meaning of this?" Welch said. "Who are you?"

"Spencer Givens, representing Ranger Ten-Wolves."

"He hasn't requested legal representation," Welch spat out.

"Let's just say I was observing in the capacity of amicus curiae," Givens said. "But now I feel compelled to speak out for proper legal edification of this proceeding."

Givens smiled over at the stenographer and gripped the lapels of his buckskin jacket with both hands. Leaning back, he began a long soliloquy about the United States Supreme Court having made it clear that absolute certainty is not the standard that officers will be judged by when using deadly force.

"As I'm sure you know, the Court ruled, in Tennessee versus Garner, that before an officer can use deadly force, he or she must have the probable cause to believe that the suspect poses a threat of grievous bodily harm to the officer or to the general public. Now this probable cause standard is a far cry from absolute certainty. Absolute certainty would require a one hundred percent belief."

Givens paused and smiled at the stenographer.

"Going too fast for you, honey?"

The stenographer smiled back and shook her head.

A ladies' man, Concho thought. He'd seen the well-known legal eagle strut his stuff in court before, but it had always been on the other side. This was as unexpected as it was entertaining.

"The Court further ruled regarding the obvious and significant danger that an officer faces in a potentially deadly shooting confrontation," Givens continued, "and it has most appropriately adjusted this probable cause standard when it comes to judging police shootings. For example, the Court further clarified this probable cause standard in the Graham versus Connor decision that an objectively reasonable police officer must possess probable cause that the suspect is a deadly threat." He paused and smiled again, this time turning toward Welch and the others. "And, I daresay, given the facts that have been related thus far by Ranger Ten-Wolves, that this threshold has been clearly established during the course of your earlier questioning. The Ranger was being fired upon by an assailant, who in turn was about to inflict great bodily harm on a fellow officer. I call upon you, sir, to acknowledge the obvious and cease and desist your spurious allegations that call into question the heroic and totally justified actions of this fine law enforcement professional."

Welch's face said it all. Given had thrust a harpoon into the man's sails. The DOJ man's head slowly sank as he looked down at the sheaf of papers in the manila folder.

Concho glanced up at Shaw, who winked. Captain Elliot was sitting back with an equally sly smile plastered across his face.

Leaning back in his chair, the big Ranger cupped one hand over his mouth to conceal his own ear-to-ear grin. The captain had obviously meant what he'd said about being on Concho's side, and had bought in a big gun to prove it. And not just a big gun—a cannon.

Meskwaa's words from earlier that morning floated back in Concho's memory like an echoing refrain.

Deception, trickery, and danger...expect that they will strike at you from out of the darkness, from behind the next corner, the next arroyo. But do not fear. You will have some help.

How had he known this?

But then again, he was wise, and Concho knew better than to question the ways of the *Chupacabra*.

CHAPTER NINETEEN

OUTSIDE THE MAVERICK COUNTY SHERIFF'S POLICE STATION the weather had grown hot and Concho almost missed the manufactured coolness of the building's interior. It still hadn't stopped him from sweating through the underarms of his white shirt and feeling like he could use a shower. He extended his hand toward Spencer Givens.

"Thank you for representing me in there, sir. What do I owe you?"

The lawyer's face crinkled with a wide grin.

"*Nada*," he said, glancing at Captain Shaw. "It's been taken care of."

Concho looked at his boss, who waved his hands dismissively.

"The good counselor and I go way back," Shaw said. "To an old traffic stop on a young attorney who'd had a bit too much to drink and was given a pass and driven home."

This was a surprise to Concho.

Givens snorted.

"It would have been bad for my image had I been forced to represent myself in court," he said. "Would have reinforced the old saying that an attorney who represents himself has a fool for a client." Givens looked askance at Concho. "Something you should remember the next time you get involved in one of these things."

"I'll certainly think about that," Concho said. "If there is a next time."

"If?" Shaw snorted and rolled his eyes. "That's like saying *if* my dog barks at the mailman again."

After shaking hands, Shaw said he needed a word in private with Concho and Givens walked over and got into the passenger side of the captain's SUV.

"I appreciate you looking out for me, Captain," Concho said.

"Will you quit saying that?" Shaw's mouth became a tight line. "I wasn't just looking out for my top man, I was doing it for the Rangers. The damn feds getting involved in this was all political bullshit. They're looking for an excuse to keep local and state agencies from policing the border."

"Why's that?"

Shaw shrugged.

"Probably because it's calling too much attention to the situation there. Anyway, this shooting thing was bullshit, but it's still going to take another day or so probably before you're officially cleared." He brought his extended index finger up and punched it against Concho's chest as he added, "So you stay outta trouble. Got it?"

"Yes, sir."

Shaw gave an emphatic nod and glanced over at the tow truck.

"And get rid of that damn thing, will ya? It's giving the Rangers a bad name. Rent a damn car, or something, if you have to."

"I'm working on it," Concho said. "But I kind of like driving it. I'm actually thinking of maybe putting in a secondary employment request form."

Shaw's mouth dropped open and then he saw Concho

chuckling. The captain snorted again, pulled up on his belt, and started heading for his SUV.

"I got to drive the esteemed counselor back to his office in San Antonio. I had somebody else pick him up early this morning, but I promised I'd buy him a steak dinner on the return trip."

"*Muchichimos gracias*," Concho said, thinking that the captain had told him not to say thank you anymore.

Shaw slapped his side and didn't look back.

As soon as Concho got back into the tow truck, his cell phone rang. Looking at the screen, he saw it was John Gray-Dove.

"You got some good news for me?" he asked.

"Good and bad news," Gray-Dove said. "Which you want first?"

"Surprise me."

"Okay. Your truck's gonna be a few more days. One of them bullets pierced the radiator and I had to order a new one. Unfortunately, it hasn't come in yet."

Assuming that was the bad news, Concho asked about the good.

"I got you a real nice loaner all set up," Gray-Dove said. "Drop by the shop and I'll give it to you."

"Sounds good," Concho said. "Real good."

"Yeah, I figured I'd better get my secondary tow truck back. I'm probably going to need eventually it since you'll be driving this loaner and all."

"Ha ha," Concho said. "I'll be right over."

After hanging up, he did a quick glance at his watch and saw it was almost noon and he was starving. He wanted nothing more than to drive to the nearest roadhouse and order a big steak, but he had other things on his mind. One was Nila. He'd asked her to go check on those mall surveillance videos and wanted to know if she'd picked them up yet, but he didn't have a cell phone number for her. She'd called him from the KTTP station earlier that morning. He started up the vehicle, shifted into gear, and eased up on the clutch. The tow truck rumbled forward with a jerking motion.

He wasn't going to miss driving this thing, that was for sure.

Shifting into second, he scrolled down to Maria's number and pressed the button to all her as he shifted into third.

The phone rang twice before he heard her luscious voice.

"I was hoping you'd call," she said.

"Why? Hawk been hitting on you again?"

She laughed. "No. Actually, since I mentioned your name and our relationship, he's been a perfect gentleman."

"That's good to know. Say, did you check on those videos for me?"

"Sure did, and in fact, your female counterpart's going over them right now in the security office."

That was good news to Concho. Apparently, Nila hadn't been exaggerating when she said she really wanted to find Peskipaatei Standing Bear.

"Great," he said. "Do you know if she's found anything?"

"No, I've been tied up with other stuff, but I can call over to the security office and ask her to call you."

"No need. Just call over there and tell her I'll be there shortly. I have to get rid of this albatross and pick up a new loaner truck."

"You're getting rid of the tow truck? Oh darn, I was hoping you could teach me how to drive a stick."

Concho thought about making an off-color joke but decided not to. Instead he told her he'd be stopping by in a bit.

"Okay," she said. "Call me when you get here, but there's a ton of corporate honchos milling around, so we'll have to be discreet."

"I'll keep that in mind," he said and terminated the call.

It's always something, he thought as he slipped the phone back into his pocket, but corporate or no corporate, that son of a bitch, Hawk, had better keep his distance from Maria.

* * *

JOHN GRAY-DOVE HAD A NICE RED CHEVROLET SILVERADO that was a couple years old but in really good shape. After handing the keys back for the tow truck, Concho thanked Gray-Dove and got inside the cab. As he started it up, the engine hummed and then the low-gas alarm sounded with a distinct squeal.

"What the hell?" Concho said. "There's no gas in it."

Gray-Dove shook his finger at him.

"You should be a detective."

Concho frowned and shifted into DRIVE.

"I'll make sure to return it back to you at the same fuel level," he said and took off.

It took him about thirty-five minutes to get to Eagle Pass Mall after stopping for gas. He filled it up, thinking that it was a prudent move.

You can never have enough gas when you need it, he told himself. Or enough ammo.

Arriving at the mall, he was amazed at the amount of traffic and parked cars, and then he remembered that the talent quest was still in full swing. He drove around to the back and found a loading zone to park in. He looked for a white SUV with the KTTP insignia on it, but saw none.

Oh well, he thought. *Maybe Nila Willow was no longer there.*

Hoping to maintain as low a profile as he could, he slipped on one of his sleeveless camo BDU blouses over his shirt. It covered the Texas Ranger star on his chest and hung down low enough that it covered the Staccato in the pancake holster as well.

Hustling up the back way, he entered the mall security office and tapped on the glass window. The pretty girl behind the glass looked up and smiled. They all knew him there, and he buzzed him in.

"Tell your guys not to put a sticker on my truck or call for a tow," he said. "I had to park in a loading zone out back."

The security girl smiled.

"They're way too busy anyway. The place is mobbed with this talent quest thing. You looking for Officer Willow?"

"I am."

"She's in there." The girl pointed to a room at the end of the corridor.

Concho strode down the hallways past a locker room and then two larger rooms. One of them had a wall that was composed of around twenty-some television monitors. Each showed images of varying sizes of the main areas of the mall and others showed vacant back corridors. A uniformed security guard sat at a small table at the center of the array of monitors, his fingers resting on something that resembled a joystick from an old video game. Off to the side, another uniformed security guard was at another table with two monitors on it. Seated next to him was Nila Willow. Both of them were staring at the television screens with intensity. Concho could see the images were slow-moving videos of lots of people milling about. Nila glanced back over her shoulder as Concho approached. Her ebony hair was pulled back in a long ponytail and she was wearing a brown, no-frills blouse and blue jeans. She had what appeared to be a Glock 21 in a pancake holster on her right hip. Her KTTP badge was on a circular leather clip-on holder right next to the gun.

"Any luck?" Concho asked.

She shook her head. "Rod here's been giving me a hand, but so far nothing. But there's a mountain of video to go through."

"Why don't you break off for now and I'll buy you lunch?" Concho said. He wasn't sure how she was going to take the offer, but he was ravenous and he also felt that he owed her a favor for all the work she was doing off-duty.

Nila Willow's eyes swept over him, as if she were carefully evaluating the offer and wondering what all it entailed. Since Maria had mentioned Nila by name, he assumed they'd already met and most likely Nila knew that he was spoken for and that no romantic overtures were being made.

She inhaled deeply and pressed a button on the remote she'd been holding. The image on her monitor faded to black.

"You up for lunch too, Rod?" she asked. "We both appreciate all the time you spent here helping to look."

Rod, who was kind of chubby and White, grinned and shook his head.

"I brought my lunch. Brown bagging it. Trying to lose some weight so I can take the Maverick County physical agility test when it comes up next time."

Concho tried to imagine the kid in a uniform sporting a badge and a pistol.

Stranger things have happened, he told himself.

Nila stood and stretched. She was rather short, perhaps five-two or three, and had kind of a stocky build, although she wasn't fat. Her face had the high cheekbones and light bronze color of a full-blooded Kickapoo. It was easy to see why Rod had volunteered to help her.

"Let's just hit the food court," Nila said. "I'll show you what I got from the phone carrier."

"Sounds good to me." Concho turned to Rod. "That talent quest thing still in full effect today?"

"Sure is. In fact, one of Mr. Hawk's men is doing a martial arts demonstration in the center court area in about twenty minutes. Should really be something to see."

Concho nodded, and he and Nila left the security office. As they walked through the back corridor toward the staircase that led down to the main mall area and the food court, he waited for her to initiate some conversation. She said nothing.

Concho remembered Echabarri laughingly refer to her as the woman of few words. Now Concho understood what the chief had meant.

The food court was packed, mostly with young people as well as a few older ones. After grabbing a couple of burgers, soft drinks, and fries, Concho and Nila finally saw an unoccupied set of chairs near the outskirts of the seating area and made their way toward it. They sat down and each of them devoured their food without speaking. When they'd both finished, Concho felt compelled to initiate some type of conversation.

"So I really appreciate you going the extra yard on this," he said. "You off today?"

She shook her head, took out her phone, and looked at the time.

"I've got to go in for afternoons." She covered her mouth as she yawned. "Have to go home and change pretty soon."

Concho felt doubly bad about her spending the morning working this case and then going in for a full afternoon shift.

"The chief going to compensate you for what you did this morning?"

"Yeah." She smiled. "He'll most likely give me one of those little, tiny gold stars that I can stick on the outside of my locker."

Concho smirked. It was good to see that she had embraced the humorous side of the cynicism that affects most law enforcement officers.

"Take it from me," Concho said, "sometimes that's all the thanks you'll get for doing a good job. Just knowing you did your best has to be enough sometimes."

She gave him a sideways glance. "In looking at this particular case, that may be all that we can hope for."

"Meaning?"

Nila took a deep breath. "I checked our juvenile records. This isn't the first time she's run away."

This fit with what Echabarri had told him, but he waited to hear what Nila had found out.

"It's her fourth time," she said. "The first three were only minor overnight excursions. Sneaking out of the house. She turned up the next day. But the last one she was gone for three days. Her and a girlfriend took a bus to Laredo. That was two months ago."

"What's the girlfriend's name?"

"Elena Navarro."

"Maybe we should talk to her."

Nila shook her head. "The family moved. I'll have to wait 'til I go in to do some digging on the computer to see if I can get their new address."

"You mentioned you had that phone carrier info?" he said.

She nodded and reached into her shirt pocket, pulling out a set of folded papers. Spreading them out on the table, she tapped the first sheet with a fingernail.

"Her phone was on and active up until yesterday morning. Then it was turned off." Her fingernail stopped under one of the numbers. "I haven't been able to identify all of these, but these highlighted ones are from a burner phone, and these two come back to a rideshare company at zero-zero-thirty-six hours."

"That matches what her grandmother told me," Concho said. "She figured Peskipaatei left their trailer sometime during the night."

"Tracing the cell towers that it pinged off of, she went someplace in the unincorporated Maverick County El Dorado area."

"That had to be her BBF's house. Holley Cameron." Concho recited the address.

Nila scribbled it down and then continued.

"There's another couple of calls to an unidentified cell. Maybe the BFF?"

Concho nodded. "Makes sense."

"She stayed there for a bit and then called another rideshare company. The next pings put her in the vicinity of the mall that morning," Nila said. "I checked on social media, but if she's on it, her account's apparently marked private."

Concho knew little about such things, but just grunted in agreement.

"I've got a list of phone numbers here," Nila said, "of the calls she made and of frequently used numbers. I'll try to see if I can run down the rest of them tonight."

"Can I get a copy of those? I can have our tech guys see what they can find also."

Her head tilted, and the dark-brown eyes scrutinized his face.

"I thought you were on administrative leave?"

Concho snorted in both amusement and frustration. Was there anybody who didn't know about his current limbo status?

"I am, but hopefully not for much longer. I had my hearing this morning."

"How'd that go?"

He shrugged. "They're always a barrel of laughs."

She didn't say anything more. He didn't think she'd had to go through anything like that, and hoped she wouldn't. But you never knew.

"Come on," he said, starting to rise. "Let's go up to the mall office and use the copier. I'll need those numbers."

"I already copied them for you," Nila said, also getting up and handing him two of the folded sheets from her stack. "Rod let me use theirs up in the security office."

Concho accepted the papers and was stuffing them into his jeans pocket when a flash of auburn hair attracted his attention and his vision zeroed in on a familiar face.

Holley Cameron.

She was walking with two friends, one male and one female.

"See that girl with the red hair?" Concho sat back down. "That's Holley, Peskipaatei's BFF."

Nila remained standing but turned her back to the three youngsters. They were all gabbing and playing with their cell phones, snapping pictures.

"Think they might lead us to her?" Nila asked.

"If she's here. She knows me, and I'm kind of easy to spot. Why don't you tag them and see where they go. I'll hang back out of sight and watch for a bit."

Nila turned and walked away without saying anything.

A woman of few words, he told himself again.

Concho waited for what he felt was an appropriate length of time and then stood. Although Nila was short, his height made it easy for him to keep a fix on her brown shirt and black ponytail. He trailed along, trying to mix with the crowd as his quarry headed to the center court area.

The ebb and flow of the throngs of people shifted like an overflowing river. Concho lost sight of Nila. He stretched to his full height and scanned the area, but it was like looking for a ripe huckleberry on a vine full of them.

Then he saw Holley holding up her phone and snapping a selfie with her two friends. They were only a few feet from him. After the click and the flash, Holley giggled and lowered the phone, only to do a double-take when she laid eyes on Concho.

The cat's out of the bag now, he thought and managed to smile in what he hoped would be a disarming gesture.

"Hi, Holley," he said, taking a step closer. "How you doing?"

Her two friends, wide-eyed and open-mouthed, edged away from her. Holley turned and started to follow, but Concho said, "Hey, wait a minute."

The girl seemed to try and quicken her step, but the crowd made a rapid exit virtually impossible.

Nila was suddenly there and stepped in front of Holley.

"Miss Cameron," she said. "I'm Officer Willow, KTTP. We need to talk to you for a minute. I think you know Ranger Ten-Wolves."

The girl stopped. Her two friends continued on their way, now lost in the crowd. Holley glanced around, the tendons in her slim neck tightening.

"What do you want?" Her words sounded almost breathless.

"Just to talk," Nila said. Her voice was calm and reassuring. "It'll only take a minute. We're trying to find somebody."

Holley compressed her lips momentarily, then said, "Penny?"

Nila nodded. "Her grandmother's very worried about her. So are we."

Holley bit her lower lip.

"Let's go over here where there's fewer people," Nila said, holding her arm out toward an isolated section with two doors leading to the interior sections of the mall.

"All right," Holley said. "But I can tell you right now, I don't know nothing."

Concho smirked at the double negative. Obviously, she was ignorant of the grammatical significance of her statement. He stepped over in front of Nila and the girl and began walking, the crowd automatically parting for him. They came to a pair of solid metal doors with small glass windows at eye level through which an empty hallway was visible. Concho knew the corridor led to one of the service areas and the back entrances to the stores on this side of the complex. He pulled the door open and stepped inside, holding it for Holley and Nila.

As the door closed behind them with a silent, pneumatic efficiency, Concho glanced toward Nila and cocked his head, as if to say, "You take it from here."

Nila evidently understood the unspoken message and smiled at the girl.

"When was the last time you spoke to Penny?" Nila asked.

Holley bit her lip again.

The girl was nervous.

"I don't know. A day of two."

"Did she call you last, or did you call her?"

"She called me." The response was quick.

Concho's previous hunch that the girl was hiding something seemed reaffirmed.

"And this was two nights ago when she came to your house?" Nila kept her voice calm and non-accusatory.

Holley's eyes widened in obvious surprise.

"How did you know that?"

"I told you, we're investigating. What did she say?"

Holley's shoulders shrugged.

"She took the rideshare to your house, didn't she?"

The girl's mouth trembled slightly.

"Tell us about it," Nila said.

"I don't know what you're talking about."

"You know that's not true," Nila said. "We're not looking to get you in trouble, but it's really important for you to tell us the truth, Holley. Penny's missing, and as I said, her grandmother's very worried. If you know where she's at, it's important that you tell us."

"But I *don't* know," she burst out. She grimaced. "I really haven't heard from her since that night."

"What was the gist of your conversation with her?" Concho asked. He had decided to stay silent no longer. If anything, his masculine intrusion might make her more likely to relate to Nila.

Holley said nothing.

"Come on," Nila said. "Tell us. You know you want to."

Holley took in a deep breath.

"Okay," she said. "She texted me real early, like one o'clock in the morning. She was outside my house. Wanted me to sneak her inside."

"And you did."

"Of course. I mean, it was nighttime time, and it was kinda cold."

"She told you how she got there?" Concho asked.

"She said she took a ride share. Told me the guy was kind of creepy and she jumped out of the car and called me."

"Okay," Nila said. "And then what happened?"

"Well, she had her Tilly bag all stuffed with clothes and things. Said she just needed to hide out until the mall opened."

"Hide out? Did she say why?"

Again, the girl's eyes drifted downward, and she said nothing.

"Holley?" Nila said.

"Okay, okay. She told me she'd met someone. A new guy. A little older, but really cool."

"She tell you his name?"

He shook her head. "But she has it real hard at her grandmother's. She won't let her do anything. He promised to take her away from all this."

"Does he have a car?" Concho asked.

Holley shook her head. "She wouldn't tell me. Said she promised not to tell anybody about him."

"Promised who?" Nila asked.

"Him, I guess. I don't know. She just wouldn't say. She was super tired and just asked if she could sleep in my room with me for a while. So we did."

"Is he from around here?" Nila asked.

Again, the girl shook her head and shrugged.

"I told you, she wouldn't say. And she made me promise not to tell anybody anything. Now I've snitched on her."

Nila smiled. "You did the right thing. She's in over her head."

"I know," Holley said. "I've been worried, too. I want her to be happy, but I don't want to lose her. I mean, she's my BFF."

"Do you have any idea who this guy is?" Nila asked. "What he looks like? Where he lives?"

Holley took in a deep breath. "At first I thought she was going to run off with Tyler, but she said no. It wasn't him."

"Who's Tyler?" Concho asked.

"Her boyfriend. Or her old boyfriend. He's not that much older, though. He's a senior, and he's on the football and basketball teams."

"What's his last name?"

"Peterson."

Concho made a note of that.

"Where's he live?" Concho asked.

Holley told him the street but didn't know the address.

It was Nila's turn again. "So then what happened?"

"We talked a little bit more and then went to sleep. I let her stay in my room. I snuck her in some breakfast when my mom and dad got up. I had to get ready for school, but it was a short day because of the talent quest. Penny called another rideshare and snuck out the back. Said she'd see me later at the mall. But I couldn't find her when I got here. I tried calling her but she wouldn't pick up."

"Let me see your phone," Nila said.

The girl handed it over without a protest.

Concho remembered Holley's intrusive father from the day before.

The asshole.

Something else caught his attention. Holley was wearing that same red bracelet that she'd had on the day before. It wasn't a fancy thing at all—a loose, hard-rubber oval that could be slipped on and off. It had some kind of design on it that Concho couldn't quite make out, but it held a vague familiarity for him.

"Whose numbers are these?" Nila asked.

Holley looked at the screen and started reciting the names. Tyler Peterson's was one of them—his home and cell numbers. Nila pulled out the folded sheet of paper and began jotting down the information.

"Like I told you," Holley said, "I tried to call her, but she's not answering."

"Is she on social media?" Nila asked.

"Yeah, we both are."

"Check her account." Nila handed the phone back to her.

"Both of our accounts are private." The girl's thumbs raced over the keys, then the space between her eyebrows crinkled.

"That's funny," she said. "It's been deleted."

"Show me the pictures of you and her," Concho said. "And Tyler."

Holley complied, and Concho told her to send them to Nila's KTTP departmental email. There was no way he wanted to use his own. The way this damn thing was shaping up, the photos were probably going to end up as part of a chain of custody evidence log.

The sound of the freight elevator descending emanated from about thirty feet away down the hall. Someone was coming from the upper office area.

Nila held out one of her cards,

"This has my contact information on it," she said. "I also wrote Ranger Ten-Wolves's number on the back. Please call us right away if you hear from Penny."

Holley took the card and said she would.

Glancing at Concho, Nila asked, "You have any more questions, Ranger?"

He started to shake his head and then stopped. He remembered where he'd seen a similar wristband that the girl was wearing.

"Yeah," he said. "That wristband. Let me see it."

He held out his big, open palm.

The girl bunched up her lips as she worked it off her wrist and gave it to him.

He studied the insignia, but it meant nothing as far as he could see. Just a yellow circle with some circles and lines running through it.

"Where'd you get this?" he asked.

Her eyes darted to the left, and then down.

"Holley," Concho said.

His voice had taken on an authoritative resonance.

Nila was staring up at him with a perplexed look.

The freight elevator noisily slammed into place and all three sets of their eyes shot toward the horizontal, bilateral doors as they began opening from a slit in the middle, like a clam shell.

"Did Penny give this to you?" Concho asked the girl.

She nodded.

"When?"

"The other night."

"Where'd she get it?"

"I don't know. She didn't say. She just told me to keep it because it was special and she wanted me to have it to remember her by. She said she didn't need it anymore."

"What did she mean by that?" Concho asked.

Holley shrugged. Several people started exiting the freight elevator.

"I don't know," Holley said. "Please, can I go now?"

Concho glanced down the corridor and saw Maria leading a pack of men. There were three of them in suits whom he recognized as corporate assholes from the meeting two days ago. Behind them were Vince Hawk, dressed in a decorated buckskin jacket and bright blue silk shirt, his redoubtable and shoeless stunt man, Jim Dandy, who was wearing some kind of black robe with a pair of dragons embroidered on the lapels, the ex-cop, Alexander Drum, and another flunky in a sports jacket and string tie. Two other guys looking like Mexican laborers carried heavily laden shopping bags.

Maria's eyes widened when she saw Concho, and she smiled.

"Can I go?" Holley repeated.

Concho pushed open the door and gave a quick nod.

"My bracelet?" Holley said.

"I'm going to hold onto that for a while," he said. "Go."

The girl frowned as she slipped through the space and as she walked Concho saw her crumple up the card that Nila had given her and toss it onto the floor.

"So much for her cooperation," he said as he let the door close on its own.

"What's with the bracelet?" Nila whispered.

"Just something I need to verify." He dropped the bracelet into the pocket of his BDU.

And if it was what he was thinking it was, Peskipaatei was in deep trouble.

CHAPTER TWENTY

Maria allowed her fingertips to briefly brush the back of Concho's hand and she led the entourage to the closed doors and made the introductions all around. The last of the corporate suits offered his outstretched palm and asked, "You're the police officer who responded to the terrorist attack here at the mall some months back, aren't you?"

The man looked soft and way out of shape and Concho was careful not to exert too much pressure with the handshake.

Vince Hawk's Hollywood smile was wide as he stepped over to shake hands as well.

"Hey, Ranger Ten-Wolves," he said. "Just the man I was looking for." His eyes swept over to Nila. "And who's this pretty lady? Oh, she armed. You part of the Rangers, too?"

"Officer Nila Willow, Kickapoo Traditional Tribal Police."

Hawk affected a surprised facial expression and then flashed his patented movie star grin again.

"Hey, I was just talking to your chief yesterday," he said. "We're going to be filming part of my new movie on the Rez. Who knows, I might be able to use you as an extra. Interested?"

She shook her head.

"Well anyway, think about it," Hawk said, turning to the guy with the string tie. "Randy, keep an eye open for Miss—I mean *Officer* Willow here. I think she'd look dynamite in a buckskin dress. A tight buckskin dress."

The smile was back in place as he clapped Concho on the shoulder.

"And you, big fella," Hawk said. "I still got that part open for you."

"No thanks," Concho said. "I got a job."

He pulled back the vest and showed his Texas Ranger badge pinned to his shirt.

Hawk emitted what sounded like a forced laugh.

Concho caught a glimpse of Maria's expression, which looked a bit nervous.

He smiled reflexively.

"Anyway," Hawk continued, "we got some things to discuss, you and me. Give me a call later, after the show, okay?"

Concho said nothing and Hawk's hand lingered on the Ranger's big shoulder. The movie star made a rubbing gesture on the meat of Concho's enormous upper arm.

"I'm serious," Hawk said. "I got something I want to talk to you about. In the meantime, how'd you two like to be part of the afternoon show? Tonto here's gonna do a martial arts exhibition. Break a few boards and stuff." He stepped to the side, exposing the rest of his entourage. Alexander Drum nodded to Concho. Jim Dandy smirked and puffed up his chest a little.

"Whaddya think, Tonto?" Hawk said. "You think you're good enough to be able to break one with this big dude holding it up in the air."

"No problem," Dandy said. "I'm so good, I could do it with him standing on a chair."

Concho noticed the man's pupils were very dilated.

"That I'd like to see," Drum said.

Dandy shot a glance at the ex-cop and then back to Concho.

"So how about it?" Dandy said. "You up for a little *Walker, Texas Ranger* stuff?"

The other man's eyes—the slight, almost imperceptible involuntary nystagmus of the irises told Concho a lot.

Cocaine, maybe?

"Another time," he said. "Another place."

Dandy blew out a stream of breath.

"Too bad they're not still filming that old TV show around here," Dandy said. "I'd like to come on it and give old Chuck Norris a real ass-whipping. But in the meantime, how about you and me put on a little sparring session out there, Ranger?"

"In your dreams, Jimbo," Drum said. "The man here's an officer of the law, and he's authorized to shoot your ass if you start causing trouble."

"Trouble's my middle name." Dandy leaned back and slowly raised his right leg off the floor, letting his limb hang suspended in the space between him and Concho. In a flash, Dandy's foot shot upward, sending two kicks in the direction of Concho's head. The big Ranger instinctively angled back, but the kicks were well out of range.

"Dammit, Jimmy," Hawk said. "Behave yourself. Would ya?"

Dandy regained his footing a second later and flashed a lopsided grin.

"Sorry, Ten-Wolves," he said. "But believe me, I wouldn't have hit you. I'm a karate man. I got excellent control."

"Lucky for you," Concho said.

Drum snorted a laugh.

Dandy shot him an irritated glance and shrugged off his robe, handing it to Drum. He stood there bare-chested, clad only in some ebony-colored pants. A black martial arts belt with yellow embroidery on it was knotted around his waist. His build was impressive, replete with impressive pecs and a chiseled six-pack. The rippling muscles glistened with a sheen of perspiration, despite the rather cool, air-conditioned temperature. He also had several tattoos on his pectoral muscles and shoulders. And Concho noticed one other thing. Dandy had an oversized flesh-colored Band-Aid on the left side of his neck.

After stepping over to one of the Mexicans carrying the bags, Dandy reached inside and withdrew a wooden plank that was approximately ten-by-twelve inches and around an inch thick.

"Watch," he said. "And be amazed."

He gripped the top of the board with his left hand, extended his arm outward, and drew back his right fist, holding it down by his waist. His right fist shot forward with a reverse punch striking the board in the center. It split apart with a resounding crack and the bottom piece skittered across the floor.

"Whaddya think about that, Ranger?" Dandy's tone was taunting, bordering on being confrontational.

Concho had just about enough of this idiot, and after a quick glance at Maria, he put his palm on the door and began pushing it open.

"Let's go, Nila," he said.

"Scared, big man?" Dandy said. He had a leering grin and his body odor was pungent, even a few feet away. Not only that, but his sweating seemed to have increased.

Nila stepped through the door and Concho started to follow but hesitated and turned back to the group.

"What's that line from that old Bruce Lee movie?" Concho asked with a smile. "Boards don't hit back?"

Dandy grunted. "You don't know nothing about the martial arts."

"Only what I picked up in the airborne rangers in the Army."

"Well, big man, I'd be glad to show you a few tricks then. We should spar sometime. I always enjoy cutting you big guys down to size and knocking you down on your ass."

Hawk interceded again, stepping over between Concho and Dandy.

"Jimmy, I told you. Knock it off."

Dandy's lower lip jutted outward, but he said nothing. He reached out and grabbed the robe for Drum and slipped it on. As he did so the Band-Aid on his neck slipped off and fluttered to the floor. Instead of picking it up, Dandy used his foot in a sweeping motion and knocked it off to the side.

Job security for the mall custodial crew, Concho thought. He saw two crusted-over, slanting, parallel scratches on the martial artist's neck.

Hawk turned back to him.

"Sorry," Hawk said. "He's just worked himself up so he can put on a good show. For the kids. They love him. He's a natural-born showman."

"I'll keep that in mind. And speaking of kids—" Concho reached into the pocket of his BDU and withdrew the framed BFF picture, holding his thumb over Holley's face as he showed it around. "In the meantime, any of you seen this girl around? She's a runaway."

Dandy took a look and then made a braying noise.

"Nah, I ain't," he said. "But I'd probably have a better chance if you had a picture of the top of her head."

Maria emitted a gasp of disgust. Hawk's face contorted and he leaned close to Dandy and whispered something harsh sounding. The martial artist compressed his lips and looked away.

Turning back to Concho, Hawk said, "Why don't you give me a copy of that? If she shows up here, we'll let you know."

"We'll look into that," Concho said, wondering if it would be an appropriate move to circulate some flyers. His gaze settled on Maria, whose eyes were tightly closed.

"Perhaps we should reschedule this event," she muttered.

"Nonsense," Vince Hawk said. "The show must go on. Just give us a minute to compose ourselves, and we'll bring down the house." His face turned ugly as he gripped the thick collar of Dandy's robe and towed him off to the corner, their heads as close as conferring lovers.

Concho watched the ungainly pair and heaved a sigh.

Maria was staring at him now, and from the looks of it, she was anything but happy.

Time for me to leave, he thought.

* * *

AS THEY WALKED THROUGH THE BACK EXIT TOWARD THEIR respective vehicles, Nila asked Concho if he thought that Jim Dandy was "on something."

He nodded.

"Coke?" she asked.

"Probably," he said. "The symptoms fit."

"I'm glad we didn't have to go to battle with him. Did you see him break that board?"

Concho smirked.

"Like I said, boards don't hit you back. Besides, there's a trick to that kind of stuff. Usually the boards are thoroughly dried out, and then you have to hit the board so your fist is parallel to the grain. It's actually easier than it looks."

"You've done it?" Nila asked.

"Only when I was a youngster trying to impress the girls."

That brought a smile to her lips.

He stopped at the red pickup and looked around. As he remembered, there was no KTTP white SUV in the vicinity.

"Where you parked?" he asked.

"Over there in employee parking. The tan Honda."

"Well." Concho placed a hand on the fender of the Silverado. "This one's mine. At least for the moment. Until I get my F-one-fifty back."

"You got rid of the tow?"

He was surprised she knew about that one. Was there anything about him that wasn't public knowledge?

"Regrettably," he said. "It was kind of a neat undercover vehicle."

Nila laughed and pulled a set of keys out of her pocket.

"That's not what I heard," she said. "But then again, I hear a lot of things."

Concho wondered what she meant by that, but he didn't inquire.

"So where do we go from here?" she asked.

Her question surprised him as well. She'd done a respectable job on her own so far, and initially she'd seemed almost adversarial. Now it seemed as though she was respecting his judgment. Could it be that she was warming up to him a little?

"The boyfriend. Peterson," Concho said. "He seems like a logical next step. What do you think?"

"True," she said. "But does that fit with what Holley told us? I mean, she said Peskipaatei told her she had a new boyfriend."

The girl's description echoed in his memory.

A new guy. A little older, but really cool.

"Maybe so," he said, "but we can't afford not to check out every lead. Think you can find Tyler Peterson's address for me from what Holley gave us?"

"I should be able to, but going over to his house to interview him might be problematic, depending on how busy we are."

"When you find it, call me. I'll go check him out."

Another wary glance of the dark eyes shot up at him.

"Are you back to full duty status?" she asked.

He wondered about that but grinned.

"Let's just say, I'm this close." He held up his thumb and index finger, holding them a few millimeters apart. "And there's something else to check on. Didn't you say that Peskipaatei ran off with another girl and they were picked up in Laredo?"

"Right. The girlfriend's grandmother lived there apparently. She dimed them out to the other girl's parents and the police picked them up."

"You got a name on the other girl involved?"

"Elena Navarro. But I don't have a current address for her.

And all we had on it was an assist other agency blotter notation and juvenile card. It was officially a Maverick County case."

"I'll give Sheriff Parkland a call," he said. "And see if Laredo can fax you over a copy of their report on it."

"You think she might be with that Navarro girl now?"

Concho shrugged.

"Like I said, we can't rule anything out. See if the computer kicks back anything concerning Elena Navarro. If we keep shaking enough bushes, maybe something will jump out."

He didn't want to use the metaphor of looking under rocks. The situation was grim enough.

"I wish we could do more," she said.

"Me too." Then, trying to sound a bit optimistic, "But at least we've got some new leads to follow."

In reality, it wasn't much to go on, and the bracelet thing was still bothering him. Nila seemed to sense that he was thinking about it.

"That bracelet," she said. "What do you think it means?"

"Maybe nothing," he said, "but the other night when I was working the border I caught some illegals—women, girls really, from Nicaragua. They all had on similar red bracelets. I've heard a lot of traffickers are using them. Sort of a color-coded way to know where to send the migrants."

Nila's teeth clenched over her lower lip.

"Yeah, I've heard that too," she said after a moment. "And a lot of young girls disappear that way, especially Indian girls. You think she might have fallen in with some sex traffickers?"

"Let's hope not," Concho said. "But we can't assume anything at this point. I'm just not liking the way this thing is shaping up."

"So where do we go from here?" She glanced at her watch. "Oh, shoot. I'm going to have to go home and shower and change. I'm working afternoons."

"Okay," Concho said. "In the meantime, if you have some

spare time tonight, check out the rest of those phone numbers on the list and get back to me. All right?"

"Will do. What are you going to do now?"

He considered his options, reached into his pocket, and withdrew the bracelet.

"Maybe I can run this down," he said.

CHAPTER TWENTY-ONE

CONCHO CALLED RAUL MOLINA AND ASKED HIM TO OBTAIN AN address for the Petersons on the street where Holley Cameron had told him Peskipaatei's ex-boyfriend lived. Molina emitted an exaggerated groan.

"You can't give me a minute's rest even when you're not supposed to be working, can you?"

"As they say, there's no rest for the wicked."

"Thanks a lot," Molina chirped. Concho could hear his friend's fingers punching the keyboard. "Okay, here it is. Now will you do me a favor and quit bothering me?"

Molina read off the listing.

"Thanks," Concho said. "I owe you another one."

"You owe me a hell of a lot more than that," Molina said and hung up.

Concho drove over to the area and stopped down the block. It was another rather well-to-do upper-middle-class area. Peskipaatei had friends who lived in high places. Was it any wonder she probably compared her rather bleak lifestyle to those with so much and ran away? Despite the monthly checks forwarded to the residents of the Rez, the young girl no doubt yearned for more—like an expensive blue and white Tilly backpack. The haves and the have-nots. The tragic cycle continued to flourish. Such was life on the Rez. He thought back momentarily to his own childhood…the poverty, the beatings…if it hadn't been for the steady guidance of his grandmother and then Meskwaa, he might have ended up missing or dead.

He hoped it wasn't too late for Peskipaatei. In her own way, she was walking between the two different worlds, just as he had.

It was still early afternoon and there was one vehicle, a blue Nissan Altima, parked in the driveway. After cruising by and getting the plate, he pulled over to the curb and picked a good vantage point from which to watch the residence. Then he took out his phone.

After spending a frustrating half hour on the phone with the border patrol trying to get hold of someone concerning the six girls from Nicaragua, Concho decided to cut through the red tape and called Maverick County trying to get Terrill Hoight. The deputy was working and on a call, but the dispatcher said she'd send him a message via the MDT to call Concho ASAP. It only took him fifteen minutes to reply.

"So you're back in the saddle again?" Concho said when his friend called.

"Almost," Hoight said. "I'm still not officially reinstated as an FTO, but I was pretty much cleared of any negligence regarding Cate. How'd you do with that shooting review?"

"Still waiting to be officially cleared, but it shouldn't be too much longer."

"I heard you had Spencer Givens defending you."

Concho laughed. "Yeah. My captain knows him. Cashed in a marker for me."

"Damn, that's great. I wish I would've had him for my bullshit hearing. But it all turned out okay."

"How's Cate doing?"

"He's still off, but he's out of the hospital. Got to get

cleared medically by workman's comp. Hopes to come back soon."

"He's a lucky kid," Concho said. "Say, you happen to get any information on those six female illegals we picked up the other night?"

"All I got regarding those chicks was a couple of Mexican names and some el dee-oh-be-ohs. Probably as phony as a three-dollar bill."

"They said they were from Nicaragua."

"Whatever. Same difference. They got turned over to some supervisor from the border patrol."

"You get the border agent's name?"

"Yeah, I think so. It's in my report, but lemme check my notebook."

Concho waited and presently Hoight gave him a name and number.

"How about that guy you arrested?" Concho asked.

"His name I do remember. Hugo Cuevas. Mexican National." Hoight read off a date of birth. "Won't do no good to check on him, though. We charged the son of a bitch with a bunch of traffic and state charges. The asshole had some fancy-ass lawyer. Bonded right out."

"If he's a Mexican National, what address did he use for the bond?"

"Beats me, but the deputy at the bond hearing said he was then scarfed up by a couple of feds."

"Feds?"

"Yep. Right after the bond hearing."

"Know who they were or where they took him?"

"Nope. I wasn't there. But I heard through the grapevine Hugo was going to cooperate."

Concho considered this and then said, "Okay, Terrill, thanks. And hang in there."

"You too."

After terminating the call, Concho called the number Hoight

had given him for Special Agent-in-Charge Fredrick Sheehan. A harried-sounding man answered after about three rings, and Concho identified himself and asked for Sheehan by name.

"He's out of the office right now," the harried man said. "Something I can help you with?"

"Maybe," Concho said, surprised that the border patrol agent had even asked. "I was involved in a stop of some illegals a couple of nights ago. Got six Nicaraguan females and a couple of bags of fentanyl."

"Yeah," the guy said, warming up slightly. "I heard about that one. What'd you say your name was again?"

"Ranger Concho Ten-Wolves."

The guy's harried tone evaporated.

"You were involved in a shooting, too, weren't you?"

"Right."

"And you iced the prick, didn't you?"

"I did."

"Good job on that, Ranger. My name's Pearsol, by the way."

"Thanks. But I need to do some follow-up. You know where those girls are being held? I'd like to talk to them as part of this case I'm working."

"You got their names by any chance?"

"Huh-un."

The harried tone returned. "I guess I can try to look them up. Lemme call you back."

Not knowing how long that would take, if Pearsol would even call back at all, Concho pressed onward.

"There was a suspect we took into custody during that incident as well," he said. "Hugo Cuevas." Concho read off the date of birth. "I was told he was in federal custody."

"The name and DOB helps narrow things down," Pearsol said. "Lemme put you on hold and I'll look it up."

The connection went silent for a good seven or eight minutes. Just when Concho began to wonder if the man was still there, he came back on the line.

"Okay," he said. "Here's the scoop, but you didn't hear it from me, okay?"

"You got it."

Pearsol laughed. "Hugo posted bond on the state charges you guys laid on him, fleeing and eluding, obstructing a police officer, PCS, unlawful use of weapon, etcetera. Some super-duper agents from the Bureau picked him up at the courthouse and brought him in, along with some high-priced lawyer who said his client wanted to flip. They purportedly worked out an agreement, and that was that." He expelled a harsh-sounding breath. "They were guarding good old Hugo at a little motel waiting for him to set up some kind of drug deal when lo and behold, the son of a bitch said he wanted to take a shower. They let him have his privacy and somehow the asshole used a bunch of towels knotted together to lower himself through the bathroom window. Somebody must have been waiting to pick him up down below. He's now officially in the wind."

"Is there a warrant out for him?"

"I don't think the illustrious Bureau boys want this all coming to light. They'll probably just put a tag out on him if and when he gets picked up on your state warrant, if and when he misses his next court date."

"Who was the lawyer?"

"Some turd named Theodore H. Marshfield. Claims he didn't know nothing about the guy rabbiting." Pearsol laughed. "Typical horseshit, but whatcha gonna do? I guess they're figuring to sweep it under the rug and if he's ever picked up they'll let you guys ram the state charges up his ass."

"Yeah," Concho said. He knew the chances of that were slim and none, and slim left town. "Any mention of the Nicaraguan women?"

"I got some names and birthdays, but they're probably phonies. They were processed and released with notices to appear."

"Processed and released? Without papers?"

Pearsol sighed heavily.

"Welcome to my world," he said. "The way things are now, their scheduled court appearance is about three years away and there's no way to keep tabs on them in the meantime. We're so swamped with illegals it's like a revolving door. Who the hell knows where they were shipped off to? Says here they had a sponsor. An *alleged* sponsor."

"A sponsor? Someone to help them get work?"

"Right. A.C. McMillan Incorporated. Based in Austin." Pearsol read off the address and phone number, and Concho scribbled them down. "You know, I seen that name before on a lot of these sponsorship applications. Mostly young females. Supposedly runs some kind of domestic cleaning services."

Concho hoped, for the sake of the six girls, that it was legitimate, but he had his doubts.

"I really appreciate this," he said. "But let me ask you something else. I remember the females in question were all wearing these distinctive red bracelets. You know anything about that?"

Pearsol snorted. "Do I? Hell, it's like playing flag football. The cartels give out these wristbands indicating whose property the illegals are. The colors correspond to various buyers and sometimes signify how long the wearers are indentured. It's just like modern-day slavery. People being bought and sold like a bunch of cattle."

The word choice bothered Concho, but he knew it was grimly accurate. He thanked Pearsol and asked him to fax or email a copy of the report to him, in care of Nila Willow's KTTP address.

"KTTP? I thought you were a Texas Ranger?"

"I am," Concho said. "But I'm currently working the case with Officer Willow of the Kickapoo Tribal Police. And—" He paused and huffed what he hoped would be interpreted as a commiserating laugh. "I'm technically off due to the shooting."

"Oh," Pearsol said. "I got ya. I'll send it right over."

After terminating the call, Concho texted Nila and said

some reports were forthcoming and asked her to hold onto them. He then debated what would be his next move. Hugo Cuevas was gone, so interviewing him was impossible unless he was rearrested at some point. Concho debated whether or not to call Della Rice, an FBI agent he'd worked with in the past and knew pretty well.

Probably not a good idea, he decided. From the sound of it, the Bureau boys had stepped on their dicks, as they used to say in the Army, and probably wouldn't be too forthcoming with any information. Besides, it was a rather vague connection to a missing Indian girl anyway. And trying to get something out of a shitbird lawyer like Theodore H. Marshfield, whom Concho had clashed with on more than one occasion, would be like pissing into a windstorm. At this point Concho figured the boyfriend, or ex-boyfriend, whatever the case might be, was a long shot, but the possibility that he might know something couldn't be ruled out. It was closing in on fifteen-forty. Nila Willow would be heading to roll call and probably wouldn't get back to him right away. He wondered if Tyler Peterson would be home from school, but didn't want to spook him. Not just yet, anyway. Deciding to take a chance, he dialed the home number they'd gotten from Holley's phone. A woman answered after three rings.

"May I speak to Tyler Peterson, please?" Concho said, trying to sound as benign as possible, which wasn't easy with a commanding voice like his.

"He's not here at the moment."

Concho considered his options, recalling the level of coop-eration he'd received from Holley Cameron's parents. Alarming the woman might lock him out of any type of future communication so he had to tread carefully.

"My name's Concho Ten-Wolves, ma'am, and I'm with the Texas Department of Public Safety. The Texas Rangers. I'd like to talk to Tyler. Do you know when he'll be available?"

"What's this about?"

Concho hesitated briefly. Out-and-out lying to her was out

of the question. After all, he was a Texas Ranger. But he decided that being circumspect would be the best tactic.

"It's about one of his classmates from school," he said, leaving it vague and hopefully routine sounding.

"Which classmate?"

"A young lady. Peskipaatei Standing Bear. Do you know her?"

"Not off hand. Is she in trouble?"

Concho debated what to say, and worried that he'd already blown his chance. If Tyler was complicit in Peskipaatei's disappearance, a call from his mother would probably send him into panic mode.

"We're trying to locate her and we're interviewing all of her friends."

"Standing Bear...she's a Native American girl?"

The woman was obviously trying for political correctness. Most of his people disdained the euphemistic terminology thrust upon them by well-intentioned White liberals in favor of just calling themselves Indians. Being a liberal could mean that the woman might harbor some anti-police sentiment, but it also probably made the likelihood of her housing a runaway less likely. He decided to appeal to her maternal instinct.

"She's actually missing from home and we're trying to locate her. As I said, we're talking to all her friends at school to see if anyone has seen her or might know where she's at."

"Oh, my god. That sounds terrible. And you think Tyler might know where she's at?"

"As I told you," he said, keeping his voice low and amicable, "we're trying to find her. She lives with her grandmother and she's very worried."

"And you think Tyler might know something?"

"We're talking to all of her friends. What time will he be home?"

"He's got basketball practice...I imagine he'll be home by five-thirty or so if he doesn't stop off at one of his friend's places."

"I see. Could you have him call me when he gets in?" He gave her his cell phone number and added in a matter-of-fact tone, "I just need to talk to him for a minute."

Her tone sounded less alarmed as she said she'd comply and Concho thanked her and terminated the call. He then called Raul Molina and asked another favor.

"Another one?" Raul said with a laugh. "For a guy who's supposed to be on administrative leave, you're racking up the overtime."

"Overtime? It's more like Concho time. Now run a computer Sound-Ex on the Peterson family." He gave Raul the address and plate number of the Altima and asked what other kinds of vehicles were registered to them.

"Okay," Molina said, "I got two of them. One's a Cadillac Escalade, bronze in color, and the other's a Jeep Gladiator. Camo colored." He read off the plate numbers.

A three-car family, but none of the vehicles as overly pretentious. Still, the family was definitely one of the haves that Peskipaatei coveted.

"Thanks, Raul."

"So what the hell you working on, anyway? This still that runaway juvenile thing?"

"Yeah," Concho said. "But it might be expanding into something else. Something ugly. I'm checking out leads."

Molina grunted. "Sorry to hear that. Let me know if you need anything else."

After terminating the call, Concho reviewed his options. At the moment, he'd taken things about as far as he could until something else popped up. He leaned back in the seat, adjusted his Stetson so it fit low on his forehead, and decided waiting on Tyler Peterson was his best option at the moment.

Hell, he thought. *Until I hear something else, it's my only option.*

Just then a Jeep Gladiator swung around the corner at the other end of the block and sped past him, heading for the Peterson's driveway.

CHAPTER TWENTY-TWO

TWENTY MINUTES LATER CONCHO WAS FEELING FRUSTRATED AS he drove back to the Rez. The lead concerning the Peterson kid had turned up virtually nothing, and Concho got the feeling the boy really had feelings for Peskipaatei. The tears flowed as Concho confronted him in the driveway.

"Holley called me," Tyler Peterson said. "Please tell me that Penny's okay."

Concho explained that he wasn't sure and tried pressing the youth for more information. What he got was of dubious value. Tyler told him that Peskipaatei had dropped him after she'd gotten back from her ill-fated Laredo excursion with Elena Navarro.

"It was just like out of the blue," he said. "She told me she couldn't see me anymore."

"She say why?" Concho asked.

Tyler shook his head and swiped at the tears that wouldn't stop flowing. The kid was white with a fair complexion and a flush of redness colored his cheeks.

"She wouldn't say. I kept trying to call her, but she blocked my calls." The youth looked up at Concho. "Please, Ranger, you got to find her."

The interview had morphed into a counseling session so Concho cut it short and got out of there with an assurance that he'd do his best. As he was driving away, his cell phone rang. Glancing at the screen, he didn't recognize the number but answered it anyway, which opened the door to more frustration.

"Ranger Ten-Wolves," Rachel Standing Bear said, "have you found her yet?"

Concho recited some of the same standard platitudes he'd used with the Peterson boy, trying to be reassuring, but not offering any false hope or promises that he might not be able to fulfill. Listening to the grandmother's tearful breakdown, blaming herself for the situation, soured his mood even more. And the remoteness of the phone connection made it even more tedious.

"What can you tell me about her last disappearance?" Concho asked. "The one where she went to Laredo."

"You know about that?" Her voice caught. "Yes, of course you do. You're a policeman. I'm sorry, I should have told you about it, but she really seemed like she'd straightened up after they brought her back. She was studying and doing good in school and everything."

She wants to be a nurse, Concho thought, *mimicking the woman's earlier claim.*

Then he felt a wave of shame come over him for doing that. The girl was all this woman had, and from the looks of it, this one wasn't going to have a happy ending. He told Rachel Standing Bear that he'd call her if he got any new information and terminated the call.

The dashboard clock told him it was 1830 and he wondered why Gray-Dove had set the apparatus on the 24-hour clock cycle.

Maybe he did it on my account, he told himself, trying to find some amusement in what was shaping up to be the last lap of a frustrating day. But still, the shooting review had turned out better than he'd anticipated. At least that had gone right.

Now if only they could get a decent lead to follow concerning Peskipaatei. He decided to swing over to the KTTP station and check with Nila to see if she'd found anything.

His phone rang again and this time he looked at the screen and smiled.

"Hey, beautiful," he said, answering it.

"Ooohhh," was her harried-sounding reply.

He sat up, worrying that Hawk had made another inappropriate pass.

"What's wrong? That son of a bitch make another move on you?"

"No, no, no," she said. Some freshness had come back into her tone. "Like I told you, since I mentioned our relationship, he's been keeping his distance."

"Then what's up?"

She heaved a sigh.

"It just turned out to be a looong day," she said, drawing out the word. "That Jim Dandy fellow's a real jerk."

A new set of concerns flooded his mind. He imagined himself wringing the lanky martial artist's neck.

"What did he do?" Concho asked. He was already slowing down, ready to make a U-turn and head over to the mall.

"Nothing to me," she said, "other than to mutter disgusting, chauvinistic comments in a low tone throughout his little demonstration. And the girls in the audience were going wild and screaming like he was some kind of a rock star so they couldn't hear any of it. He broke a lot of boards and roofing tiles."

"Those don't hit back, remember?"

She laughed.

"That's right. I felt like telling him that. Anyway, I'm done for the night and wanted to thank you."

"Thank me? For what?"

"For being a gentleman today and not knocking someone's block off. I know you wanted to."

"Maybe just a little."

She laughed again.

"Or a lot," she said. "Anyway, thanks. I had those corporate jokers there, and I couldn't have afforded having to explain away some kind of incident."

"I aim to please," he said, wondering if he was going to have the pleasure of her company tonight.

"Anyway," she said, "I'm on my way home. I'm really feeling beat and I think I'll just slip into a hot tub and then go to bed. I've got to be back early tomorrow morning and I really need a good night's sleep."

"Well," he said, "you could still come over, take a hot shower instead of a bath, and I could fix you something to eat. After that, I'd let you go to sleep."

"Right. And we both know how that plan would turn out. I really need to get some decent rest. I'm feeling exhausted and cranky."

He was silent, but he knew she was probably right. Whenever the two of them got together, the temptation for some amorous activity overrode the best of chaste intentions.

"Oh, darling, I'm sorry. Please don't be disappointed." Her voice sounded genuine. "I've been dragging the past two days and tomorrow's this big planning session with corporate. I've got to be on my toes. As much as I'd love to be with you, you know we never get much rest when we're together."

"Yeah," he said, trying to keep his tone somewhat upbeat. "That is true."

"So you don't mind?" Her tone was pleading now. "I'm just soooo tired."

He was feeling tired and hungry himself. Plus, he still had a stop to make and some heavy-duty thinking about his next move.

"Just as long as you're not trying to dump me so you can invite Vince Hawk over."

"What?"

His low chuckle brought a realization laugh from her a few seconds later.

"Oh, you," she said. "Okay, thanks. I'll call you tomorrow."

After hanging up, he stopped at a fast-food restaurant and ordered a couple burgers, several packages of greasy fries, and two large soft drinks. Then he drove over to the KTTP station and parked in front. Echabarri's white SUV wasn't in his usual spot.

At least one of us is spending a nice evening at home, he thought.

He entered the building and the afternoon records clerk, whose name Concho couldn't recall, smiled and waved him in. The door metal security door buzzed and he pushed it open with his hip and walked over to the dispatcher.

"Nila busy?" he asked.

The woman turned and shot him an exasperated expression.

"She's on a call. They've been running like crazy all shift."

Concho held up the bag of food and the cardboard tray with the drinks. The grease was already seeping through the paper bag leaving an incremental waxy stain.

"When she's ten-eight have her come in," he said. "I brought her something to eat."

The woman nodded and seconds later Concho heard Nila clearing from the call. The dispatcher told her to come into post for a visitor.

Nila acknowledged over the main radio band and then her voice came over a side channel.

"Who is it?"

"Ranger Ten-Wolves," the dispatcher replied.

"Ten-four. En route."

"What kind of call was she on?" Concho asked.

"Domestic. It's been wall-to-wall family fights since they came on."

His old training officer had told Concho that a heavy call load during a shift was all related to the barometric pressure. The higher the pressure, the shorter people's fuses, thus leading to agitation, irritation, and conflict. Concho sort of agreed but figured it also might have to do with the arrival of the monthly stipend checks that were sent to everyone on the Rez each month from the casino profits.

Give people something for nothing, he thought, and *they'll sure enough find a way to fight over it.*

He went into the break room. The station was deserted. Placing the greasy bag down on the table, he took off his hat and set it on the table far enough away from the bag to avoid any contamination. The odor of the burgers and fries wafted his way and he considered unwrapping one and eating it.

If I start before she gets here, it might look rude, he told himself.

After another deep breath, and more enticing aroma, he reached over and grabbed the bag. Just as he took out one of the burgers, he heard the electronic buzz of the front door. Replacing the burger in the bag, he pushed the entire package away and placed both of his hands on the tabletop.

The smell is probably better than the taste anyway, he thought.

Nila Willow strode into the room and made eye contact.

"What's up?" she asked.

Concho gestured toward the food.

"Brought you something to eat."

She heaved a sigh and raised her eyebrows.

It was a gesture that Concho, for some reason, was unable to do, but he always marveled at the ability in others.

Nila called on the radio that she was down on a break and pulled out the chair across from him. Her fingers tore open the bag and she thrust one of the burgers toward him, along with a bag of fries.

She didn't say anything as she unwrapped hers and then took a bite.

Concho did the same and stuffed a bunch of fries into his mouth as well. He tore open the bag some more and removed a couple packets of ketchup, tossing one across to Nila. The condiment helped offset the now cold fries. The burger was tasting a bit like cardboard as well, but that didn't stop Concho from grabbing the third one and planning to devour it.

Nila had consumed about half of hers before she said, "Thanks. This is great. We've been running from call to call since we came on. We're shorthanded and I think everybody and their brother wants to fight tonight."

"It's a barometric thing," Concho said, trying to sound matter-of-fact.

Her brow furrowed as she took another bite. When she'd finished chewing, she looked at him.

"Barometric?"

He nodded. His burger was all but gone now and he shifted some of the partially chewed food to his cheek so he could talk.

"It's complicated. My first training officer explained it all to me, but I failed to take good notes. Anyway, you had time to do any investigating?"

She frowned.

"Nothing. I've been too busy to try and run down the rest of those phone numbers, but I did manage to track down Elena Navarro's parents. They live in Crystal City."

Concho waited while she took a long sip of her drink.

"Unfortunately, her daughter ran away again," Nila said. "Been missing over a month and a half."

"Damn," Concho said. "Just what we need. Another missing girl."

"And to top off a real frustrating day, Laredo wouldn't send over the report. I called and talked to a sergeant who told me since it was a juvenile matter, I'd have to check with their youth officer tomorrow." She looked at the remnants of her partially eaten burger and muttered, "The asshole," before taking another substantial bite.

He couldn't help but smile, thinking of their initial conversation a few days ago.

"Yeah, those are the rules, all right," he said.

Whether or not she associated his statement with what she'd originally told him was unclear, but he thought he detected a hint of a smile on her lips.

"I struck out too," he said. "I doubt the Peterson kid's involved or knows anything."

"What about the bracelet? Anything there?"

She took a long pull on the straw of her soft drink.

Concho gave her a rundown of what he'd found out.

"Typical FBI," Nila said. "Rush in and take charge and then screw everything up."

He smirked. The animosity between the Bureau and the police was fully entrenched.

"I did find something else of possible interest, though," she said. "I was going to text you, but I didn't have the time."

"What did you find out?"

She held up a finger and grabbed more fries.

Concho waited while she finished chewing.

"Our buddy Vincent Hawk," she said. "Eagle Pass Mall isn't his first talent quest."

"Oh?"

"And," she started to say, but just as she was about to elaborate, the loudspeaker above them blasted with the station dispatcher's voice, "Nila, you available?"

"What you got?" Nila yelled back.

"Another domestic," she said, her voice sounding urgent. "And Timbo's going by himself."

"Shit," Nila said under her breath, rising and then yelled back to the dispatcher. "Mark me ten-eight and en route."

The call then came over Nila's shoulder mic and she radioed she was ten-seventy-six.

Ah, the joys of uniformed patrol, Concho thought, watching her hustle toward the door, wiping her mouth with one of the paper napkins.

"What else did you want to tell me?" he asked. "About Hawk?"

She made a half-turn.

"He had another one in Laredo," Nila said. "About two months ago. And there's more."

Then she'd disappeared out the door.

Concho cleaned up the rest of the wrappers and half-eaten food and mulled this latest piece of information over in his mind.

Peskipaatei had been picked up as a runaway about two months ago in Laredo—the same time of one of Hawk's talent quest events. And her cell phone put her at this one the day she disappeared.

Coincidence?

Maybe, but he didn't like coincidences.

Just when he was trying to see how all the pieces fit, his cell phone rang. The number was unfamiliar, but he answered it anyway with a generic, "Yeah?"

"Ten-Wolves?"

The voice was deep and unmistakable.

"Speaking."

"How you doing? It's Vince Hawk."

Concho said nothing.

"Hey, listen," Hawk said. "There's something I got to talk to you about."

"So talk."

"Huh-un, not over the phone. Come by my room at the hotel. Now. Tonight. It's important."

Concho tried to figure out what this was all about, but he knew he couldn't afford not to go.

"Well, whaddya say?" Hawk said, his tone sounding almost cordial now. "I'm in the presidential suite. I assume you know where it's at."

"I'm on my way," Concho said and terminated the call.

He wondered what Hawk had in mind, but figured whatever it was, the time was right for a good old-fashioned Indian-style pow-wow anyway.

CHAPTER TWENTY-THREE

ABOUT FIFTEEN MINUTES LATER, CONCHO PULLED UP IN FRONT of the Lucky Eagle Casino. The main parking lot was full, as usual, but Concho was able to find a spot on the far side of the hotel/casino not too far away from Hawk's four buses. He studied them before he got out of the truck. They were the size of Greyhounds or tour buses and were emblazoned with a circular red design on the sides. Yellow lines ran through the circle and *THUNDERHAWK PRODUCTIONS* was imprinted over the other markings in big, bold, black lettering.

After slipping on his BDU vest and locking the Silverado, Concho started for the hotel. It was a six-story structure that wound around the casino portion like a protective wall with windows. The complex was massive and had several restaurants, numerous bars, and countless gambling tables and machines inside. Most of the patrons were usually older or middle-aged White folks, although most of the employees were Indians. The place even had a well-stocked medical clinic on the second floor and Concho had used it several times when he needed some quick medical treatments, such as getting stitched up after a savage encounter. He was walking toward the hotel now at a leisurely place when he saw a heavyset figure in a pork-pie hat, dark pants, and a sports jacket but no tie, leaning against one of the grayish cement columns smoking a cigarette. The figure smirked as Concho got closer.

"An Indian driving a red pickup truck," Alexander Drum said. "You trying to be a stereotype or something."

"My other car's a Mercedes," Concho said, remembering his missed opportunity with the Camerons.

"What happened to the tow truck?" Drum asked him.

Concho was curious about how Drum knew about his previous ride but figured it must have been a topic of conversation at the mall. It was certainly no secret.

"I traded it in for a newer model," Concho said. "Why? You got a flat that needs fixing?"

Drum snorted and blew twin plumes of smoke out his nostrils.

"Hey," he said, a smile tracing over his lips, "I'll have you know that I ain't no *flat*-foot no more. I'm a *flat-out* professional security expert and bodyguard to the stars."

He punctuated his pronouncement with a laugh and tipping the small-brimmed hat in a mock salute with one hand as he brought the cigarette to his mouth with the other.

"So how'd you make out with that shooting?" Drum asked.

The heavyset ex-cop tilted his head sideways and grinned. Concho glared at him

"How'd you hear about that, Drum?"

"I told ya, call me Al."

"Okay, Al, how is it you know so much of my business?"

"I overheard a couple people talking the other day," he said. "Sheriff Parkland was one. Talked to him on the sly, cop-to-cop."

That explained how he'd heard but not his interest.

"I'm still in limbo, mostly," Concho said.

Drum blew out a cloudy breath and shook his head.

"Yeah, I know how it is. Been there myself a few times. Got in my first shooting two weeks on the job working the Second District—the projects. Armed robbery call." His index finger touched the spot between his eyebrows. "The asshole came around the corner, gun in hand, and I put one right here. My first of many such encounters."

Concho said nothing.

"I heard you been in quite a few yourself," Drum said. He was about seven inches shorter than Concho and was having a bit of difficulty matching the bigger man's strides.

Again, Concho said nothing.

"So, how many?" Drum said. "How many shootings you been in?"

"Too many to suit me."

The other man chuckled, the cigarette jiggling up and down between his lips. "Yeah, I know what you mean. I got plenty of accommodations and decorations, but every damn time that damn civilian review board would rake me over the coals. I was in eleven shootings total. It got so it wasn't even worth it putting on the uniform no more. Of course I was in detectives my last ten. When I hit the big five-oh, I pulled the pin and got into the private sector. That's where the real money is."

Taking one more drag on the cigarette, he flung the butt away from him. Concho watched it land a few feet away, its red embers creating a tiny circular burst as it struck the sidewalk.

He changed direction and stepped on it, crushing it out.

Drum's face appeared amused.

"You always like to tidy things up like that?" he said.

Concho flashed him a grin.

"Force of habit," he said. "It's been dry lately. Don't want any brush fires to start."

Drum chuckled and held up his hands, palms outward.

"Ya got me," he said. "I'll find an ashtray next time." The heavyset man turned and fell back into step beside Concho. "You're here to see Vince, right?"

"Yeah. Any idea what he wants to talk to me about?"

Drum moved his head indicating negativity.

"With Mr. Super Hawk, it's anybody's guess." Drum

reached into his shirt pocket, removed the pack of cigarettes, and shook one out. He started to put it back and then offered it to Concho.

"No thanks," Concho said. "That's one bad habit I never picked up."

"Good for you." Drum stuck the new smoke between his lips and cupped his hand around the end, flicking the wick of a disposable lighter. "I been smoking since I was eighteen, unfortunately. Got started when I was in the Army. Hey, I heard you were an airborne ranger."

"I was."

"Me, I was ninety-five B. Military Police." Shrugging, he exhaled more smoke. "Don't know what they call it now. I heard all the MOSes were all changed."

"Not eleven-bravo. It's still infantry."

Drum snorted. "You got that right. Once a grunt, always a grunt, huh?"

They came to the main entrance and Concho glanced up at the overhead sign. It was getting dark now and the red letters were glowing over the white outline of the flying eagle set beneath them. Concho grabbed the door and held it open for Drum, who nodded a "thanks" and slipped through. The second set of doors retracted with automated efficiency.

"You know the way up to the presidential suite, right?" Drum asked.

"Yeah. You coming up?"

Drum took a final drag on his cigarette, smirked, and made a show of stubbing it out in a nearby ashtray.

"Nah, I'm gonna go shoot some craps. The boss is up there waiting for you." He took out his cell phone. "I'll give him a call and tell him you're on the way up."

The elevator doors opened.

Concho held his arm in front of the retracted elevator door. "My buddy Jim Dandy going to be up there?"

Drum paused with his dialing.

"Nah, that son of a bitch is probably out trying to get laid."

His head swiveled toward Concho. "But if he does show up, watch yourself. He used to do MMA fighting and he's pretty good." Drum looked him up and down. "But you don't look like no Tinker Bell, neither. You might be able to take him. It'd be something to see."

"What name did he fight under?" Concho asked, figuring it might be worth a look-see just in case a match-up was in the cards.

Drum's face crinkled and he shrugged his shoulders.

"Some Polack name. Jimmy Lindowski or Lewinsky or some shit like that."

The elevator door started forward and jerked to a stop and retracted when it hit Concho's outstretched arm.

"Catch you later, Drum," he said as he stepped into the elevator.

The ex-cop pointed his extended index finger at Concho as if it were a gun.

"Not if I catch you first."

* * *

THE PRESIDENTIAL SUITE HAD A GOLD PLAQUE DECLARING IT AS such attached to the solid oak door. Before Concho could knock, the door swung inward and Vince Hawk appeared wearing a white terrycloth hotel bathrobe and a wide grin.

"Ranger Ten-Wolves," he said, stepping to the side and extending his arm with a welcoming gesture. "Come in. Please."

Concho noticed the man was wearing some kind of fancy house slippers, the kind you usually wore at the pool. The suite was expansive and lit by a few lamps farther inside the room. An immense chandelier hung in the center of the ceiling and numerous fancy lounge chairs and a plush sofa were opposite a large flat-screen television. A pattern of slow-moving and ever-changing colors wove over the screen and some low music played. A well-stocked wet bar was in one corner. Hawk walked over the thick carpeting toward a big Jacuzzi with bubbling water and gestured for Concho to follow. The room was pretty much as Maria had described it, right down to the two luscious girls lounging in the bubbling water. Just their heads were visible and they were both giggling.

Maria had said they'd looked young, and Concho estimated their ages to be maybe late teens, early twenties. One of them looked to be possibly Indian. Kickapoo maybe, or Navajo. The other girl was white, and had that look of a pale-skinned Scandinavian. Both were quite beautiful and from what he could tell, quite naked.

Hawk was watching Concho's reaction with a proverbial Cheshire cat's grin. He continued over to the wet bar and stepped behind it.

"What's your pleasure?" he said, setting two glasses on the top of the bar and using some silver-colored tongs to drop ice cubes in each.

Concho shook his head, trying not to look at the two girls.

"Come on," Hawk said. "Don't tell me you don't drink."

"What was it you wanted to talk to me about?"

Hawk shrugged and filled one glass with an amber-colored liquid from a bottle.

"I feel as though I need to set the record straight," Hawk said, coming from around the bar and walking over to Concho. He was tall, but not nearly as tall as Concho and Hawk had to adjust his gaze to look up at the taller man.

"Concerning what?"

Hawk glanced away and appeared to try and soften things with a sedate shrug.

"Ms. Maria Morales." He took a sip of the drink. "Believe me, if I woulda known she was your girl, I would have kept my distance."

Concho said nothing, figuring his silence would speak volumes.

Hawk shrugged again. "I mean, let's face it. She is a very attractive woman." He glanced over at the two girls in the hot tub and added, "Maybe a bit mature for my usual tastes, but nonetheless..."

The two girls giggled again. They both straightened up and sat on what must have been a submerged ledge in the tub exposing two sets of exquisite breasts. Concho saw that they each had some kind of tattoo on their abdomens.

Two red circles with yellow lines—possibly lightning bolts, running through them. It looked to be identical with the one Jim Dandy had sported on his chest.

"When I asked her up here for a drink, and then suggested we get more comfortable," Hawk said, "I got the impression that she took it the wrong way and got a little bit...irritated."

Concho recalled what Maria had told him about the incident and felt like twisting Hawk's arm around behind his back and dunking his head in the hot tub.

"What are you trying to say?"

"Just that I think she took my offer a little out of context. Sure, I was attracted to her, and, not bragging or anything, I do get my share of feminine companionship from time to time." He jerked his thumb toward the two girls in the Jacuzzi. "And I don't mind sharing. Interested?"

More giggling emanated from the hot tub.

Concho glared at them and both girls sank lower in the water so that their breasts and abdomens were no longer visible.

"Those girls look kind of young, don't you think?" he said.

"Well, you know what they say," Hawk said. "You're never too young to think about being a dirty old man."

The grin persisted until Concho told him, "No thanks."

Hawk shrugged dismissively. "A one-woman man, huh?"

"Something like that."

"So anyway..." Hawk cleared his throat. "The last thing I wanted was to do something that would piss you off. I remember you from my days on the Rez, bro. We were buds then and I hope we can be buds now. I meant it about the job offer. I could use a big, strapping guy like you in my next picture. I told you about that one, right? I'm playing Geronimo. I'm gonna be using a lot of Indians from the Rez, too."

Hawk was speaking very rapidly and Concho wondered if the man was on something. He looked around to see if he could spot any drug paraphernalia like maybe a razor and small mirror. Hawk's eyes were too dark to discern if his pupils were dilated.

"And I happened to hear that you're on suspension, or something, right?"

Again, Concho said nothing, but he wondered how his current status had become such a topic of consideration.

"All right, all right," Hawk said. "I don't mean to pry, but my point is, there's more to life than being a police officer. Even a Texas Ranger. Just ask Al Drum. He was on Chicago PD, and now he works for me, and he couldn't be happier."

"You know I talked to Drum on my way up here," Concho said.

"Yeah, right. But what I'm saying is, I do a lot of filming down in Mexico, as well as the United States. I got a good relationship with the Mexican government, but with the cartels down there, I could always use a good, competent couple of men working security for me." The hand not holding the drink fluttered as he waved it dismissively. "Nothing real dangerous, but I'd feel better having a man I know that can take care of himself."

"I thought you had Jim Dandy?"

Hawk barked out a cough.

"Yeah, Jimbo's a good dude and tough as all hell, but he's something of a loose cannon. Used to fight MMA and between you and me, I sometimes think he took one too many shots to the head." Hawk laughed. "But I love him, and once somebody hooks up with me, I take care of them."

Concho waited. The silence grew awkward between them. Finally, Hawk broke it by asking, "Well, what about it?"

Concho reached into his pocket, withdrew Peskipaatei's

BFF picture, and held it up, holding his thumb over Holley's face.

"I appreciate the offer," he said, "but no thanks. I've got other concerns at the moment. You seen this girl around?"

Hawk's frown deepened.

"Huh? No. That's the same one you showed me before."

"I wasn't sure you looked at it before." He kept holding the picture up. "But does she look familiar?"

Hawk blew out a sputtering breath, then grinned. "What's that the White man says about us? All us Indians look alike?" He snorted derisively. "If you want to give Drum a copy, I'll have him keep an eye out for her if she shows up. In the meantime, if you change your mind or that shooting thing doesn't go well, my offer still stands."

The two girls kept staring at Concho as he put the picture back into his pocket and headed for the door.

"See you around, Swooping Hawk," he said.

CHAPTER TWENTY-FOUR

THE CACOPHONY OF LOUD GAMING MACHINES AND TIPSY winners and losers blended together as Concho got off the elevator and strode through the casino. He went past the Red Sky Grill and felt a slight twinge in his stomach. The burger and fries were feeling like cardboard cutouts inside his gut and he wondered if Nila was having any of his buyer's regrets as well. The dangling silver lamp shades and cozy booths made him wish he'd come here instead of taking the fast-food option.

But life was full of choices and regrets, he reminded himself and turned his thoughts to his recent meeting with Vince Hawk. The entire conversation struck Concho as a bit weird, and Hawk had seemed a bit nervous. Concho doubted the veracity of the actor's half-assed apologia. On the phone he'd said it was "important" and that they had to talk. In retrospect, the entire thing could have easily been handled in a phone conversation. And what was with Hawk's persistent job offer of a security position? That seemed a bit out of place, too. The other day at the initial mall meeting he'd all but ridiculed Concho and now wanted to be his buddy and savior. The coup de grâce had been the actor's usage of the old "us against them" tactic when Concho had shown him Peskipaatei's picture.

The White man says we all look alike.

Appealing to the brotherhood of the underdog. As if he and Concho walked a similar path. Having grown up on the Rez, and having first-hand knowledge of Concho's situation, Hawk, of all people should have known that Concho had walked a path between two cultures, two worlds, and that put him in a class by himself.

He caught a glimpse of Alex Drum leaving the area of the crap tables. The ex-cop was busy texting something on his cell phone, the pork-pie hat pushed back on his head.

Maybe it was Hawk summoning Drum up to the suite, although Concho doubted that the movie star would want any more male company. Just then, Drum's head shot up and he looked around, and seeing Concho, he waved, smiled, and went back to his phone. Drum had seemed almost gleeful when recounting his purported officer-involved shootings, and Concho wondered how much was fact and how much was enhancement. The ex-cop exuded toughness, and Concho didn't doubt the man had been one hell of a mean cop in his heyday, but there was something about him now that bothered Concho. He couldn't quite put his finger on it, though.

Outside, the night air was cool and Concho continued toward the section where he'd left the Silverado. Hopefully, Gray-Dove would have the F-150 ready soon.

But at least I'm not driving that tow truck anymore, he thought.

He was almost to the Silverado, making his way through the aisles, when something flickered in his peripheral vision.

A hoarse whisper followed.

"Ahi esta. Cosiguele."

Spanish—there he is. Get him.

Not good.

Concho knocked the Stetson off and instinctively crouched down and slid between two parked cars, withdrawing the Staccato from his pancake holster and used his thumb to snap off the safety. He was glad he'd opted for a belt holster instead of a shoulder rig. Those added seconds to your drawing time.

A round shattered the glass of the car window next to his head as he saw a bright flash ignite about fifteen yards away. He brought the Staccato up and squeezed the trigger, firing two rounds at the fleeting silhouette that had been partially illuminated by the muzzle flash.

Had he hit him?

No way to tell at this point.

Another round thumped into the vehicle but Concho was back-peddling now rather than returning fire. Concho knew he was facing more than one adversary, but how many? And he had to be judicious about returning fire. The parking lot was usually fairly well-lit up by the overhead lights, but in this back section, the lights weren't working. Was this by design? Obviously, his opponents had been waiting for him and had come prepared. Adding to his problems, he couldn't be sure there were no civilians in the vicinity. He knew that he'd have to pick his shots and be sure of the backdrop.

Still in a crouch, Concho circled behind the automobile and headed toward the Silverado. It was higher and would offer more cover for a man his size.

Another shot went off, almost simultaneously and he heard the faint sound of glass shattering.

"*Mátalo, stupido,*" the voice shouted.

Concho rose slightly and tried to get a fix on the person doing the yelling. He saw him about thirty yards away: an obese man wearing all black, with a balaclava mask covering his face. Zeroing in on the man's big belly, Concho did a point-shoot and squeezed off two rounds. The big-bellied man grunted and hunched over.

Two more bullets plucked into the vehicle next to Concho. He turned and saw two other figures, both dressed in dark clothes and wearing masks, pointing weapons at him.

Revolvers, not semi-autos.

They didn't want to leave any expended rounds. That also

meant that he most likely had the advantage as far as ammunition.

If there were only three of them.

He dashed across the aisle and suddenly saw his truck. Reaching into his pocket, he pressed the key fob and the Silverado's lights flickered and the horn beeped. As he'd hoped, the momentary diversion was enough to catch the three would-be assassins off-guard, but only for a moment.

That was all Concho needed.

He fired two rounds at each of the other two and saw them flinch and then shuffle behind cover. A fusillade of rounds, the muzzle bursts scintillating in the velvety ambience, made Concho duck down.

He knew that he'd hit the last two of them.

Center mass, just where he'd aimed.

But they'd still moved with alacrity. While he knew that unlike the TV shows and the movies, one hit did not automatically take a foe out, the two of them looked far from incapacitated. The memory of his shootout the other night came dancing back.

Ballistic vests.

Were these guys cartel members back for revenge?

But how had they known he'd be here? And with a new truck?

The possibility of a tail that he hadn't spotted meant that they were good. Of course, he'd been so immersed in his ongoing escapades that he hadn't really been monitoring his six like he usually did.

Like I should have been, dammit, he told himself as another series of rounds slammed into the metallic cover.

Outnumbered three to one and caught with his drawers down, he knew this was going to be one hell of a firefight.

He leaned around the right rear fender and sent a fusillade of his own right back at them.

His hearing was substantially impaired due to the auditory exclusion factor, but Concho distinguished another series of rounds going off from behind him, one of them sounding like a cannon. He glanced back and saw a group of figures advancing on foot, their arms outstretched and holding weapons. Two of them were casino security guards. The third one was the lumbering figure of Alex Drum holding a massive chrome-steel revolver, a trail of smoke rising from the end of the barrel.

"*Correr*," one of the adversaries shouted. It was the fat one —the first one Concho had shot. "*Vaminous a salir de aquí.*"

They were getting the hell out of here.

Concho felt a bit of relief, but he was far from at ease.

Drum and company kept on advancing, but apparently their aim was poor. None to the three marauders slowed or showed any sign of being hit. They disappeared into the darkness. Scant seconds later, Concho discerned the sound of a vehicle revving up and peeling out. A dark van shot down the adjacent aisle of the lot and zoomed toward the main entrance/exit.

One of the security guards readjusted his aim toward the fleeing vehicle but Drum grabbed the young man's arm and pushed the gun down.

"You nuts?" Drum shouted. "You never shoot at a fleeing vehicle unless you know who all's in it."

The guard's jaw dropped and he sheepishly holstered his weapon.

Drum was making his way forward now, both arms outstretched. His revolver had a six-inch barrel.

"Hey, Concho," Drum shouted. "You hit?"

"No," Concho yelled back. Both his words and Drum's sounded like they were being funneled through a wind tunnel.

Auditory exclusion, he reminded himself, knowing it would soon pass. He pulled himself to his feet and rushed to the driver's door of the Silverado. Jumping in, he shoved the keys into the ignition and twisted to the starting position.

Maybe, if he could get rolling fast enough, he might be able to catch sight of the van.

The starter ground and ground, unable to catch. Swearing, Concho twisted the key again, getting the same result.

Drum was at the shattered passenger side window now, a wide grin plastered on his face.

"You might as well go ahead and call your tow truck buddy," he said. "You're leaking antifreeze like it's going out of style up here, and you got two flat tires on your right side. Face it buddy, you ain't going nowhere."

Concho heaved a sigh and slammed the heel of his hand down on the steering wheel.

"Jesus," Drum said. "You gonna break that too?"

His grating chuckle made Concho grind his teeth.

"Hey," Drum added. "Look on the bright side. You ain't shot and we gave as good as we got."

Concho nodded but wondered what the hell else could go wrong tonight?

CHAPTER TWENTY-FIVE

SEVERAL BRIGHT FLOODLIGHTS HAD BEEN SET UP, ILLUMINATING the once-dark area, and one of the KTTP patrol officers scampered around taking photographs with a digital camera. Nila Willow stood off to the side saying nothing. Chief Roberto Echabarri had responded and was personally supervising his personnel's processing of the crime scene. Concho remarked that it was good to see all that training he'd received at Quantico being put to good use.

"Yeah," Echabarri said. "Right. You got any idea who they were?"

Concho shrugged.

"Well, I got plenty of enemies, but I did overhear them speaking in Spanish. While that certainly doesn't rule out any locals, it could also point to the cartel. They have a score to settle with me. You find the van?"

Echabarri nodded. "Maverick County did. Stolen and abandoned and set on fire. Noticeable blood trail leading away from it, so you must have hit one of them."

"Somebody must have picked them up," Concho said. "These boys were organized. Good thing they weren't better shots."

Depends on how you look at it." Echabarri chuckled. "They sure killed your truck."

"John Gray-Dove's truck," Concho said. "And I'm dreading telling him."

On the other side of the parking lot a sea of red and blue lights oscillated in the darkness. Maverick County had sent some units to assist, but given this was KTTP jurisdiction, they stayed on the outskirts for traffic and crowd control. Sheriff Isaac Parkland had also responded once he heard that Concho had been involved. Unfortunately, so had Captain Dalton Shaw, who did not look happy.

"Dammit, Ten-Wolves," he said. "You haven't been officially cleared in the last shooting and here you are involved in another one."

"There wasn't much your man could've done, Captain," Alex Drum said, blowing a plume of smoke upward from his extended bottom lip. His fleshy face was covered with perspiration. "Those assholes were waiting to ambush him."

Shaw tilted his head to the side and regarded the heavyset ex-cop.

"And you are…?"

"Alexander Drum, at your service. CPD retired, and currently in charge of security for Mr. Vincent Hawk."

"How'd you get involved in this?" Shaw asked.

Echabarri stepped over to listen.

Drum, apparently relishing his time in the limelight, took another quick drag on his cigarette and let the smoke seep out of his nose while he talked.

"I was just coming out to check on Mr. Hawk's buses." He gestured toward the four of them. "All of a sudden, I hear a bunch of rounds going off. It sounded like Saturday night on the South Side. Ah, that's the South Side of Chicago. Anyway, once a copper, always a copper. I grabbed a couple of the security guards from the casino and we did a tactical advance. That's when we seen Concho here being shot at by three offenders. We advanced and once they got a load of Miss

Agnes here." He paused to pat and then lift the left side of his sports jacket, revealing the huge revolver dangling in a shoulder rig. "They took off like a bunch of sissies."

"I assume you have a concealed carry permit for that," Shaw said.

"I do," Drum said. "And a copy's already on file with the Maverick County Sheriff's Office, but I'll be glad to fax one over to you as well."

"I'll take one too," Echabarri said.

"Sure thing, Chief," Drum said and then snorted. "Hey, that's kind of apropos, ain't it? Chief."

Echabarri frowned and looked at Concho.

"Exactly what kind of weapon is that?" Shaw asked, still staring at Drum's gun. "It looks like a Python."

"It's what every Colt Python wants to be when it grows up," Drum said. "A Colt Anaconda. I'll have to let you fire it sometime."

Shaw thanked him and turned back to Concho.

"You got anything to add?"

Concho shook his head. "You going to need to hold on to my new weapon, sir? I've kind of grown attached to it."

Shaw blew out a long breath, took off his Stetson, smoothed back his hair, and reset the hat on his head.

"That the Staccato?" he asked.

Concho nodded.

"That's actually up to Chief Echabarri here," Shaw said. "This is technically his jurisdiction and his investigation."

Echabarri seemed flattered at the captain's endorsement. His chest seemed to puff up slightly.

"Well," he said. "I don't think we'll need to confiscate anybody's weapons at this point. It was clearly an ambush and thus a case of self-defense. Fully justified for you to shoot back when being shot at. Plus, it doesn't appear that we have any bodies laying around."

Concho felt his wave of relief growing.

"All right," Shaw said. "Ten-Wolves, I'm going to release

you at this time, but I'll expect a full, written account turned into me first thing in the morning."

"Copy that, sir," Concho said.

Shaw turned to go, but then hesitated.

"And, Concho," he said.

"Yes, sir?"

"I know it's not in your DNA," Shaw said, "but try to stay out of trouble. At least until we get this new mess straightened out."

Looks like my administrative leave's just been extended, Concho thought. *And I still have to call John Gray-Dove and break it to him about his fancy loaner truck.*

He looked over at the Silverado, which was resting lopsided due to the pair of tires being blown.

It had been a nice truck while it lasted.

CHAPTER TWENTY-SIX

THE NEXT MORNING CONCHO WAS UP EARLY AT HIS USUAL SIX a.m., but feeling tired he remained in bed for a while. He'd stayed awake most of the night watching and waiting, gun in hand, in case the cartel thugs tried to return and finish up the job. It wouldn't have been the first time his trailer had been attacked. His original home had been burned down, and this new one had suffered more than just the slings and arrows of outrageous fortune. He'd brought out his array of weapons, his 30.06 deer rifle with the Leupold VX scope, his night-vision goggles, his one remaining .45 caliber Colt Double Eagle, the Staccato, and his bow and arrows. He was determined that if his assailants came back for Round Two, he'd take the fight to them, no holds barred.

But it had turned out to be all for naught. Whoever they were, they didn't show. While other than the missing sleep, this should have given him some sort of solace, but he kept thinking about several things that bothered him about the whole incident. One was how the assailants knew about the loaner truck, and two, how did they know he'd be at the casino? The tow truck would have been about as easy to spot as a chewing tobacco stain on a white wedding dress, but nobody knew he was driving the Silverado except a handful of people. He tried to think back if he noticed a tail, but then again, you don't always see someone tailing you, especially if they're good. But if they were good, why the botched job?

He'd gone there in the red pickup and who'd seen him in it?

Drum had been one.

An Indian driving a red pickup truck. You trying to be a stereotype or something?

And the ex-cop had been taking out his cell phone...if Drum had been involved, you could damn well bet that Vince Hawk was behind it.

But then again, Drum had come to his defense.

Or had he?

Once a copper, always a copper. I grabbed a couple of the security guards from the casino and we did a tactical advance.

Concho wondered about the veracity of that statement. He remembered one of the security guards, Felix Gomez, standing there with a strained look on his face as Drum shot off his mouth to Shaw and Echabarri. At the time Concho had put it off to the kid's nervousness. It had to have been his first shootout and that was never an easy thing to go through.

Unless you're an old pro like Alexander Drum who got into all kinds of them on the South Side of Chicago.

Or so he said.

Concho knew no one in the Windy City and wondered whom he could call to check on Drum's record? Maybe Raul Molina had a contact there. He mentioned that he'd attended Northwestern University's Center for Public Safety School Staff Studies extension class down here and taught by a retired CPD lieutenant. Maybe he could reach out to the guy, if he still had the man's number.

That, admittedly, was a long shot, and at this point, all Concho had was speculation. Certainly, Drum wouldn't be the first retired cop to enhance his past and present experiences.

And he was part of the "tactical advance" with that big Colt Anaconda.

Of course for a guy who'd shot his first armed robber right between the eyes, this time he'd failed to hit anybody. Was he just a bit out of practice or had he intentionally not been trying to take out the bad guys? Or maybe he wanted to take someone else out with purported "friendly fire." If Drum had been complicit in the ambush, it wasn't difficult to connect the dots so that the arrow would point to Hawk, but what else?

Thunderheart Productions doing talent quests...attracting a lot of young girls...young girls like the two in Hawk's hot tub, tattoos and all.

A picture was starting to form and Concho didn't like it much. Could this be connected to Peskipaatei's disappearance? Or was that just wishful thinking, hoping she could still be found unharmed?

Concho figured he could speculate about it endlessly, but just for the hell of it, he made a mental note to go interview those casino security guards and see what their story might be without Drum there spouting off. He dragged himself to his desk and opened up his laptop, trying to dash out the report of last night's incident, but the words just wouldn't come.

It was closing in on 0830 when he finally gave up and fixed himself something to eat. After finishing a leisurely breakfast, switched off the news channel he'd been watching and placed the dishes in the sink. With his refilled mug of coffee in hand, he began putting away his weapons when his cell phone rang. Glancing at the screen he saw it was from the office.

Captain Shaw's voice was laced with irritation and sarcasm as he asked, "I hope I didn't wake you, Ten-Wolves."

Concho immediately remembered about the captain's directive: he wanted a full report on his desk first thing in the morning.

Oops.

"Actually, I was just about ready to head in, sir," Concho said. "I've been working on it."

The truth was that he hadn't written one coherent sentence.

"Yeah," Shaw said. "Right. And I'll bet you got a set of encyclopedias you'd like to sell me too, don't ya?"

"Sir?"

"Never mind," Shaw said, "you're way too young to understand that one." He blew out a heavy breath. "And so am I, for that matter. It was something my mother used to say when I would try and bullshit her."

The slightly lighter tone in Shaw's voice gave Concho the hope that the captain wasn't really that mad, but then the harshness returned.

"So it's nine thirty-five. What part about first thing in the morning didn't you understand?"

Concho figured the best tactic might be to go on the offensive a little, or at least offer a deflection.

"Actually, sir, I've been so concerned about that shooting inquiry that it's causing me to second guess myself. I was having trouble wording the report. It's like a mental block." He paused and then added. "I was wondering if you could give me Spencer Given's phone number so I could confer with him first."

Silence, and then Shaw snorted.

"Spencer Givens. Cut the horseshit and get your sorry ass in here, Ten-Wolves. I was all set to release you back to regular duty until this thing last night happened. Now I've got to go back and sweet-talk the brass upstairs again to convince them you're not some out-of-control Indian on the warpath. And I hate sweet-talking a bunch of empty holsters, even if they once were Rangers."

Empty holsters. Concho smiled. Captain Shaw was showing his rank-and-file Ranger roots.

"I'll be in shortly, sir," Concho said, then thought of one more thing he wanted to ask. "Say, Captain, you know anybody on Chicago PD?"

"No, why? You having some reservations about your savior, Alexander Drum, and his sidekick, Miss Agnes?"

Concho was glad to see that he and the captain were on the same wavelength.

"I've been reviewing it all in my mind, is all," Concho said.

"I have too," Shaw said. "And I sent a request about him through proper channels as a matter of routine. I'll let you know."

"Thank you, sir."

"All right, get your ass in here with that report."

Shaw didn't wait for a reply.

Concho set the phone down and finished putting away his guns, keeping out the Colt Double Eagle, the Staccato, and his bow and quiver. He took two extra magazines for each handgun. Mixing the two weapons wasn't an ideal plan. The two pistols not only had different ammunition, but the Staccato was single-action and the Colt double-single, not to mention the difference in their respective recoils. But the Colt had never failed him in a shootout, and the Staccato had earned its stripes last night.

Besides, he thought, *the way things are going I'm apt to have one of the other or maybe both of them confiscated.*

Sighing, he went to his desk and sat down, opening up his work computer again.

Maybe doing the report would help him organize his thoughts. He looked at the little wooden plaque that sat next to the laptop. Maria had bought it for him as a joke. It was a cartoon of a man sitting on a toilet reaching for an empty spool of toilet paper. The caption underneath, in bold black letters, said:

THE JOB'S NOT FINISHED UNTIL THE PAPERWORK'S DONE.

So true, he thought. *And so appropriate.*

* * *

FINISHING THE REPORT TOOK LESS TIME THAN HE WOULD HAVE figured. After emailing a copy to the cloud and to his Ranger account, he stood up and stretched. It was closing in on ten and he knew he shouldn't dally anymore before going to see Shaw. He slipped on the shoulder rig and put the Staccato in that, sliding the two extra mags in the two holders on the right side. He then put his Colt a pancake holster on his right hip, with the magazine holders on the left side of his belt. With his Texas Ranger badge in place on his chest, he donned the same camo-colored BDU that he'd worn the day before with all of his accoutrements: wallet, Texas Ranger ID, pens, mini-mag flashlight, and his TX395 Coast knife.

Once again, he felt loaded for bear.

As was his habit, before descending the steps from his front door, he did a quick glance around and that's when he saw the figure sitting in the fire pit, a wispy trail of smoke rising from the smoldering cigarette.

Meskwaa. Three visits in as many days.

Concho strolled over and took his customary seat in the largest of the lawn chairs.

"How bad's the other truck?" Meskwaa asked.

Concho glanced over at the tow truck parked in the usual space reserved for his vehicles.

"Bad enough," he said. "John Gray-Dove wasn't too happy, but he'll be getting another voucher from the state."

The old man chuckled. "You probably caused him to miss his favorite television programs last night."

"He's getting his revenge by giving me that thing again," Concho said, gesturing toward the tow truck.

Meskwaa sat in silence for a while, smoking.

Concho waited.

Finally, the old man spoke.

"Once again, you overcame the forces of darkness." He brought the wrinkled cigarette to his lips and the embers glowed brightly as he took a long drag. "But they are far from vanquished, are they not?"

"There's a lot of them."

Meskwaa nodded as he blew out the smoke.

"And what of Rachel Standing Bear's granddaughter? Any word of her?"

Concho shook his head. The weight of that unfulfilled quest was weighing heavily on him.

"She came to me," Meskwaa said. "Told me that you had pledged to find Peskipaatei. Asked me to look into the mists, to ask the spirits if you would be successful."

As the tribal shaman, or *naataineniiha*, Meskwaa was often sought out in times of conflict and trouble.

"And what did the spirits say?" Concho asked.

Meskwaa took a final drag on the cigarette. It was no more than a half-inch now, including the smoldering ash. He then pinched it out, removed the small envelope from his shirt pocket, and dropped the residual tobacco into it.

"The spirits seldom give a clear answer in matters such as this," he said. "My visions continue. They told me of much deceit, much trouble, some of which you have already seen. I also saw a small bird, the kind that is black, with the red markings on its wings..."

In his youth, Concho had considered becoming an ornithologist and had made a study of birds. This one, he knew from Meskwaa's description, was indeed a red-winged blackbird.

"The bird cried out in the darkness, unable to fly," Meskwaa said, "seeking the light, seeking freedom, but was surrounded by predators."

Concho waited for more, but Meskwaa adjusted the hat of many colors on his head and stood up.

"I am keeping you from your duties," he said. "I know you must go, but you must stand ready. You will soon learn more. The signs are there. There is a great battle coming. There will be blood."

The old man stood in silence for several seconds. Concho tried to make sense of all of what Meskwaa had told him.

"The path you have trod has always been between two worlds," Meskwaa said, "but this time those worlds will join together for a time, and the result will be much danger. You will be faced with choices. The darkness waits around the bend. Trust in yourself and the ways in which you have been taught. May *kehcimaneto*, the Great Spirit, watch over you and grant you strength."

Concho rose as well and watched as Meskwaa turned and began walking away.

"Take care," he said. "And heed the warnings of the spirits when they speak, and let their wisdom guide you."

I will try, Concho thought.

CHAPTER TWENTY-SEVEN

As Concho was driving to the office to print out and then hand over his report to Captain Shaw, he got a call and saw it was Nila Willow. He answered it immediately.

"What's up?"

"You tell me, Mr. Shoot-'Em-Up," she said. "You back in the doghouse again?"

"Ain't I always? Pretty soon the dog will be charging me rent."

"Well, I had something I wanted to tell you last night, but you took off and I didn't get the chance. And after the shooting, I didn't think it was a good idea to mention it. You looked like you had a lot of other things on your mind."

"Does it have anything to do with Peskipaatei?"

"Maybe." She hesitated. "Maybe not. I have to tell you, I wasn't too impressed with that pompous asshole, Jim Dandy, yesterday. And Mr. Movie Star, Vince Hawk, either."

"I knew you were a good judge of character."

"So what I was going to tell you last night when I had to run out to that domestic was that I did a little digging on both of them. You were gone after I got back to the station, and then with that shooting, I didn't think you'd want to hear about it."

"Find anything interesting?"

"Sort of. Six months ago, Hawk was doing one of his talent quest things at a shopping mall in Tucson. A month after that, they were in El Paso doing another one. Then, two months ago, he did still another one. Guess where."

"Don't tell me it was Laredo."

"Okay, I won't tell you," Nila said, her tone sounding oddly mirthful. "But it was. And if you remember, it was two months ago that Penny and her girlfriend got picked up there."

This explained a lot. Peskipaatei and her friend, Elena were both in Laredo when Hawk was there, and then Penny's midnight run to Holley's house and then to the Eagle Pass Mall for the first day of the talent quest.

It smacked of Hawk's involvement, but how to prove it? It was like trying to put a jigsaw puzzle together when half of the pieces were upside down or missing.

"Damn," Concho muttered. "I knew that bastard was dirty. He's involved in this somehow."

His thoughts returned to the two nubile nymphets in the Jacuzzi in the hotel. Had they been recruited at one of his talent quests as well?

He slammed the heel of his hand against the steering wheel making a sharp thump.

"What was that?" Nila asked.

"Nothing. Just taking my frustrations out on Gray-Dove's tow truck."

"You back to driving that thing?"

"Yeah, and he took particular delight last night in telling me that it was the only loaner available."

The humor seemed lost on her.

"But this is all supposition on our part," Concho said. "We haven't got anything solid that connects Hawk to our missing girl other than what could be termed a series of coincidences. We haven't got enough to even pull him in for questioning."

"Maybe," she said. "But maybe not."

That sounded hopeful.

"What else you got?" he asked.

"I did some more digging and found that a year or so ago, they were doing a talent quest in Las Cruces, New Mexico. One of their employees, a James Lewandowski, got arrested."

"For what?"

"Misdemeanor battery and get this, tattooing the body of a minor. A sixteen-year-old girl he'd *tattooed*. You remember, our buddy, Dandy, had a bunch of tattoos, right? Her father almost caught them in flagrante delicto in the back seat of the family car and things got physical. Lewandowski got out and gave him a beating, karate style before the cops arrived to arrest him. Sound familiar?"

"It sure does."

"The father tried to pursue a charge of statutory rape because he was over four years older, but the age of consent in New Mexico is sixteen and the girl refused to cooperate. They couldn't prove criminal penetration, so they just hit Lewandoski with the battery to the father and the tattooing the body of a minor charges."

"Drum told me Dandy has a Polish name."

"Un-huh. And here's where it gets real interesting." She paused. "I had to wait till this morning to talk to one of their detectives to get a picture of him, but it's him, all right. Jimbo Dandy, a.k.a. James Lewandowski. And here's the best part. He never showed up for court, so there's a warrant out for him out of Las Cruces."

Concho felt a surge of excitement. "Please tell me we're within the geographical jurisdictional limits of the warrant."

"We are. All contiguous states."

"Outstanding," Concho said. "We can pull him in on the warrant and sweat him about Peskipaatei. There are way too many coincidences for this all not to be connected."

"What if he doesn't talk? Lawyers up?"

"If he's at all street savvy, and I'm sure he is, he probably will, but it depends. Our best bet is to take him over to Maverick County and tell them to keep him isolated. Let him sit for an hour or two. In the meantime, it'll give us a chance to try and walk through a warrant to search Hawk's buses and their rooms at the hotel. We can go serve it and grill Hawk as well. Maybe take him in for investigation. He won't know what Dandy told us, and we can use that to our advantage."

"You think we have enough for that?"

"Maybe we do, maybe we don't. No harm in trying."

He was trying to sound confident, but he was anything but. The case was tenuous at best, and the clock was ticking. Out there somewhere was a young, fifteen-year-old girl who'd been missing for going on seventy-two hours. A little blue bird in the company of raptors…hopefully, it wasn't already too late.

Nila was silent for a time, and then she said, "I'm supposed to work afternoon shift."

"I'll call Roberto and ask him if you can have the night off from regular duties to help me on this."

"I've never written up a warrant."

"I've done enough for both of us," Concho said. "And I might know a judge who'll sign it. We'll have to run it by the DA first, but that's just a formality."

"If you say so." Her words sounded hesitant. "But…aren't you on suspension or something?"

"Administrative leave, but that's just another formality." Concho was almost at Ranger Headquarters. "Let me just drop off my report on last night's incident at the casino and I'll call you back."

As he pulled into the parking lot, he debated whether or not to tell Shaw about what he had going.

Maybe it would be best to play this close to my vest, he thought.

And besides, sometimes it was better to beg forgiveness than ask permission.

He took a deep breath, got out of the tow truck, and

started walking the metaphorical tightrope, already drafting the possible probable cause complaint for the warrant forming in his mind.

CHAPTER TWENTY-EIGHT

THIRTY MINUTES OR SO LATER, CONCHO HOPPED OUT OF THE tow truck at the mall when he saw Nila driving up in the KTTP SUV. He'd told her to bring one with a bump-shield so they could transport Jim Dandy, a.k.a. James Lewandowski, to the Maverick County Jail where they could keep him on ice for a while. He also told her to bring extra cuffs and some leg irons. Most likely, Dandy wasn't going down easily.

And Concho found part of himself hoping that it wouldn't. That part wanted to smash his fist into the arrogant son of a bitch's mouth. But he knew it would be better for everyone concerned if it didn't come to that. And he had Maria's position as mall manager to consider.

Nila parked in the fire zone behind the tow truck and got out of the vehicle. She was in uniform and looked very professional as she pulled out a camo-colored rucksack and slung the long strap over her left shoulder.

"You bring the stuff?" Concho asked, figuring that the handcuffs and leg irons were in the rucksack.

She patted the sack and nodded. "I got your text. And, by the way, I got Crystal City to send me over a picture of Elena

Navarro." She pulled it out of her pocket and showed it to him.

Another young, pretty Indian girl, lost in the woods.

"Come on," he said, gesturing toward the back entrance. Let's go see if we can find our quarry."

"So did your boss give you the green light to help me with the warrant?" she asked.

"In a manner of speaking."

She raised a querulous eyebrow.

Concho grinned. "He took my report, read it, and said to stay out of trouble."

"That's a green light?"

"Well, it's not a solid red, and my drill sergeant used to say that sometimes it's wiser to have to beg for forgiveness than ask for permission."

"If you say so."

They entered the back corridor of the mall and Concho stopped, rethinking their next move. As much as he wanted to march over and grab Jim Dandy by his neck and drag him out of the place, he had a sudden concern about how that would look to the corporate big shots and how it might affect Maria's standing. She'd been so overly concerned about this circus since the day it hit town, he figured he at least owed her a quick heads-up.

"What's wrong?" Nila asked.

"I want to give Maria a call first. Let her know what's going on. I'd like to handle this the easy way, if we can."

Nila rolled her eyes.

"Judging from the way that idiot behaved yesterday," she said, "there's not going to be an easy way. I've got my Taser ready."

Concho scrolled to her name and pressed the CALL button. It rang several times and went to voice mail. Seconds later, his phone buzzed with one of those standard automatic reply texts saying she was unavailable to take any calls at the moment.

She must be in a meeting, he thought. It was already close to eleven, and the mall had been open for a while. The talent quest had to be in full swing. Maybe Dandy was going to be doing one of his martial arts demonstrations again.

If that's the case, Concho thought, he was trying to goad me into a sparring match with him before. Maybe we'll get the chance now. If so, he didn't want to have to worry about his second gun.

"Let's go," he said, sticking the phone back into his pocket and then slipping off his BDU vest and shoulder rig. He was now wearing his standard white shirt with his badge pinned on his chest. Rolling up the vest into a tight bundle, he pointed to the rucksack.

"You got room for these in there?"

"I suppose I do." Nila slipped the strap off her shoulder and popped open the securing clasp. Concho saw the leg irons and two pairs of handcuffs inside. One was a standard set and the other a double-hinged model. He stuffed the BDU underneath the restraints and refastened the clasp.

"We'd better come up with a game plan," Nila said, repositioning the strap in place. "How do you want to handle this?"

Concho moved up the doors and peered through the small center windows. The interior of the place was packed, as usual, and most of the patrons appeared to be a mixture of young people and older ones.

Was everybody cutting school in the hopes of becoming a movie star? Knowing what he now surmised about Vince Hawk and Thunderhawk Productions, he estimated the chances of that were slim and none. *And slim left town,* he added mentally.

No wonder the road to Hollywood was paved with broken dreams.

Hearing a round of cheers and a smattering of applause, he pushed open the door and gazed toward the center court area. A bare-chested Jim Dandy was up on the raised platform and the two flunkies who had been carrying the bags yesterday were standing there holding the boards at arm's length.

Dandy lurched forward with a stutter-stepping motion and broke the first board with a lightning-fast sidekick. The other flunky was still holding his board out and Dandy whirled and broke that one also, using a spinning back-kick.

"Looks like I'd better have my Taser ready," Nila said. "He's good."

Concho was already designing his fight plan, should it come to blows. He'd move in close, not giving Dandy the distance he needed for his kicks. The guy was well-built and strong, but Concho had the size and most likely the strength advantage. Maria's face flashed in his mind momentarily and his desire for discretion returned. They also had the advantage of surprise. Dandy didn't know they'd come to arrest him. That could work to their advantage.

Nice and easy does it, Concho thought.

"We'll wait for his show to be over with," Concho said. "Let him tire himself out too. Once he's done, we go up and say we need to talk to him privately. We get him off to the side, inform him he's under arrest for the outstanding warrant, and cuff him. Once we get him back here, we'll lean him against the wall and apply the leg irons."

"Sounds sweet and easy," Nila said.

"Yeah, too sweet. Too easy."

They stayed where they were and waited. The karate demonstration went on for another fifteen or so minutes. Dandy invited a couple people from the audience, young pretty girls mostly, to join him on stage and attest that the boards were real. He broke a few more of them and then bowed. Vince Hawk came onto the center stage, all smiles, and gave high praise to his protégé.

"He's one of the reasons I don't need CGI in my movies," Hawk said. "No computer can do that kind of stuff."

That got another round of halfhearted applause from the crowd. They were clearly here to try out for the screen tests.

An assistant took the microphone from Hawk and announced that the applicants for the screen tests and interviews should line up at the designated marker. The crowd started shuffling that way.

Concho jerked his head toward the stage area and left the archway by the door. He and Nila kept on the perimeter of the crowd, working their way toward the stage. Alexander Drum, who was standing on the far end of the stage, caught sight of their approach and strolled over and tapped Hawk on the shoulder. The Indian movie star's head shot around and he and Concho locked eyes for a moment. Then Hawk said something to Jim Dandy, whose head also rotated toward them, the cocky smirk plastered on his face. Drum leaned close and said something inaudible to both of them. Dandy glanced back at Concho and Nila with what appeared to be a wary expression now as he slipped on a black T-shirt.

Concho and Nila were at the stairs leading up to the raised stage platform now. He didn't particularly like the positioning or Drum's apparent warning to his comrades, but at this point there was little Concho could do about it.

"Ten-Wolves," Hawk said, flashing one of his patented movie star smiles. "Change your mind and come back for that job offer? And I see you brought my favorite KTTP police officer with you. Good to see you, too, honey."

Nila showed no reaction to the comment.

"Could I talk to you guys for a minute?" Concho said, still harboring the hope that this could go down smoothly and without a fuss.

"Sure," Hawk said. "Talk."

"Down here," Concho said.

Hawk blew out an exaggerated breath and started down the steps. Drum followed him, but Dandy stayed where he was.

"All three of you," Concho said, flicking a finger at Dandy.

The man stiffened.

"Jimbo," Hawk said, "why don't you run over to your room and catch a shower. You're starting to smell kind of ripe." He glanced back at Concho. "He's got another demonstration to do this afternoon."

Concho repeated his come hither gesture, trying to keep it nonchalant, but something in his posture must have betrayed his anxiety. Dandy turned and began striding across the stage in the opposite direction.

"He's rabbiting," Nila said and began pushing her way through the throng of people still clustered in front of the stage.

Concho didn't follow her. Instead, he merely used his long legs to jump up onto the stage and began running full speed after Dandy. The other man took a quick look over his left shoulder and began an all-out sprint. Concho did the same.

They were across the stage in seconds, knocking over a tripod with a camcorder mounted on it. Various wires had been taped down onto the wooden surface making the footing hazardous. Dandy got to the other end of the stage first and took a flying leap off the edge. He landed with a catlike grace. His bare feet made slapping sounds on the marble floor as he ran.

Concho's massive form followed suit a few seconds later. People were milling about, and Dandy was about twenty feet ahead, roughly shoving them aside. Concho used his long arms to work his way through the crowd as well, but in a less violent manner, all the while yelling, "Police. Stop." He felt his hat fly off his head and his long hair billowed out behind him.

Dandy got to a cleared-out section of the center court that was devoid of mall pedestrians and stopped, glancing in both directions. About forty feet ahead of him was another solid block of people, looking almost like a human wall. Stores were on either side of the expansive corridor and a group of uniformed mall security guards stretched out like a team of defensive linemen. It was clear that Dandy had nowhere left to run. His expression changed from one of alarm to the cockiness he'd shown moments before, and he stopped and raised his arms in a boxing position.

"All right, Ten-Wolves," Dandy said, his lips curling back into a smile. "Come and get it."

"I've got a warrant for your arrest," Concho announced in a loud voice. "Surrender."

"Fat chance," Dandy said, adding a bit of profanity.

They were only about ten feet apart now and Concho remembered his fight plan. If he kept coming straight forward, it would give Dandy the opportunity to use one of his fancy kicks. The man was proficient with those, and for a moment Concho briefly considered drawing his weapon. He immediately dismissed that idea. Too many civilians would be in harm's way, and he was, after all, facing down an unarmed man. No, this had to be done hands-on.

Dandy danced forward and slammed a low roundhouse kick into Concho's left thigh. It sent a wave of pain up and down his leg. He retaliated with a sweeping left hook, but Dandy's head snapped back out of range and he slipped the punch, sending a trio of stinging punches to Concho's left side. His insides felt on fire.

Before Concho could react Dandy stepped in and delivered a triple jab, catching the left side of Concho's face. Concho again tried to retaliate, this time with a right cross and managed to catch Dandy's left side. The smaller man grunted and skipped away, circling to his own right, staying away from Concho's power side. The foot snapped upward with incredible speed and nimbleness, the ball of Dandy's foot striking Concho's solar plexus.

It felt like a battering ram. Concho had luckily been keeping his abdomen tight, and he was able to stay on his feet, but Dandy danced forward, his left jab shooting outward, once, twice, three times again, each blow smashing against Concho's left eyebrow and cheek. As he shifted away, he felt the warm flow of blood cascading down the side of his face.

Dandy's smile widened.

"I told you I'd teach you a thing or two," the smaller, quicker man said.

With that, he whirled and his rear leg, his right one, swept upward in an arcing motion, the heel aimed for Concho's head, but instead of backing up to get away from the kick, Concho stepped forward. Dandy's leg curled around Concho's body and the big Ranger seized Dandy's thigh. Off balance now and standing on only one leg, the smaller man hopped twice before Concho's left fist smashed down onto Dandy's nose. Twin torrents of blood burst forth from each nostril. Dandy was starting to shake his head when Concho drew back his fist and repeated the blow. This time Dandy's head jerked with something resembling an electrical shock and his eyes rolled upward. Concho released the leg and let Dandy slump to the floor.

Nila was there next to them now pointing her Taser at the fallen man. The red laser dot hovered on the surface of Dandy's back.

Concho looked at her and gave his head a slight shake, kneeling on top of Dandy and bending his limp arms behind his back.

"Save your cartridge," he said. "Just give me that pair of hinged cuffs and those leg irons."

Nila snapped the safety on the Taser, holstered it, and then reached into her rucksack.

"I think you're going to need a couple stitches," she said as she handed the restraints to him.

Concho glanced down at this once pristine white shirt and saw the blots of crimson dappling the front.

"It's not the first time," he said with a grin. "And it won't be the last."

His smile faded, however, when he saw the group of people rushing toward him. Hawk and Drum were in the rear, behind the group of corporate suits up toward the front. Leading the pack was Maria. She was carrying his Stetson with both hands, and she didn't look happy.

CHAPTER TWENTY-NINE

CONCHO FELT THE SLIGHT PRICK OF THE NEEDLE AS SOON-TO-be nurse practitioner, Samuel Reyes, jabbed the tip of the syringe into the skin around Concho's left eyebrow as he lay on the partially elevated operating table in the casino's second-floor clinic. Designed for treating any injured gambling patrons, Concho had sought quick, emergency treatment there many times. Reyes injected a bit more lidocaine into the wound site and told Concho to relax for a few minutes.

"Let the pain-killer numb things up," Reyes said. "Shouldn't take more than a couple of minutes. Then I'll finish cleaning it and stitch you up. Again."

Both of them had been here before under the exact same circumstances.

"Sam, I told you I'm in a bit of a hurry," Concho said. "Can't you just get started now?"

Reyes chuckled. "Who's the doctor here? You or me?"

"Okay, but at least call down to security and see if Gomez is working, would you?"

After placing the syringe on the metal tray that held the gauze, the hooked needles, and the stitching thread, Reyes stepped back and stripped off his latex gloves. He went to the phone and punched in a couple of numbers. After a few seconds, he said, "Yeah, this is Reyes up in the clinic. I need to know if Felix is working." After a pause of a few seconds, he turned his head toward Concho, smiled, and held up his left hand with the thumb sticking straight up. "Okay, have him come up to the clinic ASAP."

He hung up, went to the nearby sink and washed and dried his hands, and then slipped on a new pair of gloves.

"Too bad they don't leave a set of cards up here," Concho said. "We might have time for a game of Texas hold-'em."

"Five card stud's my game," Reyes said. "And you know I ain't going to be able to prescribe no painkillers or antibiotics for you, don't you?"

"That's why they make aspirin and Neosporin," Concho said.

Reyes sat on a stool and busied himself removing the tools from their sterilized packaging.

Concho leaned back and took in a few deep breaths, reviewing the events that had led up to him coming here. After the fiasco at the *Mall de las Aguilas*, he knew that sooner or later he'd have to call Maria and get things straightened out. As they'd been walking Dandy out, she'd gone from her initial, "Couldn't you have been more discreet?" to "Oh, my god, you're bleeding," when she saw the blood streaming down his cheek. His bloody white shirt had caused a bit of sensation with the shoppers and talent search junkies. As they'd parted, her expression was anything but friendly as she whispered, "I'll call you later if I still have a job." Concho hoped it wouldn't come to that, but knew that it could, given the caliber of the corporate buffoons he'd seen.

At least she'd given him back his hat.

The cell phones were out in force snapping pictures and probably recording videos as he and Nila walked the bloody Jim Dandy toward the back corridors at a brisk pace. The procession was flanked by an array of uniformed mall security guards. The corporate bigwigs had seemed in shock, but had mostly remained silent. Drum was silent as he strode by Hawk's side keeping up with Concho's long, purposeful strides. Hawk was all questions.

"Hey, Ten-Wolves, what's this all about? You can't just waltz in here and grab somebody, you know. Don't you need probable cause or something?"

"There's a warrant for his arrest," Nila shouted back. "Now leave us alone."

Dandy, who'd regained consciousness, snorted and shook his head, spewing droplets of blood onto Concho and Nila.

"Did you see what they did to me?" he shouted. "They beat me for no reason. I need medical attention."

"Jimbo," Hawk growled, "shut your damn mouth. I'll handle it. Just don't say nothing."

The ubiquitous cell phones continued to record and snap as Concho and Nila pushed through the doors and entered the back corridors. Hawk, Drum, the corporate bigwigs, and Maria followed along with some of the mall security.

A real fool's parade, Concho remembered thinking.

The door to the clinic buzzed as someone opened the door.

Concho instinctively rested his hand on the butt of his Colt Double Eagle as Reyes rose from the stool and looked to the open door separating the treatment room from the outer office. Felix Gomez walked in with a quizzical expression on his face.

"You wanted to see me?" he asked Reyes.

"Not me. Him."

Gomez walked over and stood next to the operating table. Concho's upper body had been elevated to a comfortable angel that would also allow Reyes to sew him up.

"I just wanted to ask you a couple questions about last night," Concho said. "And, by the way, thanks for saving my life."

Gomez grinned. "It wasn't nothing."

"It was great," Concho said. "You showed a lot of guts and bravery. I owe you."

The security guard beamed.

"Can you tell me exactly what happened and how you came to be out there?" Concho asked.

"Well," Gomez said, "me and Joaquin were on patrol, walking the casino floor, when we heard what sounded like a gunshot. At first I thought it was a firecracker or maybe a car backfiring, but then we heard a bunch more. I said to him, 'That ain't no firecrackers. Them's gunshots.' We radioed base to call KTTP and ran to the far exit."

He paused and Concho figured it was a good time to find out if what he suspected happened was true, or not.

"You see that guy, Drum?" he asked.

Gomez's lower lip jutted out then retracted.

"Yeah."

His answer was slow, hesitant.

"Where was he exactly?" Concho asked.

"He was somewhere outside, by the edge of the parking lot."

"What was he doing?"

Gomez shrugged. "I can't say for sure. We'd heard the gunshots and were sorta creeping along when all of a sudden he just showed up and identified himself as a police officer. He was talking on his cell phone."

Interesting, Concho thought. Drum was actually a retired police officer, but in an emergency situation like the one that was unfolding, he could probably be forgiven for leaving the word "retired" out. And whom was he talking to? Concho remembered the van that appeared out of nowhere and picked up the assailants. Had Drum been talking to them?

"And then what happened?" Concho asked.

"Well, me and Joaquin wanted to go find out what was happening but Mr. Drum held us back. 'Call for backup,' he said, 'Call the police.' And when we told him we already done that, he told us to stay behind him and for us to do a tactical advance."

"He tell you anything else?"

"Just that we didn't know what was going on so we should

aim high and not try to hit anybody until we knew what was going on."

Everything was adding up about like Concho had expected. The heroic ex-CPD cop had most likely been a perpetrator rather than a savior.

"We didn't do nothing wrong, did we?" Gomez asked, his lower lip jutting outward again.

"No," Concho said. "You did fine. Thanks again for your bravery and your help." He stuck out his hand and he and Gomez shook.

After the security guard left, Reyes moved in closer, holding one of the hooked needles, lined with the white-colored thread.

"Ready?" he asked.

"Ready, willing, and well-informed," Concho said. "Let's do it."

With each line of the silk thread being drawn through what he assumed were a couple of jagged cuts, he felt a slight sensation, but no pain. The real pain came when he found himself stuck in the mud as far as finding Peskipaatei Standing Bear. Seventy-two hours and counting and although he had a few leads, he still had nothing solid. Her grandmother's face loomed large in his mind's eye. He dreaded telling her that.

But maybe, he told himself, something will break soon.

Once he got out of here, the first priority would be to tag up with Nila and get started on that search warrant. If they somehow got one approved to search Dandy's hotel room and Hawk's buses, they might find something. If nothing else, it would give old Swooping Hawk something to be nervous about. But that son of a bitch didn't get to where he was by being nervous or stupid. Maybe they'd be able to break Jim Dandy. It was worth a shot, and at any rate, they had to do something. That clock was ticking double-time.

Nila came in just as Reyes was drawing the last line through and tying it off. She moved with slow deliberation to stand next to Concho's left side. Her expression was grim.

"Cheer up," Concho said as Reyes was affixing a Band-Aid

over the stitches. "It's only a flesh wound. And if you'll give me my vest out of your rucksack, it'll cover the blood on my shirt."

The joke failed to bring even the hint of a smile to her face, which set off a silent alarm bell inside Concho's head.

"What's up?" he asked. "You have trouble with asshole at the jail?"

She shook her head. "No. That went fine. I told them to keep him on ice and we'd be back to interview him."

From her expression, he knew there was more.

"He request to go to the hospital?"

"No. He said very little during intake. Just that he wanted to make a phone call."

"They let him?"

She shrugged.

"So what is it you're not telling me?" he asked, sitting up and swinging his legs off the table.

"On the way over here I got a call from Sherry," she said. "We got a reply to my type-three regarding the missing and endangered female."

Concho's heart sped up. Was this it?

Nila took in a deep breath.

"Earlier today they found the bodies of three young females all fitting Peskipaatei's description. Dumped in a remote area outside of town. They're at the morgue now."

"Shit," Concho said, reaching over to grab his hat. "Let's go."

CHAPTER THIRTY

MAVERICK COUNTY CORONER EARL BLAKE SET THE PLASTIC facial shield on the desk and ran the moist paper towel over the top of his bald head and face as he lowered his body down onto the black easy chair in his office. The chair squeaked loudly. He stared up at Concho and Nila.

"We appreciate you taking time out to see us," Concho said.

"No problem," Blake said, flashing a half-smile. "To tell the truth, I needed the break anyway. This one's a grim task."

Concho imagined it was, given the information that Nila had given him. He reached into his pocket and removed the BFF picture of Peskipaatei and laid it on the desk. He'd taped a piece of paper over Holley's face. Nila fished the picture of Elena Navarro out of her pocket and placed it down for Blake to see.

"Do either of these two girls look like any of the decedents?" Concho asked.

Blake studied the photos, pursing his lips.

"Well," he said, tapping Peskipaatei's picture, "this one is a no, but this one, I think…"

He left the sentence open and Concho and Nila exchanged

looks.

"Her name's Elena Navarro," Nila said. "She's a runaway from the Crystal City area."

"How long she been missing?" Blake asked.

"About three-and-a-half weeks."

The coroner's head rocked back and forth, and then he leaned forward and placed both hands on the desk to raise his bulk upward.

"Let's go in and you can judge for yourself," he said, taking the two pictures with him. "They were all three dropped in a shallow grave and then dug up by some scavenging animals. Some guys on ATVs found them, or at least one of them." Blake smiled sardonically. "Saw a human leg sticking out of the ground. Quite a shock for the poor fellow."

"I'll bet," Concho said. "Maverick County do a thorough search of the area in case there were more?"

"They assured me they did," Blake said. "What happened to your eye, by the way?"

"A little line-of-duty mishap," Concho said.

"That's what I thought," Blake said, walking them back into the interior where the autopsies were performed. "I've got Dr. Green assisting and she's finishing up the last autopsy. I'm sure she'd be glad to take a look at it if you want." Blake flashed the sardonic grin again. "She'd probably relish the chance to examine a patient who's still breathing."

Concho smirked.

"I've already got my stitches, but thanks anyway."

"Suit yourself," Blake said.

"You got a COD on these three yet?" Concho asked.

"They all appear to have been manually strangled. All show signs of recent vigorous sexual activity. Of course, we'll have to do tox screens on all three. Stomach contents appear to be of the standard, fast-food variety, undigested and the same for all of them."

He put his hand on the doorknob and opened the door a crack. "Ah, have you heard anything from Della lately?"

Concho shook his head.

Della Rice was an FBI agent Concho had worked with in the past. She was tall, Black, and beautiful and he suspected that Blake had a case of infatuation for her.

"A pity," Blake said. "I wonder if she'll be getting back this way soon?"

"Maybe sooner than you think," Concho said.

Blake sighed and opened the door. "One can only hope."

As they stepped into the expansive room filled with shiny stainless steel tables and numerous sinks. Three of the tables had the naked bodies of the three young women lying supine on them. All three had the customary Y-shaped incisions from chest to groin down the front of their upper torsos. The two far ones had already been stitched up, and a slender young woman in a white lab coat was leaning over the third corpse. A section of the girl's upper thigh looked as if it had been chewed off. The sides of the corpse's body were still open revealing a mixture of white rib bones and a mishmash of internal organs. The pervasive odor was powerful and sickening. Concho was used to the smell of a disemboweling and he glanced at Nila, wondering how it would affect her. He'd heard that women had a sharper sense of smell than men did but if it bothered her, she didn't show it.

"Finishing up, Dr. Green?" Blake asked. "Find anything interesting?"

Dr. Green looked up, her quizzical expression visible behind the transparent plastic shield. Her latex-gloved hands were coated in crimson.

"Oh," Blake said, "excuse my ill manners. This is Ranger Ten-Wolves and Officer Willow, KTTP. They're working a missing person case."

The doctor gave a perfunctory nod to them.

Blake strode across the tiled floor to the farthest body that was laid out on the steel table. He held the picture of Elena Navarro next to the corpse's head. Both Concho and Nila stepped over, as did Dr. Green.

The dead girl's face was still streaked with bits of dirt in a few places. Death had made the resemblance to the smiling girl in the photograph less discernible, but it appeared to be a match. Concho noticed her hands were bagged and sealed.

"This is the one that was frontally strangled," Blake said. "Broken hyoid bone, bruising on the neck, petechial hemor-rhaging. I'd say frontal attack grip by a male with strong hands."

"She had tissue under her nails?" he asked.

"Yes," Blake said, still holding the photo and looking back and forth between it and the dead girl.

"We'll need to get that to the crime lab ASAP," he said, glancing toward Nila. "You'd better call Maverick County to get a detective over here and brief him since it's their case. He'll have to take charge of the evidence."

She nodded.

"Actually," Blake said, "I expected them momentarily. They've already been called."

Concho was a bit miffed that they hadn't sent someone to be at the autopsy, but all that really mattered was that the chain of custody for the evidence was preserved.

"Once we brief them," Concho said, "we'll turn everything over to them. Then we can go see if we can get a sample of Jim Dandy's DNA."

"You have a suspect already?" Blake asked.

"We've got a couple of them and one had scratches on his neck," Concho said.

Blake raised both eyebrows and gave his head a curt nod.

"Excellent," he said.

"That one was obviously an American," Dr. Green said, pointing to Elena's body. "The other two Third World types. Most likely Hispanics."

"How could you tell that?" Nila asked. "About them not being from this country?"

"Their teeth," Dr. Green said, her breath causing a slight

fogging on the inside of the plastic shield. "She's had fairly good dental care. Those two, none."

"You can always tell a lot about a person's history by looking in their mouth," Blake said, still studying the picture and the dead girl's face. He leaned back and added, "And I'd say this is a preliminary yes on your possible runaway. What about you, doctor?"

Dr. Green stepped around Concho and Nila and stood beside Blake. After a moment, she frowned and said, "It appears to be so. Is this your missing person?"

"One of them," Concho said. "You say the other two girls are probably from Mexico or Central America?"

"That would be my guess."

"Nicaragua, maybe?"

"Maybe. Why?"

"Just wondering."

Concho stared down at the body of Elena Navarro and noticed something significant.

"Nila, look at this." He pointed to a circular red tattoo with some yellow lines running through it on the lower left side girl's abdomen near the upper edge of the stubble of dark pubic hair. She'd evidently been shaving, but not too recently. Or was the minute hair growth a result of skin shrinkage after death?

"Looks kind of familiar," Nila said. "Doesn't it?"

It was the same tattoo that Concho had seen on Jim Dandy's bare chest and on the abdomens of the two girls in Hawk's hot tub as well. He looked over at the dead girl on the adjacent table.

Same tattoo, same location.

"Does the third one have this tattoo on her?" Concho asked.

"Yes," Dr. Green said. "And I've already made a note of it."

Concho told Nila to pull out her phone and take some pictures.

"Facials and full body," he said. "And close-ups of the tattoos."

Blake and Dr. Green both stepped away from the steel table and Nila went over and started snapping photos.

Things were really starting to come together.

Concho was mentally putting together the wording for that search warrant. Of course with these latest developments, he was going to have to let the detectives from Maverick County take the lead, and they'd be more focused on clearing the three homicides than finding Peskipaatei.

For now, she remained a forlorn little blue bird, lost somewhere in the woods.

* * *

THE MAVERICK COUNTY DETECTIVE WAS NAMED TOM Madrigal, and he readily admitted that he'd recently made detective and this was his first homicide. Concho took the time to walk him through what he knew of the case and coached him on what pictures to take and what to do with the recovered evidence.

"The main thing is to place those tissue samples from under the girl's fingernails into evidence now and transport them to the crime lab ASAP."

Madrigal nodded.

"We've got a possible suspect in mind," Concho added. "A guy named James Lewandowski, a.k.a. Jim Dandy."

"Any idea where he's at?" Madrigal asked.

Concho grinned.

"Yeah, and we're going to interview him now about a different matter at your jail."

Madrigal said he'd meet them there after he finished and Concho and Nila took off. Before leaving the coroner's office he'd scanned an image of the county police seal from one of Madrigal's report forms and used Blake's computer to print out block letters below it:

OFFICIAL POLICE BUSINESS

When they arrived at the jail, he shoved the bogus sign

onto the tow truck's dashboard and parked in a yellow-curbed area behind Nila's police SUV.

"No more parking tickets," he told himself.

As they walked into the front entrance, Concho was conscious that he still hadn't changed his white shirt, and the bloodstains were visible. He did his best to pull the BDU vest to partially conceal them and made a note to change clothes at the earliest opportunity.

After explaining they were there to interview Lewandowski the woman behind the thick Plexiglas window told them to have a seat. The wait took several minutes and finally a lieutenant named Jones came out to speak with them.

"Lewandowski's no longer here," Jones said.

"What?" Concho said, standing up. "We left word to put him on ice so we could tie up a few things and come back to interview him."

The lieutenant's face tightened.

"Unfortunately, we had to release him. His lawyer showed up here with bond money and a writ. We had no choice."

"A writ?" Concho said.

Jones nodded. "It was somebody from that asshole, Theodore H. Marshfield's law firm. I'm sure you're familiar with him."

"I am." Concho gritted his teeth. "Didn't you tell him he was being held for investigation?"

"We tried," Jones said. "But not only did they have the exact amount of cash, two thousand five hundred, but Marshfield himself was down at court and managed to do a motion in front of a judge, who then authorized the release. The clerk faxed it over."

"Son of a bitch," Concho said. "What time did all this go down?"

"Thirteen-twenty or so."

That had been back shortly after Nila dropped Dandy off at the jail—when Concho was getting his stitches. Hawk must have been on the phone to Marshfield shortly after the arrest.

No wonder Dandy didn't opt for a hospital trip or anything. He knew that "the motion to fix" was in the works.

Concho glanced at his watch: fifteen-oh-five hours. Dandy had about a two-hour head start. Maybe it wasn't too late to catch him at the mall or the hotel.

They left the jail and Concho was dialing Maria, with his phone on speaker in his left hand as he periodically had to grip the steering wheel so he could shift with his right.

"Maria Morales, Eagle Pass Mall supervisor," she answered. "For now, anyway."

"You must have read your caller ID," Concho said, shouting to cover the distance to the phone.

"Yeah," she said. "I figured I'd use my full title while I still have it."

Her tone sounded forlorn and dejected.

"That bad, huh?"

"Worse," she said, then added, "Where are you?"

"I'm driving," he said, jamming the stick into fourth and finally holding the phone closer to his head. "I wanted to call to apologize and see how you were."

"Apologize? For what? Doing your job? It didn't look like you had much of a choice."

"True that, but if I had it to do all over again, I'd try to figure out a way not to put you in a bind. How bad is it?"

Even on speaker, with phone several inches away from his ear, he could hear the hiss of her breath.

"It's bad. I was informed by Mr. Otis that they're scheduling a full review of my position," she said. "Looks like I'll be looking for a new job."

He felt bad for her, but there wasn't a hell of a lot he could do.

"Word of warning," she said. "Asshole Otis said he was going to make a complaint to the Rangers about the way you handled it."

"He'll have to stand in line."

"What about you?" she asked. "Were you hurt? You were

bleeding."

"All stitched up. You'll be thinking I'm wearing white mascara the next time you see me."

In the momentary silence, he wondered when that would be.

"Stitches? Oh, my god. How bad was it? Does it hurt?"

"Only when I laugh," he said and instantly regretted mentioning laughter when her job appeared to be on the chopping block. Not knowing what else to say, he added, "Look, we'll figure out something. They won't want to lose the best mall manager the *Mall de las Aguilas* has ever had."

He heard what sounded like a huff.

"To make things worse," he said, "the idiots bonded out on the warrant. He's a suspect in this missing person case I'm working and another one that's a homicide."

"Homicide?" She sounded aghast.

"Yeah. You seen him or Vince Hawk around there now?"

"Hawk's involved too?"

"It's looking that way. But have you seen them?"

"No," she said. "After the incident, he raised holy hell with Otis; he pulled all his personnel out and just left. A lot of his equipment is still here, but the day's talent quest event was canceled."

That had to mean that Hawk was leery and worried. Maybe they could catch him at the hotel.

"Okay," he said. "I've got to try to find him. I'll talk to you later. And stay strong."

She told him she would and for him to be careful.

As he terminated the call he felt like someone had kicked him in the gut. The last thing he'd wanted to do was hurt Maria.

But time marches on, and he had other concerns, such as finding Peskipaatei and getting hold of Dandy's DNA. He called Nila, gave her a quick update on the mall, and told her they were heading for the hotel.

Maybe, just maybe, he thought.

CHAPTER THIRTY-ONE

Upon arriving at the Lucky Eagle Casino, Concho did a wide circle, checking in back for Hawk's four tour buses. His first inclination that things were going from bad to worse came when he saw the buses were gone. Coming to a screeching stop in front of the main entrance, he literally ran through the front doors and over to the registration desk for the hotel.

"Vince Hawk," he said to the girl behind the desk, holding out his Ranger identification. "He still here?"

The girl shook her head and asked if he'd like to speak with the manager on duty.

"You bet," he said as Nila walked up beside him.

Concho made a thumbs-down gesture.

The MOD, or manager on duty, was a young guy Concho didn't know. Before he could introduce himself, a tall, blond and very attractive woman came sauntering over and stood between them.

Concho smiled.

"Ms. Nolan, how you doing?"

"Better than you, obviously," Melissa Nolan said, directing her gaze at the bandage over his left eye. "What seems to be the trouble this time?"

"I'm actually trying to get hold of Vince Hawk. Is he here?"

Nolan canted her head and looked at the MOD.

He shook his head in a negative response.

"Him and all his people checked out a couple of hours ago," the MOD said.

Concho had figured as much, but still hoped for a break.

"All his people...any chance I could get a look at the room Jim Dandy was staying in?"

Nolan shrugged.

"Why not. We always want to accommodate the police, and especially the Texas Rangers. See to it."

"Okay," the MOD said, "but you ain't gonna find much."

Concho looked at him.

"What do you mean?"

"Mr. Hawk and all his people checked out a little after noon. Said he had an unexpected emergency. Apologized for not completing his original reservation and paid for the rooms to the original reservation date anyway."

"How generous of him," Concho said. "The rooms?"

"The rooms have already been cleaned," the MOD said. "Mr. Hawk tipped the maids fifty dollars each to go clean all of them right away. Told us he always did that because of his fans trying to break in and steal things for souvenirs and such. Pillowcases, napkins, you know."

Souvenirs and such, Concho thought. Like some leftover DNA on the towels or glasses.

"And I'll bet the laundry's been done, too."

The MOD nodded.

Concho muttered a curse word.

Nolan raised her eyebrows.

"Were you hoping for an autograph?" she said. "Or maybe a signed pillowcase?"

Concho didn't reply. He wondered what else could go wrong as he motioned to Nila and started heading for the front exit, pondering their next move.

Then his cell phone rang.

Glancing at the screen, he saw it was Captain Shaw.

He had a hunch that things had just gone from bad to worse.

* * *

"I JUST FINISHED TAKING A COMPLAINT FROM A MR. LAWRENCE Otis of the corporation owning the Eagle Pass Mall," Captain Dalton Shaw said. "He said you started a big fight there earlier today and beat the hell out of somebody."

"I took a few lumps, too, sir," Concho said. He was walking briskly toward the doors with Nila trailing behind him.

"Yeah? Well, all I can say is you'd better have a damn good explanation for all this, Ten-Wolves. Let's hear it."

Concho gave him a quick rundown on Dandy's arrest.

"The warrant was for what?" Shaw asked. "And out of where?"

"Las Cruces. For battery and tattooing the body of a minor."

He heard Shaw sigh.

"Misdemeanors. And out-of-state charges at that. Couldn't you have waited until a less high-profile moment? Otis said you came in there like gangbusters. And who was the female officer you had with you? He said she was waving her gun around."

"That's bullshit, Captain," Concho said. "She had her Taser out after the guy, who's a professional MMA fighter, was kicking my ass, but she never used it. No firearms were drawn, sir."

"That's not what Otis said."

"He's obviously got his head so far up his ass, he's having trouble seeing through the eye slits in his stomach."

Nila, who was obviously concerned after hearing the fabrication about her drawing her pistol, started to laugh at that one.

"Well," Shaw said, "I told him that's something he'd have

to take up with Chief Echabarri. What I'm concerned about is your involvement."

"We tried to handle it quietly, sir," Concho said, "but the offender resisted. I've got the stitches to prove it."

"Stitches?" Shaw was silent for a moment.

Concho used the opportunity to interject something more.

"Plus, he's a person of interest in the missing person case I'm working on and a homicide out of Maverick County."

"A homicide?"

Concho figured that would do the trick with an old lawman like Shaw.

"The bodies of three young females were found dumped. One of them had tissue under her fingernails, indicating she fought with her assailant. That guy Dandy happens to have a long track record with underage girls, and he's got some scratches on his neck."

Shaw was silent for a moment, then asked, "He is in custody?"

"Bonded out before we could interview him about the homicide. But we're tracking him now."

"Tracking him now?" Shaw's voice rose a few octaves. "What's this 'we' shit. You're still on administrative leave, or have you forgotten about that?"

"I was hoping for a little amelioration in view of the circumstances, sir."

"Amelioration? What the go to hell is *that* supposed to mean?"

"Any word on when I'll be reinstated to full duty, sir?"

"What the hell's the difference?" Shaw said, but there was a hint of mirth in his tone now. "You're doing more work now, when you're not supposed to, than if you were already reinstated."

"Just trying to follow my captain's example, sir."

"Cut the crap, Ten-Wolves. My bullshit meter's full. Just see if you can stay out of trouble for the next twenty-four hours until I can get you officially cleared, okay?"

"I'll do my best, sir."

"Dammit, do more than your best," Shaw said. "Don't get involved in any more of your capers until you're reinstated to full duty, and I mean none. That's a direct order. You got it?"

No promises, Concho thought, but he answered in the affirmative.

* * *

"So where do we go from here?" Nila Willow asked as they walked over to their respective vehicles.

"To get something to eat," he said, realizing that it was close to five p.m. "Why don't we just detour into the Red Grill Inn here and get a steak?"

"Sounds okay by me."

They went back inside and got a booth in the restaurant. Even though Nila was in uniform, Concho sat facing the entrance. He figured her smallish form would be pretty much hidden by the high back of the booth, and he'd been attacked too many times not to remain vigilant. Concho hadn't realized how hungry he was until he smelled the delicious aroma wafting from the kitchen area when they sat down. He ordered a salad, a steak, and a baked potato and went to work on the vegetables as soon as they arrived. Nila did the same.

"So," she said again, "where do we go from here?"

He considered this as he stuffed more lettuce into his mouth and chewed. When he'd finished masticating, he had a new idea. Taking out his cell phone, he texted Maria.

Hi. Sorry to bug you, but do you have Hawk's phone number?

It took about a minute for her to text back

I do. Why? You going to ask him for a date?

He smiled, gratified that she was able to find some levity in an overwhelmingly grim set of circumstances.

No date. Not my type. Please send it to me ASAP. Thanks.

Less than thirty seconds later, his phone chimed with another text listing Vince Hawk's cell phone number.

Concho wrote it on the paper placemat, cleared the text, and called Raul Molina.

"Hey, big man," Molina said. "Beat the hell out of any more wayward citizens lately?"

"How'd you hear about that?"

Molina chuckled. "Smoke signals. What's up?"

"I need you to ping a phone number for me."

"Okay." Molina's tone was a bit wary. "But hey, aren't you still on administrative leave?"

"It's all but over," Concho said.

"The way I heard it," Molina countered, "it's all over but the cryin'. Now what's the number?"

Concho read it off.

"Hold on."

About a minute later, Molina came back on the line.

"No dice. He must have it turned off or have his IMEI number cloaked. Whose number is it?"

"Vince Hawk's."

"Damn, didn't you just beat up his bodyguard, or stuntman, or something?"

"The guy's a suspect in a homicide. He deserved it."

"No doubt," Molina said. "But as the old Led Zeppelin used to say, the song remains the same. You back to work, or what?"

"Officially, no, but I'm closer to it than a bloodhound's wood tick. Can you periodically keep checking on that number and let me know if you find anything?"

"Will do," Molina said. "And by the way, some chick's been calling here asking for you."

"She leave a name?"

"Huh-un, but she sounded kind of young, if you get my drift."

"What's her number?"

"It was blocked. Err, you haven't knocked any young gals up, have you?"

Concho felt a current of excitement.

"Not hardly. Look, if she calls back, give her my phone number and tell her to call me."

"Roger that," Molina said, mimicking the old Army radio refrain.

When Concho had hung up he looked across the table. Nila was staring at him.

"We may be getting some kind of break," he said. "I think Holley Cameron's trying to get hold of me."

CHAPTER THIRTY-TWO

Twenty minutes later, as they were finishing their meals, the break they'd been waiting for came as Concho's cell phone rang with a blocked number. He answered it with a quick hello and was met by an initial silence, and then, "Ranger Ten-Wolves?"

The voice was young, feminine, tentative, and familiar.

"Hi, Holley," Concho said in as unthreatening of a tone as he could. "How you doing?"

He heard her hard breathing. Evidently his identification of her voice startled her. He silently cursed himself for not being more cautious. He was dealing with a flighty, nervous kid. But she had something serious on her mind.

"You know it's me?" she asked. "Who's calling you?"

"I recognized your voice is all. What's up?"

More hard breathing. The girl was torn.

He had a fish on the line now and knew he couldn't over-play things.

Kid gloves, he thought. *Nice and easy.*

Finally, she said, "I got a text. From Penny."

"Is she all right?"

"I don't think so," Holley said. "From the sound of it, she's in trouble. She asked me to come pick her up but texted I'd have to be real careful."

That sounded very problematic.

"Did she say where she was?"

"No. I don't think she knows. She said her and a bunch of other girls are in a big building somewhere. They took their phones and their clothes and won't let them go out."

It sounded like a stash house.

"She texted that she stole one of their phones to text me. She's afraid to call for fear they'll hear her. She says they're real mean."

The urgency factor was shifting into overdrive. Concho spoke with slow deliberation so as not to alarm the girl.

"Okay, Holley, you did the right thing calling me." His thoughts shot back to her crumpling up the card Nila had given the girl at the mall.

Lucky break.

He asked her to read the number off to him and she did so.

"All right, Holley, you're doing good." Positive reinforcement, he kept telling himself. Nice and easy does it. "Here's what I need you to do."

He gave her the standard instructions of not trying to call Peskipaatei back, but if she did re-contact her to say that help was coming and try to find out more information on where she was. "Above all, tell her to leave the phone on and in a place where no one will see it. Got it?"

"I think so."

"Good," Concho said. "And call me back if you hear from her. Now I need you to give me your number so I can have Penny call you when we find her or in case I need any more help from you. Can you give it to me, please?"

Holley recited her number and Concho scribbled it down.

"Okay, you're doing good. Now I need you to forward me those texts. Can you do that?"

"Yes."

After he received them he thanked her again and said he'd be in touch.

"You'll find her, won't you?" the girl asked.

"I'll do my best," he said and terminated the call.

Nila had her notebook out and was scribbling down all the information, her face the picture of excitement. Concho was already dialing Molina's number.

"I take it she called you?" Molina said.

"She did," Concho replied. "And I need you to ping a phone number for me, Raul. I'll need a triangulation ASAP. Exigent circumstances."

CHAPTER THIRTY-THREE

CONCHO WEIGHED THE CONSEQUENCES OF DISOBEYING A DIRECT order from Captain Shaw as he loaded his body armor and bow and arrows into the tow truck. He'd considered taking his Remington 30.06 rifle but the Gray-Dove's substandard vehicle had no place to properly secure it. He still felt well-armed with the Staccato and his Colt Double Eagle. Fifty-two rounds of 9mm and twenty-five of .45. Plus, he had twelve arrows in his quiver.

Pretty much, as he'd said before, loaded for bear.

But Meswkaa's last warning still haunted him.

There is a great battle coming. There will be blood.

Concho straightened his Stetson on his head and the edge of his hand inadvertently brushed over the bandage causing him to wince.

There's already been some blood, he told himself. I wonder how much more is going to be spilled? And whose?

He slammed the door and stood outside, looking up at the night sky. A myriad of stars twinkled against the vast velvet backdrop. It was going on eighteen-thirty and he'd heard nothing from Molina or Holley Cameron. He'd sent Nila back to the KTTP and called Echabarri to explain what was happening. The chief promised to send whatever units he could spare when the time came. Concho had also touched base with Sheriff Parkland and briefed him as well, asking if he could look into getting some backup units lined up.

"If possible, Terrill Hoight and Detective Tom Madrigal," Concho said. "They're familiar with me and with the situation."

Parkland said he was on it.

Now all there was little to do but wait. He reached into his pocket and fingered the bracelet he'd gotten from Holley. He thought about the other girls he'd seen wearing them.

Property rights, Pearsol had said, to tell the cartels who the girls belonged to.

His fingers curled over the hard-rubber bracelet and crushed it into a ball. Its resilience was intact, and it quickly snapped back into its original shape.

And the clock kept ticking.

As it turned out, he didn't have to wait long.

Holley's call came first.

"She just texted me," she said. "I told her everything just like you told me."

"Good, Holley. What did the text say?"

Her voice was reticent.

"She...she said..." Silence. "She told me she didn't have much time left and thanked me for being her BFF."

"Forward that to me," Concho said.

"I already did, but—"

When she didn't say anything else, Concho asked, "What?"

"You're going to find her, aren't you?"

Once again, he said, "I'll do my best."

That was getting to be a habit.

His phone vibrated with an incoming call and he saw it was Molina. Terminating the call from Holley, he answered quickly.

"What's up, Raul?"

"Okay, I just got a half-assed triangulation for you, but it's anything but definitive."

"Where is it?"

Molina sighed. "Like I said, it's indistinct. I've got a weak signal bouncing off a couple towers, and it looks to be originating in the old Cummins Industrial Park."

That was a huge area composed of a slew of large empty warehouses in an unincorporated area of the county about ten miles from Eagle Pass. It had been vacated after an industrial accident at a chemical plant and accompanying massive fire. The entire area had been declared a hazmat scene and all of the remaining businesses pulled out. A few buildings were now used for storage by a trucking firm, but most of the structures stood empty.

But not too empty, Concho thought.

It was isolated, deserted, and the perfect place for a stash house.

He thanked Molina and was about to hang up when his friend said, "Hey."

"What?"

"You want me to roll you some backup?"

Concho remembered Shaw's admonition of earlier that day.

"Not right now," Concho said. "I'm working with some other agencies, and besides, I'm still on administrative leave, remember?"

"Yeah, right." Molina chuckled. "Well, whatever you do, watch your ass, okay?"

"Roger that," Concho said, harkening back to the radio protocol he'd used during his days in Afghanistan.

He was on the phone to Echabarri and then to Parkland as he was rolling and shifting through the gears.

"Christ," Parkland said. "That's a pretty big area. I'll see who I can get, but I've got most of my people tied up on a train derailment that's turned into a hazmat scene."

"Tell whoever you can spare to be on the lookout for a big,

dark-skinned Indian wearing all black body armor, a Texas Ranger badge, and war paint."

"What the hell did you just say?" the sheriff asked.

"It's red war paint," Concho replied. "Like I said, send Hoight if he's available."

He hung up and continued driving at a high rate of speed.

CHAPTER THIRTY-FOUR

CONCHO CUT THE LIGHTS ON THE TOW TRUCK AS HE COASTED up to the main entrance to the industrial park. A huge sign was posted on one side of the driveway.

PRIVATE PROPERTY. NO TRESPASSING
PROPERTY OF A.C. McMILLAN INC. ENTERPRISES.

A.C. McMillan...the same company that border agent Pearsol had mentioned was sponsoring the migrants. Domestic workers.

Yeah, right.

The park was surrounded by a twelve-foot-high cyclone fence with triple strands of barbed wire strung along the top. There was an abandoned gate shack in place just outside the large gates, which were closed and secured by a chain and heavy-duty padlock. Concho got out and surveyed the area.

Beyond the fencing, a cluster of large buildings spread out along a series of asphalt roadways. There were no perceivable lights visible anywhere. He listened and heard the occasional sound of traffic coming from a nearby interstate, but inside the fencing, things looked deserted. Taking the chain between his fingers, he estimated the sturdiness of the linkage. It appeared to be chrome steel, which meant that it wasn't going to be an easy task with a bolt cutter. The lock, too, was as thick as a small brick and its hasp looked equally formidable. He did notice that the lock was hanging on the inside of the fencing, which told him that it had been locked from the interior.

Probably once Hawk's stretch limo had been driven through.

Or his buses.

Concho jumped back into the tow truck and backed it up about ten yards from the secured gate. He untucked the hooked end of the winch cable and slipped it over the chain. Going to the controls, he worked the lever of the winch drawing the cable tighter and tighter. The chain held for longer than he thought it would, but finally the crossbeam of the fencing broke and gates swung open. Disconnecting the hook, Concho rewound the winching cable and got back into the truck. As he drove through the opening, pushing the battered gates even farther apart, he stopped and considered the situation.

He couldn't afford to wait for the backup and didn't know where, in this sea of two, three, and four-story structures, they were holding Peskipaatei. And Holley had mentioned other girls.

His thoughts turned to the three bodies in the morgue.

They were all somebody's daughters.

No, he couldn't wait.

As he shifted into gear, he was struck by another idea.

Shifting to neutral and applying the emergency brake, he got out and shoved both of the gates farther open. Then he went to the rear of the tow truck and took out four flares. After twisting off the cap of the first flare and striking the rounded end, the sulfur ignited with a sudden hiss, raining sparks and a bright flame. Concho repeated this with the other flares, setting each one down on the surface of the entranceway forming a big, illuminated arrow.

That should be easy enough for Maverick County's finest to follow, he thought and got back in the truck.

The clock was ticking.

He knew he had to move. After taking off the shoulder holster, he slipped his body armor over his black T-shirt, pinned his Texas Ranger badge on the strap, and slid back into the shoulder rig, securing the straps to his belt to ensure stability. He placed his Stetson on the passenger seat of the tow truck, crown-down for luck, and reaching into the leather tote sack he'd placed there earlier. After removing a small yellow tin can, he twisted it open and dipped his index and middle fingers into the red ochre. Drawing his fingers across his prominent cheekbones, he left two sets of parallel lines under each eye.

Now he was ready for battle.

Red war paint.

There will be blood.

* * *

IT TOOK CONCHO ONLY A FEW MINUTES TO FIND WHAT HE figured had to be the target building. After winding his way through the wide, street-like aisles, he heard a faint drumming sound. With the lights still out and the window down, he drove toward the sound. The thrumming grew louder as he approached, and then the vibrating generator came into view. It was off to the rear of a large, three-story brick-and-mortar structure.

He took out his cell phone and texted Nila, describing the building's location.

I've lighted the target with flares, he added and slipped the phone back into his pocket without waiting for a reply.

If only I had a radio, he thought.

But such was not the case for a Ranger on administrative leave he added mentally, allowing himself a grim smile.

You go with what you've got.

The building had several windows, but they were boarded

up and had bars over them. A sturdy-looking metal door, devoid of rust, was adjacent to the machine. Getting out of the truck, he crept over to the door and twisted the doorknob.

Locked.

Looking upward, he saw a dome-like globe mounted on the soffit.

A camera.

And how many more were there?

This increased the urgency factor.

If someone was monitoring the camera system, they might already know he was there.

But now they were about to go blind.

He grabbed the bow and took out one arrow. After sighting in on the camera, he let it fly.

The solid piercing sound told him all he needed to know.

Scratch one camera.

He grabbed his last flare, ignited it, and tossed the burning stick down on the aisle-like street.

Hopefully, his backup would arrive and see it before it burned out.

Grabbing the large crowbar from the rear of the truck, he went to the steel door and examined the lock. Working the beveled edge of the crowbar between the door and the jamb, he shoved the bar backward and the door groaned in protest before giving way. Inside, an unlighted hallway was visible. Concho dropped the crowbar onto the ground, picked up his bow and quiver, and fitted the night-vision goggles on top of his head, leaving them in the up-position.

Removing another arrow from the quiver, he nocked it in place as he moved down the hallway. It was dark, but the brightness of lights shone from the other end. The place had power and was well-illuminated.

A discordant modulation of voices became audible.

"You're just going to have to wait. We got some more filming to do first."

The speaker's voice was unmistakable.

Vince Hawk.

Concho crept closer to the end of the hallway. He could see this section was slightly higher than the main floor.

The smart plan would be to reconnoiter and try to locate Peskipaatei, secure her, and maybe try to sneak her out.

But Peskipaatei had texted "girls." Plural.

There was no telling how many there were.

Too many variables, he thought.

A guttural utterance in Spanish followed, and Hawk's voice replied, louder and more forceful.

"Don't lay that Spanish shit on me, Hugo. You know we got a deal."

Hugo?

Hugo Cuevas?

This was shaping up to be an old friend's reunion.

"And we got *la policia y la migra* on our asses, too. We gotta move out now, *chingado.*"

"Hey, beaner," another man said. "Don't you be talking to the boss that way or I'll kick your ass."

That voice also had a familiar ring to it: Jim Dandy.

Concho got to the end of the corridor and flattened against the wall, dropping the quiver by his foot. His elevated vantage point gave him a good view of the area below opened to a very large room, perhaps fifty yards long with stacks of oil drums and piles of lumber scattered throughout. Twin rows of overhead lights hung from a ceiling that was about sixty feet high. The expansive room was filled with what appeared to be makeshift rooms constructed of wood. Many of them had only three walls and were well-furnished with brightly colored wallpaper and plush furniture. Most of the furniture appeared to be long couches or beds. There were sophisticated-looking cameras positioned on tripods in front of a couple of them.

Porno sound stages, Concho thought.

Farther down the way, Hawk's four tour buses were parked by a series of massive overhead doors.

Doing a quick peek, Concho surveyed the rest of the area.

Hawk and Jim Dandy stood about fifty feet away with their backs toward Concho. Opposite them were a group of Mexicans. Concho recognized the diminutive Hugo Cuevas standing in front of five others. Alexander Drum stood off to the side, leaning against a stuffed chair looking amused. Several more men were next to him. Concho recognizes some of them as Hawk's entourage at the talent quest.

"*Chinga tu madre*," Cuevas muttered. "We gonna leave now and we taking *las chicas* with us."

"Like hell," Hawk said. "I told you, we got scenes to film. And one of my clients down your way wants another snuff film. He's already paid for it."

Another snuff film?

Three dead girls, all strangled. The son of a bitch.

Cuevas looked about to reply when another man, a White guy, ran up to the group.

"Boss," the man said, breathless. "Our cameras just went dead in back. I think we got company."

Hawk's head swiveled around and barked an order at Drum.

"Go check it out. And Jimbo, get the bitches and load 'em into the bus."

Dandy turned and trotted off.

Concho tried to melt back into the shadows but his movement gave him away.

"There he is," somebody shouted.

A bullet zinged off the wall above Concho's head as he crouched down. Two guys were running toward him, their arms outstretched and holding guns.

Another shot sounded as fire leaped from a big semi-auto one of the running men was holding.

Drawing back the bow, Concho let his nocked arrow fly. It struck one of the running men with the guns in the chest just below the throat. He did a stutter step, reached for the shaft, and twisted to the ground.

"Ten-Wolves," Hawk shouted. "Get him. Kill him."

Slipping off the night-vision goggles and dropping the bow, Concho withdrew the Staccato. He leveled the weapon and fired off four rounds in quick succession. Two more of the rushing men tumbled to the ground. Hawk was running toward the row of three-walled rooms. Drum was crouching down beside a stack of lumber, and Jim Dandy was sprinting to the far wall, beyond the row of porno sound stages and toward the area where the buses were parked.

Concho fired a round at Drum, causing the heavyset ex-cop to seek cover behind the wood.

Another pair of bullets hit the wall by Concho's body.

It was time to move. If he stayed where he was, he'd be picked off.

Holding the Staccato out to his side as he ran, he fired off several rounds as cover fire while sprinting in the same direction he'd seen Dandy going.

He had to get to the girls. Hopefully, his backup would be here soon and hear the shots. But until then, he was on his own.

How many shots had he fired?

In the excitement, he'd lost count, but he was sure it was at least eleven or twelve.

Good old seventeen plus one, he thought. Not time for a combat reload just yet.

He pivoted and crouched behind a metal dumpster.

A bunch of rounds pinged off the metallic surface.

Crouching and leaning off to the side, Concho saw Hugo and three of his thugs advancing, their guns outstretched and firing.

Cuevas's mouth twisted into a vicious grin.

Concho aimed and fired, and a millisecond later, he saw a red mist blossom from the back of the Mexican gangster's head. He dropped like a stone. The thugs had grouped themselves too close together and Concho was able to pepper the other three with well-placed shots.

The slide of the Staccato locked back.

Concho pressed the mag release button, and as the magazine dropped to the floor, he slammed a new one in place. Not seeing any immediate potential threats, he ran at a quick pace toward the line of buses. Zigzagging through the clutter of stacks of lumber, oil drums, furniture, and various boxes, he managed to come to a walled-off section of offices. One of the substructures had solid walls, and he figured that must be where the girls were being held.

He stopped and took cover by a stack of boxes.

Not cover, he decided, noticing the flimsiness of the construction. Only half-assed concealment at best.

The door opened and Dandy came partially out. He was holding a gun in one hand, a blue steel revolver, and his other hand was wrapped around a young girl's upper torso. She was naked, except for a pair of underpants, and looked terrified.

Concho glanced in the direction he'd just come.

Nobody in sight yet, but Drum and Miss Agnes were out there.

Dandy moved forward, dragging the girl with him.

"Come on, bitch," he muttered.

The girl's breath came and went with huffing sounds.

Taking a deep breath, Concho edged around the corner of the boxes and zeroed his aim on Dandy's head.

He thought about issuing a warning but decided the risk was too great.

The front sight aligned between the V-shape of the rear sights, level across the top, and he squeezed off the round.

Dandy's head jerked back and then forward and his body went limp, the revolver tumbling from slack fingers as he collapsed.

The girl screamed, and Concho ran forward and shoved her back into the room.

He saw at least twenty young girls, all mostly nude, clad only in panties and clutching each other in terror. Numerous plastic buckets were stationed around the room.

"Texas Ranger," Concho said, then realizing most of them

probably didn't speak English, he added, "*Soy policia. No se preocupen.*"

His voice sounded strange. Far away, like it was echoing down a long hallway.

Auditory exclusion, he realized—from all the gunshots.

"*Señor*," one of the girls said, "*¿No nos recuerda?*"

It was one of the six from Nicaragua that he'd rescued that first night. She was still wearing one of the red bracelets.

He was about to reply when he saw her face twist in alarm.

A second later, he felt the sting of pain as something hard slammed into his back and right shoulder.

He whirled and saw Vince Hawk wielding the long 2 x 4. Hawk's handsome face was a twisted caricature as he raised the piece of wood over his head to deliver another strike. Stunned, Concho tried to lift his arm to shoot, but his body was for some reason, moving in slow motion. A flicker of a wickedness gleamed in Hawk's eyes but as he stepped forward one of the girls grabbed a plastic bucket and hurled the liquid contents into Hawk's face. It appeared to be urine.

He hesitated and coughed.

Three more girls ran forward, their fists beating down on his face, neck, and back. Two of them grabbed the wood from his hands and rammed it against him.

Concho shook off whatever momentary paralysis he'd felt and stepped forward.

"Let me do that," he said and smashed his left fist into Hawk's face.

The Indian movie star stiffened, staggered backward, and sat down heavily on his backside. Holstering his weapon, Concho flipped him over onto his stomach, wrenched his arms behind his back, and used the handcuffs from the pocket of his vest to secure Hawk's wrists.

"Get your hands off me," Hawk said. "You don't know who you're messing with."

"Well," Concho said, "I know you're no Geronimo."

He stood and went to the door, gun in hand.

Drum stood there with a smirk on his face holding his oversized revolver down by his leg.

Concho immediately raised his Colt Double Eagle and pointed it at Drum.

"Don't move and drop your weapon," he shouted.

Drum held out his hands let the big Anaconda drop to the floor.

"No argument from me," he said, cocking his head toward the right. "FYI, *Kemosabe*, the cavalry's here."

Concho could hear voices now shouting out orders using a loudspeaker and announcing a police presence.

No more gunshots.

"Drum, kick your weapon over here," Concho said. His hearing was starting to come back.

The ex-cop complied and then grinned, keeping his hands elevated.

"Like I told ya, I'm smart enough to know when I'm licked. And besides, I'm low down on the food chain here. I figure that gives me a good shot at turning state's evidence and getting off with a light sentence or maybe even a cushy place in wit-sec." His lips parted in a smile. "So whaddya think?"

"Stranger things have happened," Concho said.

He studied the faces of the girls in the room, and one popped out at him. She stood staring at him, her arms across her bare breasts. She has the circular red tattoo on her lower abdomen. It had some translucent coating over it suggesting it was recent.

"Are you Peskipaatei?" he asked.

She nodded.

"Your grandmother's worried about you."

"I know," she said.

The smiling face in the BFF picture was there, but there was something different now—a total loss of innocence now around the eyes.

Nila Willow was going to have her work cut out for her.

CHAPTER THIRTY-FIVE

TWO DAYS LATER, HE WAS LYING ON HIS STOMACH ON THE BED in his trailer with Maria next to him, and they were both completely naked.

"Oooh," Concho said. "Yeah. Right there. That's the spot."

"This is a terrible bruise," Maria said.

He felt her fingers dancing over his back and shoulder.

"You got that right," he said.

"So," she said, "the mighty wolf got clobbered by the hawk."

"You should've seen the other guy."

"And those girls threw a bucket of...?"

"Yep."

She giggled. "I wish I could have seen that."

"Too bad nobody had a cell phone handy. They could have used it as a poster for the next talent quest."

She giggled again.

He felt her warm legs straddle him. He glanced over and saw the potted plant he'd bought her for Valentine's Day and wondered if she should just leave it here.

"So our buddy Mr. Otis backed off once the news of Hawk's arrest got announced, eh?" he asked.

"Totally." She started kneading his back. "And Peski—how do you say her name again?"

"Peskipaatei. It means blue."

"Whatever. She's back with her grandmother?"

"Yeah, and hopefully a bit wiser. Nila's sort of acting like a big sister to her."

Maria sighed as she continued rubbing his shoulder.

"I hope she can straighten the poor girl out."

"Me too," Concho said.

"All's well that ends well," she said. "Isn't that what they say?"

"That's how Shakespeare put it." He felt himself getting aroused by her massage. "But since I'm scheduled to get off administrative leave tomorrow, you know what I want?"

"What?"

He twisted his head so he could look up at her.

"I really want to turn over," he said.

Her smile was wickedly delicious. She leaned down and kissed his cheek.

"Why don't you do that?"

A LOOK AT: GUNSLINGER
THE COMPLETE WESTERN ADVENTURE
SERIES

**FROM THE AUTHOR OF THE FAST-PACED AVENGING
ANGELS SERIES COMES A NEW KIND OF WESTERN
HERO.**

Fourteen-year-old Connor Mack dreams of a life full of adventure—while he's stuck plowing, doing chores, and being worked to death on a half barren family spread in East Texas. He plans to one day flee the beatings delivered by his hulking older brothers and lazy pa. But he knows when he does, he has to take his twin sister, Abby, with him.

Connor gets his chance when River Hicks, a man wanted for the murder of a policeman in Fort Worth, rides into town with a pack of bounty hunters on his trail. As the gun smoke clears, and Connor has killed men for the first time in his life, he knows this is his and Abby's time to escape their life of abuse.

Knowing the law will soon be on their heels, they follow Hicks—an outlaw driven by his own demons and deep secrets, which somehow involve the Mack twins.

Conner has a lot of learning and growing up to do…and he has to stay alive to do it.

Read along across nine action-packed books as odds are defied, relentless dangers are faced, and treacherous journeys of self-discovery are navigated in an attempt to carve out a life of freedom in several gripping tales.

Gunslinger: The Complete Series includes *Gunslinger: Killer's Chance, Gunslinger: Killer's Fuse, Gunslinger: Killer's Choice, Gunslinger: Killer's Train, Gunslinger: Killer's Reckoning, Gunslinger: Killer's Brand, Gunslinger: Killer's Ghost, Gunslinger: Killer's Gamble, and Gunslinger: Killer's Requiem.*

AVAILABLE NOW

ABOUT THE AUTHOR

Michael A. Black is the author of 36 books and over 100 short stories and articles. A decorated police officer in the south suburbs of Chicago, he worked for over thirty-two years in various capacities including patrol supervisor, SWAT team leader, investigations and tactical operations before retiring in April of 2011.

A long time practitioner of the martial arts, Black holds a black belt in Tae Kwon Do from Ki Ka Won Academy in Seoul, Korea. He has a Bachelor of Arts degree in English from Northern Illinois University and a Master of Fine Arts in Fiction Writing from Columbia College, Chicago. In 2010 he was awarded the Cook County Medal of Merit by Cook County Sheriff Tom Dart. Black wrote his first short story in the sixth grade, and credits his then teacher for instilling him with determination to keep writing when she told him never to try writing again.

Black has since been published in several genres including mystery, thriller, sci-fi, westerns, police procedurals, mainstream, pulp fiction, horror, and historical fiction. His Ron Shade series featuring the Chicago-based kickboxing private eye, has won several awards, as has his police procedural series featuring Frank Leal and Olivia Hart. He also wrote two novels with television star Richard Belzer, I Am Not a Cop and I Am Not a Psychic. Black writes under numerous pseudonyms and pens The Executioner series under the name Don Pendleton. His Executioner novel, Fatal Prescription, won the Best Original Novel Scribe Award given by the International Media Tie-In Writers Association in 2018.

His current books are Blood Trails, a cutting edge police procedural in the tradition of the late Michael Crichton, and Legends of the West, which features a fictionalized account of the legendary and real life lawman, Bass Reeves. His newest Executioner novels are Dying Art, Stealth Assassins, and Cold Fury, all of which were nominees and finalists for Best Novel Scribe Awards. He is very active in animal rescue and animal welfare issues and has several cats.